HEARTS HEAL IN HAITI

Book Three In

Ladies in Lab Coats Series

By
Sally Burbank

HEARTS HEAL IN HAITI

Book Three: Ladies in Lab Coats Series
By Sally Burbank

COPYRIGHT 2021 All right reserved
Woodmont and Waverly Publishing

Hearts Heal in Haiti is a work of fiction. All characters, events, and the medical clinic where Grant and Allison worked are products are the author's imagination and do not refer to any person alive or dead. All rights reserved. No part of this publication may be reproduced, distributed, or transmitted in any form or by any means without the writer's written permission.

www.sallywillardburbank.com

ISBN: 9798753336460

Contact the publisher at:
Woodmont and Waverly Publishing
207 Woodmont Circle Nashville, TN 37205
Cover Design: Najla Qamber Designs
Editor: Candie Moonshower

OTHER BOOKS
By Sally Burbank

FICTION:

Can You Lose the Unibrow?
More Than a Hunch

NON-FICTION:

Patients I Will Never Forget
The Alzheimer's Disease Caregiver's Handbook: What to Remember When They Forget

ANTHOLOGIES:

Chicken Soup for the Soul:
~The Power of the Positive
~Hope and Miracles
~Miracles Happen
~Laughter is the Best Medicine
~Readers' Choice 20th Anniversary edition

DEDICATION:

This book is dedicated to my wonderful in-laws, John and Lois Burbank, because of their years of supporting both my writing and hard-working missionaries around the globe like those depicted in *Hearts Heal in Haiti*.

I hit the jackpot when I married Nathan and won them as a part of the package.

John and Lois, I love you both to Haiti and back!

ABOUT HAITI:

If I had to pick one word to describe the people of Haiti, it would be resilient. Why? Let's explore the history of this beleaguered Caribbean Island, and you will understand why.

The native citizens of Haiti were South American Indians from the Arawak and Taino tribes who settled the island that later became known as Hispaniola.

Christopher Columbus first explored the island and left Spanish settlers there in 1492. But by 1625, French colonists inhabited the island and grew wealthy from sugar and coffee profits produced off the backs of hard-working African slaves. In fact, the 1788 census showed that the island's 25,000 French colonists owned a whooping 700,000 African slaves.

Inspired by the message of the French Revolution, Haiti's slaves revolted, and after a thirty-year struggle, they gained their independence in 1804. Most of the Europeans left the island, (or were killed if they didn't!), so Haiti is now largely inhabited by the descendants of African slaves.

A long string of corrupt and inept leaders has ruled the island, and most of the financial aid granted by the United States and other countries has been misappropriated. Sadly, average Haitian citizens received nothing and remained destitute.

Haiti's most recent Prime Minister, Jovenel Moïse, was assassinated in his home on July 7, 2021. Haiti now has an interim Prime Minister, Claude Joseph, until the next election.

The July assassination and subsequent political upheaval couldn't have come at a worse time, because Haiti was slammed with a 7.2 magnitude earthquake just a month later, on August 14, 2021.

Over 2,000 died, and another 12,200 were missing, injured, or homeless. Many are now desperately trying to flee to the United States.

Despites its troublesome political record, Haiti has its' strengths—namely, natural beauty. It is the most mountainous island in the Caribbean with much of the island located over 4,000 feet high. The tallest mountain, Mount Selle, towers the island at 8,773 feet.

Sadly, Haiti is the poorest country in the Western Hemisphere with $4/5^{th}$ of the population living in abject poverty and $3/5^{th}$ unemployed or underemployed. Two-thirds of Haitians are farmers who grow cassava, plantains, bananas, yams, cocoa, papaya, maize, mangos, and rice. Three-fourths of Haitians lack running water, and $2/5^{th}$ are illiterate, especially in the rural areas.

Homes are usually two-room dwellings constructed with mud walls and floors and a roof of thatched grasses or corrugated metal. The kitchen is often located outside, and the bathroom is a latrine dug in the ground.

While poverty is rampant in the inner mountainous regions, tourism brings in big bucks along the coastline, thanks to the island's crystal blue waters, breathtaking beaches, and affordable prices. Cruise ships love to stop at Labadee, where talented Haitian artisans tempt the tourists to part with their money.

Because Haiti's inhabitants originated from Africa but were owned for two hundred years by French Catholic colonials, half of Haitians practice some form of Catholicism, but most worship with a mixture of voodoo and Catholic traditions. In fact, Haiti is the only country in the world that recognizes voodoo as an official religion.

Many organizations work tirelessly to improve conditions in Haiti. I personally donate to World Vision, LiveBeyond, and the Joseph School.

LiveBeyond is an organization started by a Nashville physician. It provides free schooling, medical care, and an orphanage. Their work is the inspiration for this novel.

LiveBeyond provides top-notch medical care and services—(far more advanced than the imaginary clinic depicted in my novel!) Should you want to explore donating to LiveBeyond, look them up online at: http://livebeyond.org

You can also financially support them by mailing donations to: LiveBeyond, 1515 Ave South, Suite 200, Grand Prairie, Texas 75050.

The Joseph School is a Christian school with a mission to raise up ethical future leaders in Haiti—not unlike Joseph from the Old Testament. Information can be obtained at:
http://thejosephschool.org
(615) 724-6073

All profits earned from the sale of this novel will be donated to the Joseph School and LiveBeyond ministries.

CHAPTER 1

Dr. Grant Stockdale III would gladly trade in his BMW for a few hours of uninterrupted shut-eye. He trudged from the Surgical ICU toward the hospital elevators as the last twenty grueling hours of hospital rounds and operating without a wink of sleep drained what little energy he had left. But decent rest would have to wait, as Dr. Morrison had requested a private meeting with him. Excitement, fear, and a mug full of high-octane coffee swirled in his stomach. He wiped sweaty palms on his lab coat.

Maybe all the years of hard work will finally pay off.

Two of his classmates, Thomas and Jeremy, caught up with him on their way to the cafeteria.

"I'll bet he wants to offer you the Chief Surgical Resident position," Thomas said.

"Duh!" Jeremy agreed. "Nobody else has Grant's grades. Or Board scores."

While grateful for their endorsement, Grant couldn't squelch his fear he might lose out to an infuriatingly skilled classmate who matched his competency in every way.

"Morrison could just as easily pick Allison Smith," he said, voicing his worst fear. "She and I have identical grades and board scores."

Thomas snorted. "Allison Smith? She's barely five feet tall and probably weighs less than an EKG machine."

"What does that have to do with anything?" Grant snapped, his lack of sleep catching up with him.

Thomas met his gaze head-on. "Let's be real. A short, beautiful woman like Allison couldn't possibly command the respect from newbie interns that a tall athletic guy like you could."

Jeremy elbowed Thomas. "Besides, the interns would all be too busy drooling over Allison to pay attention to their scalpels. Might be dangerous."

Grant rolled his eyes. Seriously? With the thousands of well-qualified doctors Johns Hopkins could have chosen, how had they settled on Neanderthals like Jeremy and Thomas?

Thomas whacked Jeremy's arm. "That comment was low—even for you, Dyson. They can't discriminate based on height—or lack thereof. Right, Grant?"

Grant refused to respond to the inane question.

As they entered the elevator Thomas said, "You know, with all the emphasis on equal opportunity for women, minorities, and LGBTQ these days, if Allison matches you in every way, Morrison *might* feel obligated to pick Allison over you just because she's a woman."

"You're right," Jeremy agreed. "How long has it been since they picked a woman for Chief Surgical Resident?"

Grant's stomach plummeted. He hadn't even considered that possibility. Had all his years in the OR and library been for nothing?

When they reached the cafeteria, Grant's colleagues wished him luck then beelined toward the tantalizing aroma of crispy bacon and fresh-brewed coffee. Grant's stomach growled as he headed toward Dr. Morrison's office, but breakfast was out of the question until after his meeting.

As he rounded the corner away from the cafeteria, he reminded himself to play it cool. Act surprised. Express what an honor it would be to serve as Chief Surgical Resident.

But don't act too surprised, he mused, as he reached Dr. Morrison's office. No flapping of the hands or covering of the face in feigned modesty and shock like some newly crowned Miss America. Calm, confident, but humble.

The secretary gestured toward the door of Dr. Morrison's executive office. "He's expecting you, so head on in."

Grant's hands trembled as he turned the knob. Was he in for a huge letdown or the biggest honor of his life? He forced himself to suck in a deep breath.

"Have a seat," the bespectacled, balding Dean of Surgery said, gesturing with his beefy paw toward the chair in front of his intimidatingly large mahogany desk.

Grant sat down with the posture of a military recruit and forced himself to smile.

Dr. Morrison shuffled some papers on his desk then got to the point. "You probably know why I called you in here today."

Grant offered a slight shrug but said nothing.

Dr. Morrison cleared his throat and then continued. "I want to discuss the Chief Surgical Resident position with you."

Yes! Grant forced himself not to grin like a hyena on happy gas.

Dr. Morrison continued. "Grant, you are a brilliant and committed surgeon. Your grades, test scores, and evaluations are at the top of your class, so obviously, you're in the running for the position."

Grant's heart jolted. In the running? What did that mean?

Dr. Morrison's eyes bore into Grant's. "I'll be frank. Allison Smith's academic performance is tied with yours, but she also has an impressive record of humanitarian work. She volunteers at the homeless shelter and has participated in a medical mission trip to Guatemala."

"What does that have to do with being the Chief Surgical Resident?" Grant couldn't help but inquire.

Dr. Morrison shifted in his chair. "A Chief Resident is supposed to be a role model in every way to our interns and residents. Johns Hopkins has a long tradition of serving the poor."

Grant couldn't stop himself. "So, you'd pick Allison over me because she's put in a few hours of volunteer work?" He gripped the arms of his chair as righteous indignation coursed through him. Had he busted his butt off all these years to lose out just because Allison had clipped toenails or bandaged up a few scrapes on alcoholics at the homeless shelter?

He'd graduated summa cum laude from Harvard, while she'd graduated from the University of Vermont—hardly equal to an Ivy League institution! Okay, she *had* been Valedictorian of her class and clearly matched him in medical school and residency test scores, but rumor had it her father raised cows and pigs and chickens in the sticks of Vermont. Certainly not the usual background of a Chief Surgical Resident at America's most prestigious medical school.

He immediately scolded himself for his elitist thoughts. Snobbery—the very trait he despised when he heard comments like this from others at his parents' country club. How many times had he jumped his grandfather's case for judging people on pedigree instead of merit?

If Allison won the position, how he dreaded the comments his family would make. He could hear them now:

"You must not have studied enough," his father would accuse. His grandfather, a surgical dinosaur with values dating back to Hippocrates, would shake his head in disgust. "You lost out to a woman who didn't even graduate from an Ivy League?"

Grant raked agitated fingers through his hair. His father paid for all his college and medical school expenses, but with the exorbitant tuition checks came high expectations—namely, that Grant would rise to the top of his class, just as his father and grandfather had.

And now he had let them down. He hung his head in shame.

They'll be so disappointed in me.

As though reading his mind, Dr. Morrison said, "Grant, I know your family has a long tradition of serving as the Chief Surgical Resident at Johns Hopkins." He chuckled and added, "Your father and grandfather are practically institutions around here." His eyes bore into Grant's with surprising kindness. "I understand completely the pressure you feel to keep up the family tradition."

Grant glance up, surprised Morrison had any idea the weight riding on his shoulders.

Dr. Morrison leaned forward and steepled his fingers. "I'd also be remiss not to acknowledge all the generous donations the Stockdale Foundation has made over the years to the Johns Hopkins medical community."

"We *did* fund an entire science building, along with a huge parking garage," Grant couldn't help but point out.

Dr. Morrison removed his glasses and cleaned them with a silky square he withdrew from his lab coat pocket. As though deep in thought, he continued his cleaning ritual until Grant's heart was one step from needing a cardiac ablation.

Get on with it! Are you giving me the job or not?

Grant forced himself to inhale slow deep breaths.

Finally, Dr. Morrison hooked his glasses around his ears and tucked his cleaning cloth back into his pocket. "I can't, with a clear conscience, offer the position to you. Not if Allison matches your achievements *and* has extended the Johns

Hopkins tradition of providing care to the less fortunate. Choosing Allison would also demonstrate our institution's commitment to provide equal opportunity to women."

Had political correctness reared its ugly head and bit him in the butt? No matter how hard he studied, would he be punished for being a white male from a wealthy family?

Although he felt he deserved the position, if serving the poor mattered, then Allison clearly deserved it *more* than he did—with or without his prestigious Harvard degree.

Grant stood to leave avoiding eye contact. "I appreciate your time and for letting me know I was a top contender."

He hurried toward the door. If Dr. Morrison had already chosen Allison over him, why hang around and have it smeared in his face?

Dr. Morrison jumped to his feet and extended his hand like a stop sign. "Grant, wait! My decision isn't final. You're still in the running."

Grant turned and raised upturned palms. "If Allison has performed all that volunteer work, how can I possibly compete? Plus, she can pull out the woman trump card."

Dr. Morrison smiled. "I'm glad you asked. You can compete by going on a twelve-week medical mission yourself.

Grant stared back at him dumbly. "But I'm already signed up for a plastic surgery rotation that starts next week."

"Your plastics rotation is purely elective, so you can easily switch to the three-month Surgical Missions in the Tropics rotation."

Grant stared at him in shock. "How would I find a rotation like that with so little notice? Surely all the slots are already filled."

Dr. Morrison grinned. "I was hoping you'd ask."

He opened his desk drawer, pulled out a pamphlet, and handed it to Grant. "Haiti, that's where. They are desperate for doctors, especially surgeons."

Grant's head jerked up.

Haiti?

Surely, he'd misunderstood. Insufferable heat, mosquitos, political unrest, poverty, crime. No one in his right mind would go there. He eyed the brochure and couldn't stop himself from blurting, "You seriously expect me to go to Haiti?"

"Only if you want to become Chief Surgical Resident." His expression turned serious. "Grant, I can't justify giving you the position over Allison unless you start demonstrating sufficient charitable hours on your résumé."

Grant scratched the back of his neck too flummoxed to think clearly. There had to be an out clause. "But I-I don't speak Spanish," he stammered, desperate for any excuse to bow out.

Dr. Morrison smirked. "Considering the Haitians where you'll be serving speak French Creole, that won't be a problem."

"Oh, right." Grant thumped his forehead embarrassed he'd stumbled over such a basic geography fact. So much for his pricy Harvard education.

"Years ago, Haiti was a colony of France," Dr. Morrison reminded him.

"Yes, of course. I remember now," Grant mumbled. Hoping to save face he added, "I operated on a gangrenous gall bladder and a ruptured appendix all night, so I'm afraid my geography game is a little off this morning."

Grant opened the pamphlet and half-heartedly rifled through it, dreading even the thought of spending three months in a humid place where voodoo and vipers were commonplace.

"You *do* have an up-to-date passport, don't you?" Dr. Morrison frowned. "If not, it's a deal-breaker."

"Yes, and I know it's current because my family took a ski trip in the Alps at Christmas."

Dr. Morrison's brow rose. "The Alps, huh?" His lips twitched. "Guess it's time to trade in your ski parka and goggles for mosquito netting and sunblock, huh?"

Grant did not find it funny. Not one bit.

"I'll warn you. Haiti is not for the faint of heart. It's hot and humid and one of the poorest countries in the world. Thanks to that devastating earthquake in 2010, over 230,000 people died. Then another hit in 2021, and they've never recovered."

"Yes, I've read conditions are deplorable."

Dr. Morrison shook his head. "Pitiful, really. Orphans, poverty, and devastation everywhere."

"Doesn't the U.S give them a ton of financial aid?"

"Yes, but unfortunately, the Haitian government is corrupt, so the money gets misappropriated, and the people who need it most are often left with nothing." He picked up his coffee mug and swallowed a swig before continuing.

"Adding insult to injury, Haiti suffers from staggeringly high unemployment and crime rates."

Grant's shoulders sagged. This was sounding worse and worse. Why would he consider going to such a horrible place? Picturing his father and grandfather's disappointed faces, however, he forced himself to say, "Sounds like they need capable doctors. I will give your suggestion careful consideration."

Envisioning three months in a sweltering inferno with no air conditioning, Grant promptly rejected it.

Dr. Morrison cleared his throat and chewed on his lower lip, as though debating whether to say what was on his mind. Finally, he came out with it. "Grant, you've had a privileged life with luxuries and opportunities others can only dream of. It's time you see how the rest of the world lives."

He rose from his desk. "Grant, I'm not recommending this assignment as a punishment or merely as a means for you to clinch the Chief Surgical Resident position. I want you to do it for *you*." Gripping both of Grant's shoulders, his eyes bore into Grant's. "This experience will enrich your worldview in a way a plastic surgery rotation never could. You'll return a changed man. A better man. I promise."

Grant nodded then browsed through the brochure with more deliberation. The pamphlet displayed a rudimentary surgical clinic with a doctor and several bedraggled but smiling Haitian patients.

"I'll need time to digest all this before I make my decision," Grant said, hoping to defuse the pressure.

Dr. Morrison shook his head. "You don't *have* time. You'll need hepatitis A and typhoid vaccines along with a prescription for malaria prophylaxis. Also, check your hepatitis B antibody titer to make sure you don't need a booster shot. Same for polio, measles, and tetanus. And since stray dogs roam everywhere in Haiti, it wouldn't hurt to get vaccinated for rabies."

Rabies? Typhoid? Malaria? Yeesh! Haiti was a regular Petri dish of disease.

He scratched the back of his neck as he tried to absorb what Morrison was demanding of him. "Between the thugs, tropical diseases, and rabid dogs, will I even make it back alive to become Chief Surgical Resident?"

Dr. Morrison chuckled. "We haven't lost a resident yet."

Grant's eyes widened. "Yet?"

He patted Grant on the back and offered him a reassuring smile. "Come now, Grant. Plenty of doctors have served in Haiti and made it back to the States safe and sound."

Grant must have looked unconvinced because Morrison added, "Look, I wouldn't send you there if I thought you wouldn't make it home alive."

Grant chewed his lower lip mulling over the repercussions of a rotation in Haiti.

"I'll need your decision by tomorrow so I can let Dr. Jones in Haiti know if you're coming."

"I'll do it," Grant said before he could come to his senses and bow out.

Dr. Morrison's head jerked up. "Really? You're sure?"

The words already weighed Grant down like the bulky luggage he'd soon be dragging into the Baltimore airport, but if serving in Haiti could land him the coveted Chief Resident position, what choice did he have? He owed it to his father and grandfather.

Dr. Morrison grinned and slapped him on the back. "That's wonderful news? You won't regret it. I promise."

"I hope not, but either way, Port-au-Prince, here I come."

As he exited Dr. Morrison's office, he was too stunned to watch where he was going and collided straight into Allison Smith. He nearly sloshed her coffee all over her lab coat.

He groaned. Allison Smith—the *last* person he wanted to see right now. Thanks to her goody-goody charity work, he'd be stuck sweltering for three long months in a mosquito-infested hellhole. He mumbled an apology.

"Hi, Grant," she said with that perky tone that made every nurse on the surgical ward adore her.

He wanted to snap, "Drop dead!" but he forced himself to suppress the ugly words. Instead, he muttered a cursory hello and strode by too upset to offer so much as a cursory smile.

* * *

Allison turned and stared at Grant's back as he stomped away from her toward the resident call rooms.

What was up with him? He'd glared at her as though he hated her. She racked her brain to think of something, anything, she could have said or done to offend him.

Coming up with nothing, she decided to give him the benefit of the doubt. Maybe he'd been up all night with a challenging patient. Perhaps he'd gotten some bad news. Besides, wasn't Grant Stockdale III known for being temperamental when things didn't go his way? A head nurse once jokingly told her that Grant Stockdale suffered from SRKS—better known as Spoiled Rich Kid Syndrome.

While Allison couldn't deny Grant came out of the womb with a crystal baby bottle in his mouth, she had to grudgingly admit he studied and worked harder than anyone else in the program. Sure, he donned expensive clothes and drove a pricy sports car, but no one could claim he limped through medical school and residency on the Stockdale name alone.

Unlike the snarky nurse, Allison often glimpsed over-the-top kindness and dedication from Grant—like the time he stayed an extra night in the hospital because he'd given his word to a fireman that he wouldn't leave until the man's wife was out of danger from her touch-and-go surgery. Even when Allison coaxed Grant to go home and get some sleep and let her take over the case, he'd refused to leave. "No, I promised Mike I'd stay until his wife was in stable condition, and Stockdales always keep their word."

Her respect for Grant had pole vaulted to a new level that day. But today, he'd plummeted back to an entitled SRKS brat who probably thought he was above conversing with her.

God forbid he waste a moment of his free time on a poor farmer's daughter from the backwoods of Vermont.

He deserves a swift horse kick in the shins.

Fanning the flames of her resentment, she charged down the hall toward the hospital elevator wondering if Grant had been in Morrison's office brown-nosing for the coveted Chief Resident's position—a position she secretly wanted herself.

Not that Grant had anything to worry about. With the Stockdale name, he was a shoo-in for the position, even if her grades and recommendations were just as good. Or better, if you included all the charity work she performed.

But since Grant's father and grandfather had been Chief Surgical Residents and had even paid for the medical school parking garage, how could they *not* pick Grant?

She mashed on the elevator button with unnecessary force. No point getting her hopes up. How could she compete against a member of the Stockdale dynasty?

A twinge of guilt stabbed her for her seething bitterness. Until she had walked a mile in his Brooks Brother wingtips, she didn't know the hurdles he jumped or the burdens he bore.

She resolved to quit judging him and start praying they could somehow develop a cordial professional relationship in their final months together at Hopkins. Besides, she needed to get busy packing—for her upcoming trip to Haiti.

CHAPTER 2

Allison released another yawn and forced herself to shuffle one foot in front of the other into the aisle of the Boeing 737 that had just landed at the Toussaint Louverture International airport in Port-au-Prince, Haiti. After operating into the wee hours of the morning to save an elderly patient, she was now thirty-six hours without sleep and could barely keep her eyes open.

Catching some sleep on the plane proved impossible due to a baby in the row behind her shrieking at decibels loud enough to induce hearing loss. When she managed to doze off despite the deafening racket, the baby's older brother entertained himself by kicking the back of her seat and jarring her awake.

As she lugged her unwieldy carry-on suitcase out of the plane and toward the terminal, a suffocating wave of heat and humidity slammed her. The pungent odor of one especially sweaty passenger assailed her nose as he walked by. Allison held her breath to keep from gagging.

Lord, give me strength and a heart softened and ready to serve others.

She meandered to the "recuperation des bagages" to collect her luggage, then snaked through an endless line of bedraggled travelers all waiting their turn to be interrogated at customs.

After an hour of inching along at the pace of a constipated snail, she reached the front of the line barely able to keep her eyes open, let alone remain standing.

She'd read in her Haitian travel book that locals appreciated those who attempted to speak their language, and it might make sliding through customs without a hitch more likely. Maybe her four years of high school French would pay off.

As she approached a sour-faced customs officer, she offered him a smile and a cheery, "Bonjour."

The customs officer never cracked a smile. Instead, he barked out in heavily accented French Creole, "Avez-vous des drogues illégals dans votre valise?"

It sounded like, "Do I have elegant drogues in my suitcase?"

Because she had greeted the customs officer in French, he assumed she spoke the language fluently.

She chewed on her bottom lip desperate to remember her senior year of high school French.

What the devil was a drogue?

She mopped the sweat dripping from her forehead as impatient eyes glared down at her. What would happen if she just denied having any elegant drogues? After all, if she didn't know what they were, odds were, she didn't have any, right? She stammered, "Je ne l'ai pas apporte des drogues."

He managed the slightest hint of a smile and nodded. "Bien. Avez-vous apporte des armes avec vous?"

Ready to keel over from exhaustion, her thoughts became jumbled, her thinking off-kilter, and she only heard the word arms. She glanced down at her arms and frowned.

Was this a trick question to see if she'd answer honestly?

She replied, "Yes, I brought my arms with me."

The customs agent's eyes widened, and two security guards suddenly charged out from behind closed doors, snatched up her two suitcases, and escorted her none too gently into a small room where her suitcases were opened and thoroughly searched.

Socks, panties, pajama bottoms, bras—nothing was off limits. When they dumped boxes of sanitary napkins and tampons onto a wooden table and pawed through them, she wanted to crawl into her suitcase and slam the lid. Anything to avoid their prying, accusatory eyes.

Not finding anything after their cursory inspection, they explored again, this time looking for hidden compartments.

Finding none, the two intimidating masses of muscle and gun belt glared at her with crossed arms. "Où sont vos armes?"

She lifted up her left arm and pointed at it with her right index finger. "Ici! Voici ma armes."

The two customs agents looked at each other with puzzled expressions and then rolled their eyes in disgust. "Bras. Ce sont vos bras."

Allison recoiled. *They want my bras?*

She'd heard about the corruption of the Haitian government, but she hadn't expected this. Were they wanting her to bribe them to leave her alone? Were bras in short supply in Haiti? What would constitute an acceptable bribe? Or should she take off her bra and hand it to them?

Clearly now beyond delirious from her thirty-seven hours without sleep, she didn't realize how ridiculous her reasoning had become.

She quickly removed her bra by unhooking it in the back and slipping the straps off underneath her T-shirt. She dangled her bribe at the customs officer then leaned against the table to avoid collapsing into a heap of exhaustion.

One of the customs officials seemed to finally figure out the problem and said in broken English, "Armes. Bang, Bang." He imitated the motion and sound of a firing gun with his fingers.

Oh, course! Weapons. As in Hemmingway's book, *Farewell to Arms*. Duh!

She hung her head. No wonder they had pawed through her suitcases so thoroughly. She had confessed to bringing illegal weapons into the country! Guns! "Pardonnez-moi," she mumbled, her cheeks hot with shame. "Je ne comprend pas."

What had possessed her to attempt French after eleven years with no practice—especially after thirty-seven hours with no sleep? Plus, "illegal guns" was hardly in her French 101 textbook.

The agent struggled to explain further. "Bras." He paused as though trying to think of the English word. Failing, he thumped on one of his arms with an exaggerated motion and then on the other. "Mon bras." He then made an exaggerated motion of handing her brassiere back to her with his arm outstretched. He turned to his fellow customs agents and smirked.

Swell. I'm now the laughingstock of Haitian customs.

So bras meant arm, not brassiere. She must have been ill the day body parts were taught in French class.

Note to self: when asked a question by a Haitian customs officer, just shake your head no at every question. No drogues. No arms. No whatever else they came up with.

Thank goodness they hadn't tossed her in a Haitian jail to rot. Out of curiosity she asked, "What does drogues mean?"

The customs agent rubbed his chin. "Her-o-in, marry-juana, co-caine," he said in a thick accent. He then pretended to inject drugs into his elbow crease to demonstrate.

Thank goodness she'd shaken her head no on that one, or they might well have tossed her in a dank cell and thrown away the key.

Why hadn't she simply informed them she didn't speak the language? That stupid tourist book advising her to speak French nearly landed her in jail.

A wave of complete exhaustion overtook her. She leaned against the wall, her eye lids now heavier than medical school tomes. She shut her eyes savoring the moment of respite. Her head bobbed, and for a second, she fell asleep until she felt the none-to-gentle shake of the customs officer.

"Mademoiselle?"

She jolted. "Pardonnez-moi. Mon erreur."

The customs agents stuffed everything back into her suitcase and escorted her out of the dingy interrogation room. They stamped the necessary forms and papers allowing her to leave with her bags.

As she walked away with what little remained of her pride, she overheard one officer comment, "Américain— stupide!" It didn't require a Rick Steves translation dictionary to figure out what that meant.

Once she had dragged her overstuffed, and now poorly packed, tattered suitcase toward the exit of the airport, she peered around looking for a short, toothless black man named Jean-Pierre that the director of the hospital had supposedly sent to transport her to the site of the mission.

Jean-Pierre was supposed to be holding a sign with her name on it. Except he wasn't here.

She stood on tiptoe and scanned the sea of ebony-skinned men who milled about the airport. Many were short and missing teeth, but none held a sign with her name on it. What now?

She glanced at her watch. Two o'clock—the exact time he was supposed to meet her at the airport.

With no phone or internet access at the remote medical missions' site, she couldn't call or e-mail the medical clinic.

What if he didn't show up? She tried to ignore the growing panic that churned in her gut.

She wandered outside the airport in case Jean-Pierre was waiting next to his truck. No luck.

What now? Maybe she should inquire at the information desk if Jean-Pierre had left her a message.

When she re-entered the airport, she noticed three ruffians eyeing her. Swell. She grabbed her luggage and dashed to stand next to a uniformed security official. Surely they wouldn't rob her in front of an armed officer.

After the thugs wandered away, she located the information desk, and thankfully, the woman spoke English. No one had left her a message. She clutched her suitcase and decided she had no choice but to wait for Jean-Pierre to show up.

From her mission trip to Guatemala, she remembered that Central Americans took a more leisurely approach to time than did Americans. Most didn't own a watch. Her driver might not show up until two-thirty or even three.

After her intimidating customs interrogation, she released a weary sigh and collapsed into the only unoccupied seat—a plastic chair with a large crack. When she twisted in the seat the crack pinched her bottom. No wonder no one else wanted this chair.

With thugs milling around the airport, she did her best to stay awake, though she knew she had briefly nodded off several times. At least with the security officer close by, no one had dared to steal her luggage.

Every few minutes she scanned the airport and wandered outside to look for Jean-Pierre. So far, no trace of him—and no sign with her name on it.

A bead of sweat meandered its way down the side of her face. *Whew! It is hot down here.*

She stood to scout out a bathroom.

That's when she noticed someone who resembled Grant Stockdale. She stared at the man. It *couldn't* be Grant. He'd told her last month he'd signed up for the plastic surgery rotation.

No surprise there! Probably Mr. Moneybags was already drooling over the handsome salary he could earn performing facelifts, breast augmentations, and nose jobs on the political elite in the D.C area.

No way would Mr. Donated-a-Science-Building reduce himself to three months in Haiti when his idea of roughing it likely entailed a week with no housekeeper to scrub his marble-tiled bathroom floors or launder his designer jeans.

As the man strode in her direction, she couldn't help but stare. Either Grant had an identical twin, or it *was* Grant.

She stared as he approached. It *was* Grant. Had his plastics rotation fallen through? Could Dr. Morrison have somehow persuaded him to take this elective instead?

Hmm. Perhaps that's why he acted so grumpy when she'd seen him outside Morrison's office last week. The Dean must have bullied him into signing up for Haiti! She had to smile.

She couldn't imagine Grant Stockdale III living in such oppressive heat and squaller. Three long months with no air conditioning, smartphone, or Internet connection? No cook, maid, or fancy BMW? Talk about a shock to his system!

Her sophisticated classmate sure looked out-of-place as he strolled through the airport. Perhaps she should say hello and inform him their ride was nowhere to be found.

She rose from her chair dreading the awkward encounter. Besides working on surgical cases together, she and Grant never hung out together outside of the hospital. They were from social circles miles apart, and they both knew it. Grant attracted beautiful women who hung on his every word.

She was convinced these gold diggers only wanted a piece of the Stockdale name and fortune, but since she didn't know the hearts of the women—or Grant—she tried not to judge.

Despite the gaggle of attractive nurses and unit clerks who clucked around him as though he were a celebrity, Grant never seemed to show a particular interest in any of them. His demeanor was always polite, but he remained detached and analytical, as though immune to the adoring brood who swirled around him like contestants on *The Bachelor*. She'd overheard a classmate complaining she'd asked him out, and they'd gone to a movie and dinner, but he never reciprocated the offer.

He'd certainly never shown any interest in her. Not that she had any right to expect it, coming from her background. Men like him never settled for women like her—a lesson she'd learned the hard way.

She released a sigh.

If she was forced to work with Grant for three months, she might as well get the awkward first interaction over with.

Grant stood next to his luxury Louis Vuitton luggage and glanced around the airport as though looking for someone. Jean-Pierre, no doubt. He glanced down at his Burberry watch and frowned.

Mr. Punctuality was in for a rude awakening when he was forced to adapt to the relaxed standards of this part of the world.

She suddenly noticed the same three thugs who had earlier swirled around her eyeing Grant. If he wasn't careful, he'd be robbed of that ritzy watch and pricey luggage. Didn't he know better than flaunt his wealth in such an impoverished country?

He was asking for it! As she rushed toward Grant to warn him to take off his expensive watch and hide it, she couldn't help but appreciate what a handsome figure he cut.

His muscular chest streamlined down to narrow hips, and his long legs were showcased to perfection in tailored trousers. A chiseled chin and aquiline nose projected confident masculinity. Black curls dancing across his forehead softened his erudite profile, while large, expressive eyes—the color of dark chocolate—radiated intelligence. And talk about a perfect smile! Even his walk exuded sophistication.

True confessions: she'd had a crush on Grant for four years now, but after her disastrous relationship with Alexander, she had no business thinking she'd ever stand a chance with a man as rich as Grant. Best keep things strictly professional.

No way would a Stockdale settle for a farm girl whose brief claim to fame was her one-year stint as "Miss Orleans County Dairy Queen." And don't forget her hometown of Coventry took in all the trash for the entire state of Vermont. Even if the Stockdales knew nothing about "Mount Trashmore", they'd probably already selected the perfect mate for Grant—the debutante daughter of a pharmaceutical dynasty who attended their elite country club, or the daughter of a college president.

The thugs descended on Grant and were now only a few yards behind him. His impending danger jerked her thoughts back to reality and she shouted, "Grant! Look out! Thugs behind you."

The three burly brutes pounced on Grant. One kept his hand over Grant's mouth, and another reached for his watch. A third grabbed his luggage.

Allison let out a blood-curdling shriek to draw the attention of the security officer. When he looked in her direction, she pointed toward the thieves. The officer sprang into action shouting and raising his gun.

Before he could intervene, however, Grant slammed his elbow into one thief's solar plexus leaving him bent at the waist and howling. He stomped on the foot of the second thief, who pulled back hopping on his good foot and clutching the injured foot. Then Grant whipped around with a karate kick and landed the third would-be luggage thief on his back.

The thugs caught a glimpse at the security officer running toward them with his gun extended, and they bolted for the exit. The officer charged after them in hot pursuit.

Grant brushed off his shirt as though trying to rid himself of any vestiges of his encounter with his assailants. He then spun around to face her wide-eyed. "Allison Smith? What are *you* doing in Haiti?"

O-kay! Is that how they'd taught him to greet people at that hoity-toity prep school he attended? Phillips Exeter, wasn't it? How about a thank you for warning him about the thugs!

She controlled her tongue and responded, "Apparently, I'm signed up for the same Tropical Missions elective as you. I thought you signed up for Techniques in Plastic Surgery."

Grant averted his eyes. "You and me both. Unfortunately, Dr. Morrison insisted it would broaden my horizons to see how the destitute of the world live. He claims I'll return a changed man." Grant etched imaginary quotation marks with his fingers around the words 'broaden my horizons' and 'changed man'.

He gestured toward the airport exit where the assailants had escaped. "If those thugs represent Haiti's idea of hospitality, my 'changed man' may come in the form of a neck fracture or cracked jaw."

"I certainly hope not. In fact, I'm hoping those thugs are the end of our misadventures. My first hour here wasn't so great, either."

He raised a quizzical brow. "Really? What happened to you?"

"Let's just say I nearly landed in a Haitian jail before I figured out the word 'drogue' means drugs and 'armes' means weapons. Honestly, I was so exhausted from not sleeping a wink in thirty-seven hours, I couldn't remember my high school French worth a flip."

She then shared her embarrassing gesture of offering the customs agent her brassiere.

He roared with laughter. "What a story! Cheer up, if push came to shove, I would have bailed you out."

She crossed her arms. "Gee, thanks, Grant. Good to know I wouldn't rot in Haitian purgatory forever."

She eyed him suspiciously. How had *he* made it through customs so quickly? Had he bribed the agents with a hefty wad of cash? Maybe with his pricy Harvard education, he was fluent in French and six other languages.

When she asked if he was proficient in French, he responded, "Not a bit. I took Latin all four years of high school, and then four years of Chinese in college."

She put her hands on her hips. "So how come *you* didn't get dragged into an interrogation room and forced to have your unmentionables pawed through?"

He offered an infuriating shrug. "I just kept saying 'no' to whatever they asked. I didn't have a clue what the questions were, but I nodded as though I understood."

She harrumphed. "That's what I get for trying to impress them with my French. What was I thinking? I haven't spoken it since I was seventeen." She thumped her tourist book. "This useless book said if I attempted to speak their language, it would endear me to the locals. Ha! It nearly landed me in jail!"

He rubbed his chin, unable to hold back a chuckle. "Sounds like Haitian hospitality left a lot to be desired for both of us. I far prefer the pineapple smoothie and orchid lei I received from a shapely hula dancer when I first arrived in Hawaii last year. Now that's *my* idea of hospitality."

"Here in Haiti, we'll have to replace the pineapple smoothie with a bottle of mosquito repellant."

"Right! Even if it doesn't protect us from mosquitoes, we can spray it into the eyes of future ruffians," he said with a wink.

She pantomimed squirting the bug repellant into the eyes of the three thieves. "I may be reduced to using bug spray to protect myself, but you relied on karate. Where'd you learn all those self-defense moves?"

"Harvard," he said, dragging his luggage closer. "I took an elective in self-defense for my P.E credit."

"I was impressed, and I bet your professor would be proud of your performance today." She scowled. "Far more than my high school French teacher would be of mine."

His expression soured. "Actually, he probably would have flunked me."

Noting her shocked expression, he explained. "Lesson number one in self-defense? Don't set yourself up as easy prey." He shook his head as though disgusted with himself. "I meant to tuck my watch into my pants pocket when the plane landed, and if I'd had more than a week's notice that I was heading to Haiti, I would have purchased some beat-up luggage like yours at Goodwill. Something no one would want to steal."

He must have seen her insulted expression for he put up a hand. "Wait! That came out wrong. I meant…"

"Oh, I know what you meant," she snapped, arms crossed.

Here she thought they were getting along great—like friends commiserating about their dreadful experiences at the airport—and he had to bring up their obvious wealth difference.

He thought she was low-class. Like everything she owned was from Goodwill and beneath the highbrow Stockdales with their designer clothes, hoity-toity luggage, and pricy watches.

He might be rich, smart, and gorgeous, but Grant Stockdale III was a jackass. An arrogant, full-of-himself jerk. With a capital J!

CHAPTER 3

Grant reached for her arm. "Allison, wait. I don't think you do understand what I meant. I meant, if I didn't want to call attention to myself, I shouldn't have brought fancy luggage. You were the smart one. You brought every day, beat-up bags. I didn't mean it as a put-down, Allison. Honest."

She wasn't sure she believed him, and the "beat-up bags" were all she owned! And yes, she *had* purchased them at Goodwill! But since he'd apologized—sort of—she decided to let it go. Since she'd always felt poor and unsophisticated next to this privileged Adonis, perhaps she *had* overreacted. Besides, they had to work together for the next three months. Might as well not start off on bad terms. She forced herself to smile. "Apology accepted."

She glanced around the airport then up at Grant. "Have you seen any signs of our driver?"

He raked a hand through his hair. "Jean-Pierre? Afraid not, but I've read Haitians aren't as strict about punctuality as we Americans."

He held up a paperback travel book about Haiti and thumped it. "I tried to learn as much as I could on the plane."

She pulled out a copy of the exact same book from her carry-on and waved it back at him. "Ditto."

"Brilliant minds think alike, I see."

"In fact, "I've been practicing my French Creole." She cleared her throat. "Bonswa mwen rele Allison."

He responded, "Mwen rele Grant."

"Perfect. At least we can introduce ourselves, though I didn't find the Creole word for appendicitis or incarcerated inguinal hernia. Did you?"

"Come to think of it, no," he responded with a chuckle. He glanced at his watch and his lips thinned. "If our driver never shows up, we may not *need* to know any Creole terminology." He crossed his arms. "An hour late. Isn't that unacceptable, even for a laid-back country like Haiti?"

She shrugged and glanced around once more, hoping to see Jean-Pierre and his sign.

"You know, I read in my tourist book about these colorful mini-buses called tap-taps. Maybe we could take one of those to the mission site.

Grant's brow rose as though questioning her sanity.

"Did you miss the paragraph where the State Department recommended *not* riding in tap-taps? Apparently, they're ridiculously overcrowded, mechanically unsound, and owned by a horrendous driver with a track record for accidents."

She tapped her foot in annoyance. "Okay. You have a *better* idea? There's no internet and no cell phone access at the mission site, so we can't call and find out where our driver is. I, for one, have no intention of spending the next three months at the airport—or walking to the clinic."

Grant raked a hand through his hair tousling his curls. "Let's give the guy one more hour, and if he hasn't shown up by then, we'll look into hiring a private driver."

A scruffy man reeking of body odor dragged a burlap sack bulging with clothes past them. Grant scrunched his nose. "That smell is so strong it almost knocks me over."

"Almost as foul as the abscess I operated on last week."

He nodded. "A fringe benefit of our occupation, I'm afraid."

Allison smiled. "Cheer up! If we get short on anesthesia at the mission, we can always resort to extreme body odor to knock people out."

He pointed at her. "Bingo."

Grant glanced around the airport again, wishing, praying, this Jean-Pierre character would magically appear holding a sign with their names on it. Lollygagging around a stifling hot airport with thieves ready to rip off his luggage had become intolerable. After eight years of medical school and residency at a frenetic pace, sitting around the airport doing nothing left him feeling like a caged cheetah. He paced back and forth.

Where was Jean-Pierre?

Idle time gave him too much time to think. And worry. Now that Allison had signed up for the Haitian trip as well, would it ruin his chances for the Chief Resident position? Plus, he had never performed surgery in such primitive conditions.

Would the surgical suite be sterile? Would they have the necessary scalpels, suction, cautery, and sutures?

What kind of anesthesia did they use in a rural third-world country? Did they resort to biting on nails or whiffing ether? Worse, he'd never had to diagnose appendicitis or diverticular abscesses without the luxury of a CT scanner. What if he screwed up and killed somebody?

"Grant, sit down and relax." Allison patted the seat next to her. "We'll be putting in long hours soon. Besides, pacing won't make Jean-Pierre appear any sooner."

"Relax? I'm losing my sanity sitting around this stifling airport with nothing to do."

She patted the plastic chair next to her and ordered, "Sit down! You're driving *me* crazy with all that pacing."

The chair looked like it had been salvaged from a dump, but he flopped into it and did his best to sit still. Within five minutes, his leg thumped like a bass drummer.

She pushed down his thigh forcefully. "Stop that! You make me nervous with your jiggling."

He forced himself to stop—for a minute or so.

She reached over and gripped his hand. "Grant, what are you so anxious about?"

Besides being dumped in a country where he didn't speak the language, was nearly robbed, and now had no ride to some half-baked surgical clinic? Besides not knowing if he'd wind up tolerating all the heat and deprivation for nothing if Allison was chosen for Chief Surgical Resident instead of him? Not a thing!

Not wanting to look like a wuss, he shrugged. "I'm just not used to sitting around doing absolutely nothing, that's all."

She must not have fallen for his lame excuse because she said, "Look, I'm nervous about these next three months, too. No CT scanners. No internet. No pathology lab. I feel like we're practicing in the dark ages."

"Right up there with bloodletting and medicinal leeches," he agreed.

He was grateful he wasn't the only one terrified to make surgical decisions without the benefit of advanced X-rays and laboratory support.

"We'll just have to do the best we can and obtain second opinions from each other until we bolster our confidence." She smiled up at him. "I'm glad I'll have you there to consult with on difficult cases."

Truthfully, he also liked the idea of discussing challenging cases with Allison before diving full speed ahead with a scalpel.

While peeved at her for potentially swiping his Chief Residency position, he couldn't deny Allison was a levelheaded, competent surgeon. In fact, if he had to be stuck in Haiti for three months, she was the one surgeon from their class he'd most trust to collaborate with on challenging cases.

"On a positive note, Dr. Morrison said since we won't have to compete with all the other residents and interns and for cases, we'll get to perform lots of surgeries in the next three months. We'll get loads of practice."

Grant shrugged, unconvinced. Before he could stop himself, he muttered, "We won't have to compete with all the others because none of them were stupid enough to sign up for this rotation."

She popped him on the arm. "Hey! I signed up for it, and I'm not stupid! We need to focus on the positive, so we don't get discouraged from the heat and primitive conditions."

"You're right." He rubbed his arm and retorted with a grin, "I'm positive I don't like sitting around in a sweltering airport."

She wagged a scolding finger in his face. "I mean it, Grant! No complaining. Remember—positive attitude."

He rolled his eyes but couldn't help but smile at her schoolmarmish tone.

After a lag in the conversation, Allison said, "It's clear you don't want to be here, so why did you sign up, anyhow? Did your plastics rotation fall through at the last minute?"

He offered a non-committal shrug. No way could he tell her he only signed up to swipe the Chief Surgical Resident position from her!

Undeterred, she pushed further. "Couldn't you just tell Dr. Morrison you weren't interested? There must be other electives available."

He sucked in a deep breath as he pondered his response. He shrugged and then resorted back to Dr. Morrison's claim that it would broaden his worldview and make him a better man.

Narrow eyes bore into his. Her raised eyebrow suggested she didn't buy a word of it. Thankfully, she said nothing.

He glanced at his watch again, stood, and stretched before insisting, "I'm afraid Jean-Pierre has stood us up. Why don't we see if we can drum up a taxi or a private driver?"

"You have any Haitian money?"

He patted his backpack. "Right here. I exchanged five hundred dollars for gourdes once I made it through customs."

They rounded up their luggage and lugged it outside the airport. Four run-down tap-taps painted in elaborate swirls of garish orange, turquoise, and neon green sat parked in front of the airport. Every tap-tap was crammed with passengers. Worse, the back of one van had no door. Instead, two planks of plywood stuck out the back with even more passengers sitting on the planks! What if the driver had to slam on his brakes? All those plank passengers would land in the middle of the road. The rickety old van held at least fifty people, all crammed in like pickles in a jar. No way would he ride in one of those.

As though reading his mind, Allison said, "Why don't I ask at the information desk if there are any private drivers? You wait here and guard our luggage. Since I speak a bit of French, it makes sense for me to inquire."

He nodded. In the ten minutes she was gone, he'd seen donkeys, horses, pedestrians, mopeds, and a ton of rickety bicycles traveling on the potholed road. An overcrowded tap-tap maneuvered around a three-ring-circus of travelers.

Allison returned with a glum expression. "The lady said the two private cab drivers were already hired out for the day. She predicted it would be hours before either returned."

Grant muttered under his breath. At this point, he was ready to fly back home and call off this fiasco. At least he could tell Morrison he'd been *willing* to go. Surely that would count for something, wouldn't it? Maybe he could debride foot ulcers at the homeless shelter to win Morrison's favor instead.

Just then, a rickety Ford truck pulled up to the curb, and a short smiling man with missing teeth hollered with a thick accent, "All-i-son Smith and Grant Stockdale?"

Allison and Grant looked at each other and grinned.

Jean-Pierre.

An aria by Andrew Lloyd Weber would not have sounded as sweet as Jean-Pierre's voice calling out their names.

They waved then dragged their luggage to his dilapidated truck. Jean-Pierre opened the back to accommodate their suitcases. After hoisting the luggage into the bed of the truck, he smiled and gestured for them to get in.

Allison offered to let Grant have the front passenger seat since the legroom was greater. He willingly obliged. He'd been cramped during his long flight from Baltimore, and he didn't relish being squashed again during the long drive to the clinic.

Jean-Pierre attempted to start his ancient Ford truck three times. A sputtering and rattling engine released a plume of putrid exhaust. Finally, the rumble of an engine turning over brought the vehicle to life.

The driver patted the dashboard of his truck and with a grin cooed, "Good girl, Angelina. You did it."

He'd named this dilapidated rust bucket Angelina? Little Angel. It was anything but! Grant eyed the guy suspiciously. Was he deranged? On drugs? Were they safe to ride with him?

He glanced to the backseat to read Allison's reaction. Worried eyes stared back at him. Since the ancient truck had struggled to start, would it manage to traverse the hundred-plus miles to the surgical clinic without conking out?

They could end up stranded in the middle of nowhere with those mangey rabid dogs Dr. Morrison mentioned roaming around the countryside to keep them company.

The truck released a backfire as loud as a gunshot and then jerked into motion. With a carefree smile, Jean-Pierre said in broken English, "I sorry for your bad wait. Angelina tire go, how I say it?" He gestured with his hands a circle becoming deflated.

"Flat," Allison said. "You got a flat tire on the way?"

He nodded. "Oui. Flat tire make Jean-Pierre late. Very late. So sorry."

As the truck meandered around several bicycle-powered carts and tap-taps, Allison reassured him, "You're here now. That's all that matters."

He offered a warm smile, and despite his delay and beat-up vehicle, Grant found himself warming up to the guy. While obviously poor, he exuded happiness.

As the truck jostled over ruts, potholes, and trash in the road for several miles, Jean-Pierre informed them he'd worked for the clinic for five years. In broken English, he told of how proud he was of all the mission had accomplished for the locals, and what a great boss Dr. Jones was. "He good man. Very good man."

They jostled on past miles of dilapidated shacks—some no larger than his family's pool table. A wave of guilt pricked his conscience that he lived so comfortably when barefoot children dressed in little more than rags ran in and out of tar paper shacks with collapsing rooves. The stench of raw sewage running in the ditch next to the road assailed his nostrils.

An entire hillside was landscaped with hovels and fallen shacks, each seemingly worse than the last.

Two boys, probably no older than eight, emerged from a house made of empty cardboard boxes duct-taped together. The children smiled and waved at Jean-Pierre. The older man offered them a wave and then tossed out a loaf of bread and a box of crackers stashed underneath the seat.

As they drove on, Jean-Pierre's expression turned sober. "Poor boys. No Momma. No Papa. All alone."

"But they can't be more than eight. Who looks after them?" Allison asked, her expression horrified.

"They twelve. No food. Makes them small, oui?"

Grant turned back and stared at the boys. No one should have to live like that—least of all children. On impulse, he opened his carry-on, pulled out some gourdes and tossed a handful toward the boys.

The boys ran toward the truck, grabbed the money, and hollered, "Merci," with huge smiles on their faces.

Allison made no comment about his spontaneous gesture of compassion. Instead, she asked Jean-Pierre, "How many orphans are there in Haiti?"

His face puckered as though not understanding.

Allison rephrased her question, this time speaking French.

"Thousands. The earthquake, women die having baby. No doctor. No money. Many, many children no parent."

Allison's eyes pooled with tears. "It's all so overwhelming. So much poverty."

Jean-Pierre seemed to get the gist of her comment. "Much sadness, oui? Dr. Jones wants to build home for children. No money to build yet, but we feed as many as we can."

Grant's heart inwardly wept at the memory of those two small boys so grateful for the little bit of money he'd tossed their way.

Surely if people at his parent's country club, charitable foundation, and Women's Aid society at church saw all this, they'd be more than glad to contribute toward an orphanage. He'd see what he could do once he returned to the States.

Twenty minutes into their bumpy journey, Jean-Pierre turned into a driveway that was so rutty it left Grant having to hold on for dear life to avoid whacking his head on the passenger window.

Angelina rumbled to a stop in front of a storehouse of some kind, and Jean-Pierre jumped out. "I get supplies. Back soon."

"I'll give you a hand," Grant offered. As he climbed out of the truck, he noticed his front passenger door was missing its bottom hinge. The door hung by only a rusty upper hinge. Hoping he didn't knock the door off completely, he shut the door carefully.

Allison's door wasn't much better. She had to lift it and slam it gingerly to make it close at all.

"How old do you think this junkheap is?" he whispered to Allison.

She circled the truck and inspected it. "I'm guessing it was made in 1996."

He lifted a brow. "How would you know that?"

She smiled impishly. "You forget—I'm a farmer's daughter. My dad had one just like this once. They hold up really well, though Dad finally traded his in for a newer model a few years back."

Jean-Pierre returned with a rickety dolly loaded down with bandages, disinfectants, bags of IV fluids, and medications. He arranged and then rearranged the boxes.

Try as he might, the supplies would not all fit into the bed of the truck. Hands on his hips, he shook his head in defeat. "Three more boxes, but no fit. I must come back tomorrow and get them."

Judging from the deplorable condition of the truck, Grant didn't want to risk any necessary surgical supplies not making it to the clinic—especially since they would need the supplies to operate.

As though reading his mind, Allison said, "Grant and I can both squeeze next to each other in the front seat. If we do that, all of the supplies will fit in the back seat where I was sitting."

Jean-Pierre's face brightened into a wide grin. "You do that for Jean-Pierre?"

Allison assured him that while the truck was cramped, they would be comfortable enough to make it to the surgical clinic. Grant concurred.

Jean-Pierre and Grant packed in the three extra boxes of supplies where Allison previously sat.

If no one breathed or moved, the boxes might make it to the clinic in one trip—providing Angelina cooperated.

Jean-Pierre grinned and rubbed his hands together with a gesture of satisfaction. "This good. Very, very good."

As Allison attempted to sit next to Grant in the front seat crammed against the door with the missing hinge, Grant worried the door might fall off and she'd fall out.

"There's no bottom hinge, and the top one is all rust," Grant whispered to her. "It can't withstand any weight on it at all, or you'll likely land in the ditch. He patted the top of his legs. "As tiny as you are, you can just sit on my lap. It will be safer than either of us leaning against that door."

Eyeing the foul-smelling sewage flowing in a gutter no more than two feet from the side of the road, she readily agreed.

She may be from a town that recycled trash, but she drew the line at landing in raw sewage! "I sure don't want to end up down there," she whispered back, motioning with her head toward the sewage.

She climbed in and sat primly between his legs with her back rigid and pulled as far away from Grant's chest as possible.

Despite her obvious unease with the cramped seating, she informed Jean-Pierre, "I'm fine," and gave him a thumbs-up sign.

Angelina stalled out twice, but on the third try, with much coaxing and encouragement from Jean-Pierre, she jolted to life, and they were off.

At first, Allison did her best to sit with as little body contact between them as possible, but as the truck jerked to avoid a pothole or dog, Grant instinctively pulled her tight against him so she wouldn't slam her head against the dashboard or passenger door. Not wanting her to get the wrong idea, he whispered, "I'm not being forward. I just don't want you getting a concussion when Jean-Pierre darts around dogs and chickens in the road."

As though accepting that it was dangerous to sit so primly, her body relaxed, and she leaned against his chest. He wrapped his arms around her waist to hold her securely in position.

Grant knew from talk amongst his classmates that any attempt on their part to make it to second base with Allison was always quickly thwarted. Secretly, he admired her convictions, and truth be told, when it came time to pick a wife, he'd far prefer one who hadn't made the rounds of all his buddies and classmates. Or been the brunt of Jeremy's locker room talk. Thomas labeled Allison the "Ice Queen".

Grant suspected it had more to do with her moral principles than frigidity. After all, he daily witnessed how compassionate she was with all her patients.

Surely someone like that would be warm and loving once she met a man she trusted and loved. Someone who wasn't just trying to gain bragging rights.

Not that it mattered to him. Since they would be working together closely for the next three months, it would be far safer to keep their interactions strictly professional, anyhow.

While Allison was pretty—beautiful, even—in a wholesome, Kansas-corn-queen way—he appreciated that they had always worked together as colleagues—professionals—with no hidden agendas or ulterior motives.

Unlike his recent interaction with a classmate, Catherine. She had invited him over to her apartment to work on a class presentation about colon cancer awareness.

When he'd arrived, she'd greeted him at the door in a slinky, low-cut mini dress that left little to the imagination. She'd then offered him a glass of wine and scooted inappropriately close to him on the couch as they reviewed their PowerPoint presentation.

While Jeremy—and probably eighty percent of his male classmates—would thank their lucky stars a woman as beautiful as Catherine had thrown herself at him, Grant felt manipulated. And completely turned off.

Catherine had invited him to her apartment on false pretenses. Was she going for bragging rights that she had been the one to bed the impenetrable Grant Stockdale?

More times than he cared to admit, Grant overheard nurses and female classmates talking about what a "catch" he was because he was from an established wealthy family, or because he was good-looking and smart. He didn't want someone to choose him because of superficial values like wealth, attractiveness, or even IQ.

Was it too much to want someone to love him for him—even if he was poor, nerdy, or merely average in looks or IQ?

Perhaps it was a pipe dream, but he wanted a marriage like his parents had—based on love of family, shared hobbies, community service, faith, and supporting one another. While his mother had given up her career as an ICU nurse after Grant's older sister was born, his father always treated her as an equal, so she was a loyal and devoted companion.

People always told him being wealthy, well-educated, and handsome were blessings, but sometimes Grant wondered if anyone liked him for him. Especially women. He was tired of being ogled at, whispered about, and treated as though he were some lottery prize. Consequently, he remained aloof and suspicious of a woman's motives.

In some ways, a three-month retreat to Haiti with an above-board colleague who clearly had no romantic designs on him would be a nice change.

Jean-Pierre suddenly slammed on the brakes to avoid hitting a staggering pedestrian with a rum bottle. Jarred out of his musings, Grant wrapped his arms around Allison's shoulders tightly to keep her from being flung onto the windshield.

"Thanks," she whispered in his ear.

He could feel her body relaxing against him, as though she knew she could depend on him to keep her safe. Strangely, her simple trust in him stirred up both a desire to protect her and a stronger desire to maintain her good opinion of him.

With that in mind, he wrapped his arms more securely around her shoulders and whispered, "Don't worry, I'll keep you steady."

As the Ford bumped along, he found himself enjoying his newfound role as protector.

Her small body fit against his perfectly, and the enticing aroma of coconut that emanated from her hair made him want to hold her even closer.

The warmth of her thighs pushed against him was arousing, but he forced himself to keep his hands wrapped chastely around her shoulders. He couldn't, however, resist inhaling another whiff of her coconut shampoo.

I could fall for a girl like Allison.

His heart jolted. Where had that crazy notion come from?

While he'd always found Allison spunky and attractive, he felt sure she held a low opinion of him—like she believed all the jokes about him being a spoiled rich kid.

He'd always tried his hardest to prove he had not gotten where he was solely because of family connections. He studied harder, worked longer hours, and did everything in his power to prove he wasn't at Hopkins due to family connections alone. But the rumors persisted, and no doubt Allison believed them.

Although…he frequently caught her staring at him when she thought he wouldn't notice. If he turned to acknowledge her, she always darted her eyes away, and her cheeks would flush. He suspected she found him attractive, but for whatever reason, unlike Catherine, she'd never acted on that attraction.

It was just as well if they would be working together for three months in tight quarters.

When the truck jutted over a huge rut in the road, Grant cradled her tightly against him, and her head bounced on his chest.

When they reached a road sign informing them they still had another eighty kilometers to go, Grant groaned. At this rate, it would be dark before they arrived.

He sucked in a deep breath and savored the intoxicating smell of Allison's hair. It sure beat the reek of the raw sewage flowing in the gutter next to the road.

As Grant wrapped his arms snugly around her, Allison tried to ignore the feeling of safety those strong arms evoked. After her dreadful customs interrogation, and her fear she was stranded at an unsafe airport, she had to admit having Grant there to face the challenges with her felt comforting.

She tried to ignore the feel of his thighs pressed against hers, but she couldn't ignore the heady rush of whiffing his woodsy—and no doubt expensive—aftershave. Then again, even the cheapest of colognes would be a vast improvement over the stench of raw sewage flowing down the ditches of many a shantytown.

As she leaned back against Grant's chest soaking in the safety of his arms, she felt her eyelids droop as though made of brick. Her hectic all-nighter in the OR, her long flight and customs interrogation, followed by her endless wait for Jean-Pierre had finally caught up with her.

I'll just rest my eyes for a teeny tiny second...

* * *

"Allison? We're here."

A whispered voice drifted into the sedated crevices of her foggy brain, but she ignored it.

Go away and let me sleep.

The voice, more insistent now, was accompanied by gentle shaking. "Allison? Time to wake up."

She forced one heavy eyelid to open and then the other. Reality slammed her when she realized not only had she cradled against Grant with her head snuggled on his chest, but she had also somehow wrapped her arms around his waist.

Good Lord! How had that happened?

She bolted upright and attempted to straighten her hair. "I-I'm sorry for lying on you like that."

He eyed her futile attempts to fix her hair and grinned. "I'm afraid after the day we've had, your hair is a lost cause."

She felt her cheeks flame. Had she really slept snuggled up to him? What if she'd snored, or worse yet, drooled on him?

"How long have I been sleeping?"

He shrugged. "A little over an hour."

Flustered, she turned away from him and attempted to open the dilapidated passenger door.

"Here, let me get that for you," Grant said, lifting the door handle and pushing carefully until its rusty hinge creaked open.

He leaned in and whispered, "Be careful getting out, or the door will fall off."

"That's why I leaned on you so much," she whispered back, hoping to save face. "I didn't want to land in the ditch." With any luck, he'd believe that was the reason for her way-too-chummy posture.

He nodded. "Smart girl."

She crawled out of the truck. "I'm sorry I fell asleep on you like that. I must have been a total dead weight."

He shrugged. "No big deal. It's not like you're an elephant."

"Gee, thanks, Grant! Nice to know I'm one step above a pachyderm in your estimation."

He winked at her. "I do have a way with the ladies, don't I?"

She crossed her arms in mock outrage. "Don't you, though!"

He climbed out of the truck then carefully lifted and closed the broken door.

Jean-Pierre walked around to their side of Angelina and with a flourish of his arm said, "Voila, the Missions!"

Allison eyed a rutty dirt driveway that led to a surprisingly cheery yellow-brick surgical clinic. A stone's throw away from the clinic stood a small brick house.

While a far cry from the opulence of a Hopkins facility, at least there was no raw sewage flowing nearby.

As they strolled toward the front door, a massive iguana ambled along the side of the driveway. It stopped to stare at them as though curious then ambled on his way as though more interested in snagging up a fallen mango for his dinner than meeting new guests.

"Wow! Look at that iguana!" Grant said, pointing at the alligator-sized lizard. "I have never seen one that big."

"Oui. He live near clinic for years," Jean-Pierre said in his broken English. "We call him Fred."

Grant and Allison looked at each other and smiled.

Fred?

The front door opened, and a distinguished, grey-haired man with a trim moustache and a huge smile rushed out and extended open arms.

He looked friendly enough. She hoped he was competent, or she was in for a long three months.

CHAPTER 4

"Welcome! We're so glad to have you join us, Allison. I'm Dr. Jones, the director of the clinic." He pulled her in for a warm hug then turned to Grant, and with a quizzical expression asked, "And who might you be?"

Grant froze. Had Dr. Morrison not gotten word to the clinic that he was coming?

"Dr. Morrison said he notified you I was joining the surgical team for three months."

"I didn't get the message, but it's still wonderful news!" Dr. Jones clapped his hands in glee. "There is so much to be done around here. We always need more surgeons."

"But you had no idea I was coming?" Grant asked, still flummoxed.

Dr. Jones chuckled. "News makes it into the history books before it meanders to our little clinic. With no phone or internet service, we have to rely on snail mail, and it is sketchy at best. Usually Jean-Pierre picks it up at the Post office every couple of weeks." He shook Grant's hand warmly and insisted, "Trust me, we are delighted to have you join us."

"So you actually need two surgeons?" Grant pressed, hating to swelter in this insufferable heat for three long months doing nothing.

Dr. Jones made eye contact with Jean-Pierre and the two men roared with laughter. "You think we can use two surgeons instead of one, Jean-Pierre?"

"Oui. Some days, need ten surgeons."

Grant nodded in relief.

A plump, middle-aged redhead entered the doorway and welcomed them with a warm smile. "Hi, I'm Judy Jones, and I have prepared a mini-feast for your first day in Haiti." She gestured for them to come in. "You, too, Jean-Pierre. You earned a hearty meal by picking up our American friends and the clinic supplies this afternoon."

Jean-Pierre gratefully obliged and joined Grant and Allison as they walked into a cozy living room.

Judy offered them sanitizing wipes to clean their hands. "I'm sure you're both dusty and exhausted from your long trip."

Grant glanced over at Allison and grinned. "Some of us are more exhausted than others. One of us took a long nap in the truck."

Judy turned to Allison with wide eyes. "You were able to fall asleep on that awful road? With all those ruts, it's practically a roller coaster."

Allison shrugged. "I've trained myself to sleep anywhere."

"Since your hours are erratic as a surgeon, that's a desirable trait to have," Judy mused.

"My father once found me asleep on a pile of hay after my parents had looked over an hour for me."

"Really? How old were you?" Judy asked.

Allison flushed. "Eleven."

They all laughed.

"I'm glad you can fall asleep easily because conditions in the cabin aren't exactly the Ritz-Carlton," Judy confessed.

"Luckily, you'll be so tired, you'll be grateful to lie down at all," Dr. Jones mused. He offered his wife a mock glare. "And the sleeping conditions aren't *that* bad. We provide a mattress, pillow, blanket, and mosquito netting. What more could they want?" he asked with raised palms.

Judy rolled her eyes. "Give me a break! A college dorm room is more luxurious."

Grant played along. "What? No Jacuzzi? No silk sheets? No foil-wrapped chocolate on my pillow?" He stood and motioned his arms as though pretending to leave. "I'm out of here."

Judy chuckled. "No hot water either, I'm afraid. Your showers consist of either buckets of cold water dumped over your head, or a swim in the creek that's a short distance from here. You'll quickly learn to appreciate that creek. The water feels cool and refreshing when it evaporates off you on a hot afternoon."

"I'll bet," Allison said.

Grant internally groaned. For him, a shower—the hotter the better—was the only way to start a day. It woke him up and relaxed his muscles. But hey, if Dr. Jones had adjusted to cold showers, so could he. Surely, he could endure anything for three months.

Just then, a small Haitian boy with huge brown eyes exited the kitchen and came into the room. He glanced up at Grant and Allison as though assessing if they were friend or foe. He hid behind Mrs. Jones and then peaked around her to check out the new guests.

Allison squatted down to the boy's level and gestured toward herself. "Hi, I'm Allison." Mrs. Jones introduced the boy as Raphael.

"He's one of Haiti's many orphans, and he lives next door, so I try to look out for him. I invited him to join us for dinner."

Mrs. Jones bent down and gave Raphael a hug. "I didn't have to do much persuading to convince you to join us, did I?" she said with a wink, as she mussed his hair.

Raphael nodded with an adorable toothless grin.

"Tell them what we're serving as a main course tonight, Raphael. I'll bet they'll love the pain patate we made for them, don't you?"

"What's that? Grant asked, praying it wasn't fried gophers or guinea pigs...or worse.

Judy said, "It's a sumptuous pudding made with cinnamon and sweet potatoes."

"I knew I smelled cinnamon," Allison said. "And garlic, maybe?"

"Yes," Judy said. "Good nose. It's the garlic in the legim."

"Legim?" Allison said. "Is that some kind of dried bean soup?"

"You'd think so from the name, but it's actually a vegetable stew with eggplant, cabbage, and spinach spiced with garlic and hot peppers."

"It sounds delicious. I can't wait to try it."

Judy pointed toward a dilapidated but functional large wooden table with folding chairs. "You can sit anywhere you'd like. Just grab a seat, and Raphael and I will go get the first course."

Grant pulled out a chair for Allison and gestured for her to sit. Her widened eyes suggested she wasn't used to men treating her with such chivalry.

After years of his mother drilling it into him to "treat a lady with respect," the gesture had been automatic, and he hoped Allison hadn't read too much into it.

He sat next to Allison praying the somewhat wobbly chair would hold his weight. He inhaled the enticing aroma of garlic and hot peppers. His stomach rumbled, as the last thing he'd eaten today was a packet of pretzels in the airplane hours ago.

Raphael placed cups of pink juice next to their plates with a shy but adorable grin.

"Merci," Grant said, using the tidbit of French he'd learned on his long flight.

Raphael smiled and then scurried back to the kitchen.

Allison picked up her glass, sipped it, and then turned to him. "Yum! Guava juice. Try it."

Grant swallowed a swig, and the sweet, cold beverage assuaged his parched tongue and throat. Before he could stop himself, he'd consumed half a glass.

Judy came in with a platter of white rice with black bean sauce. She ladled some onto Allison's plate. "Diri kolé ak pwa," a mainstay of Haitian cuisine. "Raphael will serve up the legim."

Grant polished off the two spicy entrees delighted he hadn't been forced to eat rooster feet, pig intestines, or something equally nauseating. He'd read in his tourist info that the locals often ate goat meat. He only hoped if he was served kabrit, as it was called in Haiti, he wouldn't know it was goat. *Just tell me it's chicken.*

He remembered the conversation he'd had with a missionary to Africa who had eaten beetles as a part of the local cuisine.

"To refuse would be considered rude," the missionary insisted. Rude or not, Grant would not eat bugs. Period. He decided that day missionary life was not for him.

Allison wiped her mouth with her napkin then exclaimed, "Judy, everything was delicious." She patted her stomach. "That totally hit the spot."

Judy rose from her seat. "I hope you saved a little room for bananes pesées."

Allison grinned. "If you force me, I suppose I could cram in a few bites. I wouldn't want to be rude, or anything."

"Certainly not," Judy agreed, reaching for Allison and Grant's dinner plates. "Raphael, while I clear the dinner plates, you bring in the dessert."

Judy stacked the dirty plates and forks and carted them into the kitchen.

Meanwhile, Dr. Jones poured them each some more guava juice. "I never tire of guava and mango. They grow on the trees right outside, so we get them fresh every day." He smiled and added, "One of the many perks of living in Haiti."

As Grant swallowed another swig of the refreshing juice, he had to admit it was delicious. Good to be reminded there was more to Haiti than abject poverty and raw sewage.

Raphael returned with two plates of bananas drizzled with a caramel sauce and placed them in front of Grant and Allison.

"Did you help make this, Raphael?" Grant inquired.

He stared at Grant blankly then looked up to Dr. Jones to interpret.

After he heard the Creole interpretation, Raphael nodded, "Oui. J'aidé."

Grant pulled out another phrase he'd memorized from his French phrase book. "C'est délicieux."

Raphael stared at him blankly. Allison giggled and then corrected Grant's French pronunciation by repeating the word properly. Grant practiced until he pronounced it correctly.

Dr. Jones patted Raphael on the back. "The meal you helped prepare was delicious." He turned to Grant. "Raphael wants to open a Haitian restaurant someday, so Judy is teaching him how to cook."

Judy came in with a pot of decaf and poured some into their mugs. "I'm also teaching Raphael to speak English, aren't I?"

He grinned and said in a thick accent, "Yes, I learn to talk English."

"Very good," she said patting his shoulder.

After savoring the sweet, syrupy banana dessert and decaf, Judy said, "I'll bet after your long trip here today, you two are exhausted. Why don't I show you to your sleeping quarters?"

As he rose from the table, Grant suppressed a yawn. It had been a long day, though he dreaded what kind of bed and mattress he might have to endure. At least they would have mosquito netting, though he knew before the three months were through, he'd be willing to trade in his sister for one night on a king-sized bed in a comfortable room with air conditioning. Even now, at ten p.m., the temperature felt muggy.

Judy gestured for them to follow her into their sleeping quarters. Allison and Grant picked up their suitcases and followed her out of the house and down a narrow rocky path about a quarter mile away to a small cabin.

Judy creaked opened the door. "I didn't know until tonight there would be two of you, so I need to retrieve the room divider that will separate the room into two. That way, you each get your privacy."

Grant glanced around the tiny cabin. The bed reminded him of a cot provided in army barracks or college dorms. Judging from the length of it, he'd have to sleep in a fetal position, or his feet would hang off the end. One perk—at the corner of the cabin stood a bathroom with an actual flush toilet and rudimentary shower, though he shivered when he remembered the water temperature would be cold.

Judy handed them each a full set of towels. She then opened two screened windows. "You'll want to let in as much breeze as possible. I promise you, the temperature does drop at night, though in the beginning, the heat takes getting used to."

Allison released a hearty yawn. "Is the water in the bathroom safe for me to brush my teeth?"

"Yes. We installed a water purification system to make it safe, but in all honesty, it has a strong chlorine flavor, so you may prefer the bottled water I left for you on the sink."

Judy then demonstrated how the mosquito nets worked. "Be sure to use these nets every night. Even though you're on malaria prophylaxis drugs, you know what they say: 'An ounce of prevention is worth a pound of cure.'"

Grant offered to assist Judy in putting up the floor-to-ceiling cardboard partition that separated their beds in the cabin.

When the divider was up, Judy bit them goodnight and informed them breakfast would be at seven.

Once the sound of Judy's footsteps disappeared, the awkwardness of their sleeping arrangements hit him. While the partition offered privacy for dressing, she would hear him if he snored—or worse yet—flatulated.

He inhaled a weary breath. He'd just have to make the best of it. This was going to be a long three months.

* * *

Allison opened her suitcase and unpacked her jeans, shorts, and scrubs into the bottom drawer of a dilapidated dresser. "I'll leave the top drawer for you, Grant."

She eyed the flimsy cardboard partition and frowned. This was so awkward. She'd had no idea she'd been sleeping in the same room with Grant Stockdale. What if she snored...or worse yet, backfired? Grant would hear it. Talk about embarrassing!

"You mind if I use the bathroom first?" she asked. "I'm dying to scrub off all this sweat and grime."

"Tell me about it," Grant agreed. "I feel grubby, too, but you go ahead. I'll gladly procrastinate getting drenched with a bucket of cold water."

As Allison wandered into the bathroom carrying her travel-size soap, coconut shampoo, toothbrush, and toothpaste, she braced herself for the onslaught of water probably cold enough to induce heart failure. She shut the door behind her trying to psych herself up for the frigid onslaught. "Who knows? Maybe it will feel refreshing," she mumbled to herself.

Putting off the inevitable, she first brushed her teeth with the bottled water.

She then figured out how to use the rudimentary toilet by pulling on a string. No more delaying. It was time to get the shower over with.

She held her breath as the icy water slammed onto her head and chest like an icy tsunami. She let out a loud squeal.

"I heard that," Grant hollered from the other room. "You're not increasing my excitement about taking a shower."

Shivering, Allison quickly scrubbed off the layers of sweat, dirt, and grime with the washcloth and soap Judy had provided, starting with her face and neck and ending with her filthy feet. Now thoroughly covered with soap, she lathered in her rich, coconut shampoo, massaging it into her scalp. She braced herself for another deluge of cold when she reached for the rinse bucket. Sucking in a breath, she dumped the bucket of cold water over her head to rinse off the shampoo. Still a bit sudsy, she dumped a third bucket over her body.

Thankfully, the third bucket was merely cold and not bone-numbing. She must be getting used to it.

She rubbed herself dry with her towel then squeezed out the excess water from her hair. She then flipped her head over and wrapped her hair into a turban. After pulling on her tattered terry cloth bathrobe, she suppressed the thought that if she'd known she and Grant were going to be sharing a bedroom, she would have splurged and purchased a satin robe.

One that wasn't terry cloth and threadbare. No doubt her tattered robe would only reinforce his belief that she was trailer trash who bought her clothes from Goodwill. Not that it made any difference. She wasn't his type.

She emerged from the bathroom with her hair tightly coiled in a turban and her terry cloth bathrobe tied snuggly around her waist.

"Dare I ask?" Creases of worry wrinkled across Grant's forehead.

"Think invigorating when the first bucket of water slaps you in the face. A better choice of words than bone-chillingly frigid."

He winced. "I have a feeling we're going to have to come up with a whole lot of creative word choices before our three months are over." He glanced around their sparse accommodations. "Judy was right. This room isn't exactly the Hilton."

"A-ya, but *we're* choosing to call it cozy." Allison slipped off her turban and began combing out her hair.

"Cozy? Try cramped, stiflingly hot, and with beds designed for midgets like you," he said with a devilish wink.

She turned with her hands on her hips. "Hey! I may be short, but I am *not* a midget! I'll have you know I am five feet one inch tall. Technically, to be a midget, you must be under four feet nine inches. Besides, the term midget is now politically incorrect. You're supposed to call them little people."

He grinned. "Maybe so, but compared to me, you're a midget." He raised his index finger. "Excuse me, little person."

She pointed her comb at him. "Good things come in small packages, and don't you forget it."

He laughed. "Touché! Actually, this scrawny bed makes me wish I was a little person." He thumped the mattress with his hand. "My feet will hang over the edge by a good four inches."

She clucked her tongue. "Tsk, tsk. Guess that's the price you pay for being tall, dark, and handsome." As soon as the words exited her mouth, she felt her cheeks flame.

Why had she blurted that out? She wanted to dive under her scrawny bed and hide. Recovering quickly, she quipped, "Well, two out of three, isn't bad."

"Ouch!" As though digesting her insult, he frowned. "So, you don't think I'm handsome?" He puffed out his chest and flexed his biceps in mock attempt to mimic Mr. Universe.

She rolled her eyes and offered a noncommittal shrug hoping he would believe it when she said, "Guess I never really noticed you one way or the other."

"Same here," he retorted. "Never gave you a passing glance. It's good to know we can work together with no risk of a romantic relationship developing, especially when we are confined to such tight sleeping quarters. It'll keep things simple and professional between us."

"Absolutely," she agreed, working out an especially challenging tangle with her comb. Hoping to get the conversation on to safer topics, she commented, "We should be grateful we have a flush toilet in our room. I had envisioned we'd be stuck with a smelly, fly-ridden outhouse."

Grant wrinkled up his nose. "Thank God for toilets! In my book, they're the greatest invention ever made."

Allison laughed. "Right. Forget spaceships, automobiles, computers, and telephones. Give Grant Stockdale a flush toilet and a shower and he'll be happy."

Eyeing the bathroom he teased, "Speaking of showers, I hope you didn't clog up the drain with all your filth and grime."

Arms akimbo she scolded, "Excuse me! That was most unchivalrous of you. I far prefer the charming Grant Stockdale."

"The Grant Stockdale who pulls out my chair at the dinner table over this rude man who comments on my filth and grime."

He chuckled. "I'll keep that in mind, Allison. Can I redeem myself by telling you I love the smell of your shampoo? It makes your hair smell like coconuts."

She tried to suppress the thrill of knowing there was something about her he didn't find objectionable. Then again, even trailer trash washed their hair.

"How did you discover I use a tropical shampoo?"

"I could smell it when you fell asleep against me in the truck. Your head was right under my nose." He shrugged. "It smelled nice." As though embarrassed to have made such a personal remark he added, "Either that, or it just beat the stench of raw sewage and decaying roadkill."

She offered him a mock glare and pointed her comb at him. "Nice to know I'm one step above roadkill. Always the charmer, aren't you, Grant!"

As she completed her combing, her thoughts meandered to the hour she'd napped nestled in his arms.

He had always seemed so elusive, and yet here she was sharing a cabin with him and teasing and swapping insults—like old friends.

She had to suppress a smile. Hard to believe the high and mighty Grant Stockdale III would be sleeping in a rudimentary cot in a tiny, hot cabin in Haiti less than five feet away from her. The whole thing was awkward and scary and...dare she say it...thrilling.

That she found Grant attractive went without saying. Any woman with two functioning eyeballs would notice Grant Stockdale. The man could be a model.

Working together in such tight quarters for three whole months with no other classmates to distract them would change their relationship. But the question was—into what? She hoped they could develop a deep friendship. Since he'd made it clear he viewed her as little more than a midget-sized colleague, fantasies of anything more developing between them would only lead to heartache, as she'd learned the hard way with Alexander.

One glance at "Mt Trashmore" and Grant would no doubt utter snide remarks behind her back. And imagine what his snooty country club parents would think of her hometown.

She'd overheard cutting remarks whispered behind her back often while in college and medical school. Not wanting more of the same in residency, she'd resolved to tell no one about her humble hometown. "I'm from northern Vermont," was all she would say. Somehow, the word got out anyhow.

When people joked that Coventry was little more than a dump for the whole state of Vermont, Allison had to bite her tongue. She loved her father's farm, with its gentle black and white Holsteins dotting the lush green pastures. She loved the panoramic mountain views that graced nearby Lake Willoughby. The lush crimson and pumpkin and canary yellow maple leaves that lit up in autumn was world renowned.

Snobs could laugh all they wanted, but the citizens of Coventry were unpretentious and hard-working. Salt-of-the earth types. Many had good-paying jobs because of that landfill. Plus, much of the revenue the tiny country town made from being the state's dumping grounds had paid for Allison's—and many of her high school classmates'—college tuition. She had graduated from medical school debt-free. So how could she feel anything but gratitude for the practical people of her hometown who placed their children's future ahead of their pride.

But no way could she share her love for her humble hometown with a blue blood like Grant Stockdale III.

She was about to remind Grant it was his turn for the shower when a loud snore erupted over the partition between them.

She couldn't help but smile. Besides surgical skills, their residency had apparently taught them both to fall asleep in two minutes flat, no matter how uncomfortable the bed or hot the room. Since he hadn't had the luxury of a long nap on the trip from the airport like she had, he was no doubt exhausted. She'd let him sleep. He could shower in the morning.

She crawled into bed and released a hearty yawn. Morning would come soon enough, and from what Dr. Jones said, she and Grant would be in for some grueling hours. She'd better get some shut eye while she could, as who knew what tomorrow would bring?

CHAPTER 5

Grant groaned at the irritating jabs on his back. Yes, the mattress was short, but did it have springs poking into him, as well? Hoping to get comfortable, he rolled onto his side and willed himself to reach sweet oblivion again.

"Grant. Wake up!" He heard a frantic voice seeping through the fog.

Okay, this was no bedspring. Someone was poking him and shaking him violently.

"Grant! Wake up! We need you. There's an emergency."

He pried his eyes open to see Dr. Jones' addled face.

Grant rubbed his eyes and blinked then forced himself into a sitting position. Still tired from the long flight and laborious drive to the clinic, he had to remind himself to act pleasant when his exhausted body wanted to scream, "Buzz off and let me sleep!"

It wouldn't do for word to get back to Dr. Morrison that Grant was moody and difficult to work with—then he could kiss his hopes for the Chief Resident position goodbye forever. "What time is it?" he asked, his voice raspy.

"Three in the morning," Dr. Jones replied. "Unfortunately, we have a life-threatening emergency that can't wait until morning."

Grant climbed out of bed yawning. "Appendicitis?" He arched his back, arms stretching toward the ceiling.

Dr. Jones snorted. "I wish. It's a pregnant woman with grand mal seizures who's so swollen her husband says he can't even see her ankle bones."

Grant's heart jolted. He was a surgeon, not an obstetrician. He'd never treated a pregnant woman with a seizure.

"How far along in the pregnancy is she?" he asked, grasping for more information.

Dr. Jones ran a hand through his rumpled hair, "The husband says he thinks she's near full-term."

Allison rounded the partition between the beds already dressed in scrubs. "If she's swollen and having seizures, it sounds like eclampsia, don't you think?"

"Probably. Any idea what her blood pressure is?" Grant asked, hurrying toward the bathroom with his scrubs and a towel.

"Afraid not," Dr. Jones replied. "She's still at her house. The husband came here to tell us about her."

Grant stopped with his hand on the bathroom doorknob.

"Wait. Why didn't he bring his wife?"

"He doesn't own a car, and he didn't dare make her walk for fear she'd have another seizure on the road. He was hoping we could deliver the baby at his house."

"At his house? If she's eclamptic, she'll need a Pitocin drip to induce labor immediately," Grant pointed out.

Allison shook her head. "Wrong. If she's having seizures, she needs a magnesium drip, IV Valium, and an immediate C-section. She and the baby will die in the time it would take to induce labor with Pitocin." She turned to Dr. Jones. "Is this a first pregnancy?"

"No, it's her fourth."

Grant and Allison made eye contact, each mirroring their mutual concern. If the woman died, three children would be left without a mother.

"I've never done a C-section by myself," Grant admitted. "They let me hold retractors while someone *else* did one during my third-year obstetrics rotation. And they grilled me about the different layers of the abdomen while *they* were cutting, but I'm hardly a competent obstetrician."

Dr. Jones opened his arms wide and shrugged. "You two are all I have. I'm an internist, not a surgeon."

Grant's heart went into overdrive. "There's no obstetrician anywhere around who could perform an emergency C-section? Someone better qualified than we are?"

"Port-au-Prince is the closest city, and you know from your trip here what a long drive that is over rutty dirt roads." He shook his head. "Unfortunately, most of the time, women like this die in childbirth. Along with the baby."

"If we're not Board-certified obstetricians, is it even legal for us to attempt a C-section?"

Allison put a hand on his shoulder, her face resolute. "Grant, there aren't any obstetricians, and mid-wives aren't legally allowed to do C-sections. If we don't operate, she and the baby will die."

He paced the cabin rubbing his chin as he weighed their options. If he attempted the surgery and she died, there would certainly be probable cause for a lawsuit, as he was completely unqualified! Did people sue for malpractice down here?

As soon as the thought crossed him mind, he dismissed it. Of course they didn't sue for malpractice in remote parts of Haiti. They couldn't afford to feed their kids, let alone fund a pricy attorney.

As though sensing he was weakening, Allison grabbed his arm and shook it gently. "We can do this, Grant."

"How do you know?" he demanded.

"Because we *have* to. If we don't, the mother and baby will die. Three children will be left with no mother."

He stared at her dumbly. Allison was seriously thinking of performing a C-section when neither one of them had ever done one unaided before? But if they refused to operate, the woman and her baby would die. What a choice!

"I suppose we should at least *attempt* to save her life," he heard himself say against his better judgment.

"What do we have to lose? I, for one, can't face those three little kids and tell them their mother died because I was too chicken-livered to try and save her."

Okay. When she put it like that...

Allison pressed on. "Look, I'll give myself a quick refresher by glancing through the obstetrics textbook I brought with me."

He stared at her in shock. "You brought an OB textbook?" They were surgeons and not obstetricians.

She shrugged. "Always best to be prepared. Since we're out here in the boonies, I had a hunch we might end up with a tubal pregnancy or emergency C-section." She smiled. "I just didn't think it would be five hours after we arrived."

"I'm impressed," he admitted.

She shrugged. "I had more time to research healthcare, or the lack thereof, in rural Haiti than you did."

She turned to Dr. Jones. "Am I going to have to operate in the woman's house, or can we somehow get her here? I'd feel better doing the surgery in a sterile environment with suction and cautery."

"Plus, she needs a magnesium drip and IV Valium to treat the status epilepticus," Grant added.

"I agree," Dr. Jones said. "Thankfully, Jean-Pierre and the husband just left in Angelina to go fetch her."

Grant's stomach dropped. If his wife and baby were in fetal distress, he sure wouldn't want to rely on that rust-bucket-of-a-truck to get him to the hospital.

"How far away do they live?" Allison inquired, digging through her suitcase until she found her obstetrics textbook. She brought it to her lips and kissed it. "Boy, am I glad I tossed you in at the last minute," she said to the book.

"Two miles," Dr. Jones replied.

"Wait! The husband ran two miles at three o'clock in the morning over those God-awful roads to get here?" Grant said.

Dr. Jones extended his arms with a grin. "Welcome to Haiti!"

Grant could only stare at Dr. Jones in disbelief. This desperate man had run two miles in the middle of the night. He'd left his pregnant and seizing wife at home with three children. What must that have been like—not knowing if his wife would even be alive when he returned? What a predicament!

"Okay, I'll do it," Grant said, against his better judgment. Allison was right. How could they let the woman die without even trying to save her? Not, when three little kids would be left without a mother.

"Not looking like that, you won't! You're a grubby mess because you fell asleep before your shower last night."

She eyed him up and down then smirked. "You need to scrub off all that filth and grime before you set foot in my OR."

Remembering his own joke last night about her clogging up the drain with her filth and grime, he chuckled and pointed at her. "Touché, Allison."

"Besides, a cold shower will wake you up," she added. "Meanwhile, I'll review the pelvic floor anatomy and surgical techniques required for a C-section. By the time Jean-Pierre returns with our patient, you'll be clean, and I'll be well-versed in performing a C-section. You can be my assistant and watch for bleeders or nerves that shouldn't be cut."

For a moment, he almost let his pride get in the way and insist he should be the lead surgeon and she could be his assistant, but he had to accept what Allison said made sense.

Plus, if it had been left up to him, he would have wormed out of doing the C-section altogether. Allison was the one who insisted they try—and the one wise enough to pack an obstetrics textbook.

As he dashed toward his cold shower, he mumbled, "What have I gotten myself into?"

* * *

Allison slammed her obstetrics textbook shut, closed her eyes, and mentally reviewed the exact steps of a properly performed C-section. Good. She had it down. Time to check out the surgical suite and prepare for surgery. She hollered into the bathroom for Grant to meet her in the surgical suite when he was dressed.

She and Dr. Jones tromped the rocky path from the sleeping quarters to the surgical suite using a flashlight to guide the way.

"Do you have any vials of magnesium sulfate to treat her eclampsia?"

"Yes, along with IV Valium."

"Stupid question, but who is our anesthesiologist?"

Dr. Jones chuckled. "You're looking at him."

She stopped and turned to stare at him. "I thought you were an internist."

"I am, but I completed post-residency training in anesthesiology for nights like tonight. For elective surgeries, I have an anesthesiologist available every Thursday, but on weekends and nights, I'm on my own."

"What about the babies? If one of them is in fetal distress, do we have a baby incubator? Oxygen? Suction? A pediatrician?" she rattled off in succession counting on her fingers.

"Yes, yes, yes, and no. We use a bulb syringe to suction the babies, but you're looking at the pediatrician as well as the emergency anesthesiologist."

Allison's heart did a nosedive. She could only hope he'd learned the necessary skills through real life training to make up for his lack of board certification.

Dear Lord, be with us tonight and give us your wisdom to provide the best possible care for this woman and her baby.

When they entered the surgical suite, she released a sigh of relief. Earlier, she'd envisioned operating on a kitchen table with a Swiss army knife and the poor woman biting a nail to keep from screaming, but this surgical suite had a modern stainless steel operating table, overhead lamps, and an array of every surgical instrument she could possibly need.

"Wow! This is great!" She circled the suite soaking in the bounty. "You have more amenities than I dreamed possible."

"A benefactor donated money to pay for all of this," he said with a sweep of his hand. "We are very blessed."

Grant entered the room in scrubs, his hair tousled and wet but his body free of the thick coat of dirt. Like Allison, he eyed the suite and grinned. "Not bad! Not bad at all! You'd think we were back in the states."

"A wealthy woman in Bethesda, who insists on remaining anonymous, donated over two hundred thousand dollars to build this clinic, and she also endowed the necessary supplies and medications."

"She must get great satisfaction in seeing the tangible results of her donation," Grant commented.

"I suspect she does." He smiled. "She's also trying to raise money for us start a group home and school for orphans and abandoned babies. Obviously, that will require another hefty endowment, as we don't want to take kids in and then run out of money before they are grown."

"Good point. How close to full funding are you?"

Dr. Jones shrugged. "It depends on how many kids we take in. But for a home with twenty-five children, we're about half-way there."

"How much money to reach full endowment?" Grant pressed.

"My accountants say another two hundred thousand to build and furnish the home and school."

"But how much to guarantee you can feed, clothe, parent, and school the kids until they reach adulthood?"

Dr. Jones released a sigh. "Another half-million per year, I'm afraid."

Allison whistled. "That's a lot of money to raise when you're down here trying to care for patients."

"Plus, you're in the boonies with no internet to assist with fund-raising," Grant pointed out.

"Exactly. It makes fundraising using the usual channels next to impossible."

"Sounds like you need a team in the U.S to take this over for you," Grant said.

"I do. Mrs. Halli—" He stopped himself. "Oops! I'm not supposed to say her name. My anonymous benefactress is generous, but older than Methuselah. She doesn't even own a computer."

Grant paced around the suite checking things out and then eyed his watch. "When do you think Jean-Pierre will arrive with our patient?"

Dr. Jones released a sigh. "That depends on if they can convince the woman to come."

Allison pulled back in shock. "If she and her baby will die without proper medical treatment, why would she not be willing to come in?"

Dr. Jones cleared his throat as he hung a bag of Magnesium sulfate on an IV pole. "I don't know how much Dr. Morrison filled you in on the local customs and religious practices of rural Haiti, but in the poorest, most uneducated areas, there is still a great reliance on voodoo, witch doctors, and appeasing the spirits."

"You're kidding! People still go to witch doctors?" Allison exclaimed.

"Afraid so, and unfortunately, a local, self-appointed witch doctor named Louis Villemort has convinced many of the locals that coming to this clinic will bring them bad luck because it will anger the spirits."

Grant scratched his forehead. "Why would seeking decent medical care anger the spirits?"

"Louis preaches that using Western medicine and not relying on his hocus-pocus and magic potions will anger the Ewa spirits and will rain bad fortune on the family."

"Great! So, we're the bad guys?" Grant said, his shoulders sagging.

Dr. Jones put up a hand. "Don't blame me. I'm just the messenger. Haitians can be very superstitious, and many have been indoctrinated to believe that when anything bad happens to them, it is because someone has angered the spirits, and that only he, the witch doctor, can appease the Ewa."

Grant resumed his pacing. "So now *we're* the bad guys? Any more cheery news to make my night?"

The creases in Dr. Jones' forehead deepened. "No more cheery news—just more bad news, I'm afraid."

Allison's head dropped. "Dare I ask?"

Dr. Jones sucked in a deep breath and released it. "Not to put any additional pressure on you, but the outcome of this surgery will spread throughout the community. If things go badly, the witch doctor will use it as proof positive that relying on Western medical procedures angered the spirits and caused the woman and her baby to die."

Allison's stomach twisted. This surgery was extremely high risk already with a mortality rate near 50%—and that was under the care of a trained obstetrician!

With the long delay in getting to the clinic—let alone her probably marginal nutritional status and prenatal care—the mortality rate was likely closer to 75%. She contemplated the repercussions of operating on, and then losing. the patient. It would certainly mar the clinic's reputation.

Should she renege on doing the surgery? The whole thing sounded like a lose-lose proposition.

Grant resumed his caged panther pacing while thinking out loud. "If that baby isn't delivered ASAP, the mother and baby will definitely die. How is that our fault?"

Dr. Jones raised upturned palms. "You're preaching to the choir. Obviously, *I* know a magnesium infusion, IV Valium, and emergency C-section is her only hope."

He continued. "I'm only warning you because I want you to understand why the patient may act leery or even afraid of you."

"Swell!" Grant growled and resumed pacing.

"The husband told me the witch doctor came over and did his chants and incantations and whatever else a witch doctor does, but instead of getting better, his wife got worse and had another seizure. After the witch doctor left, the husband ran to our clinic as a last-ditch effort to save his wife's life."

"That took a huge leap of faith on his part," Allison pointed out.

"Desperation, more likely," Grant corrected.

"What can we do to allay their fears?" Allison asked.

Before Dr. Jones could answer, Jean-Pierre and a thin, short man stormed in carrying a very pregnant woman who seemed completely out of it—clearly sedated from her last grand-mal seizure.

Was she already in a coma? That would up the mortality to 90%. What a lousy start to their rotation—a dead woman and a dead baby.

Jean-Pierre informed them the woman, named Fabiola, had a grand mal seizure in the car on the way to the clinic. She was now unarousable, but still breathing. Allison and Grant made eye contact and transmitted the same unspoken message: "There's no way this woman will make it out of here alive."

They quickly transferred Fabiola to the surgical table where Allison noticed her legs were so swollen she had no visible ankle bones. Judging from the size of Fabiola's protruding abdomen, Allison guessed she must be at least at the end of her eighth month, so hopefully, they weren't dealing with preemies. They tugged off her clothes and put on a hospital gown.

Dr. Jones applied a tourniquet and searched for a viable vein. After scrubbing with alcohol, he inserted an IV.

"I'll bolus the Magnesium Sulfate and Valium and get a drip infusing," Dr. Jones said. "We don't need her seizing in the middle of our C-section."

Allison noted Grant's eyes widen. Clearly, he had thought about that terrible possibility. Neither had she. Operating when someone is shaking like an earthquake? Thanks, but no thanks.

He turned to Allison. "Get a baseline blood pressure. With eclampsia, her pressure is bound to be through the roof."

"I'll get her temperature," Grant said, as Allison wrapped the blood pressure cuff around Fabiola's arm and the machine pumped the pressure up to 240. Her heart momentarily stopped when the pressure registered at a whooping 230/125. She shared the sky-high reading with Dr. Jones. His brow creased with worry. "We need to hang a bag of Nitroprusside to get her pressure down."

He explained to Allison how to mix the Nitroprusside and get the bag hanging. "Start with 0.3 ug/kg/minute and titrate up until her systolic pressure is below 130." He eyed the patient and said, "I would guess her ideal body weight when not pregnant is around sixty kilos, so we'll start the drip at 1.8 ug per minute. Check her pressure every minute until we get it down."

Grant pulled the thermometer out of her mouth. "Good news here. Normal temp at 98.6, so at least we don't have an infection on top of everything else."

Allison noticed the patient's husband standing nervously in the corner biting a thumbnail. She could only imagine how terrified he was, especially since, if his wife died, he'd be left to raise three children by himself. Allison smiled at him, and as she began mixing up the Nitroprusside drip, she said in her best French, "We are doing everything we can to save your wife. I am praying to my good God to help us." Or at least that's what she hoped she'd said.

The man nodded and offered the slightest hint of a smile.

Good, maybe she'd said it correctly.

Once the Magnesium sulfate, Valium, and Nitroprusside were infusing, and Fabiola's blood pressure lowered, Dr. Jones said, "It's time we get that baby out."

Grant cautioned, "Wait. Now that the mother is medically stable, shouldn't we check out the heart rate of the baby and make sure we still have a viable baby?"

Allison felt her chest tighten. She hadn't even considered the baby might already be dead from the strain of eclampsia. If the baby died, she and Grant would likely get blamed by the witch doctor. She forced herself to inhale a deep breath. Worrying about the possible negative repercussions would only distract her. She needed to stay focused on the things she could control. Namely, performing a proper C-section.

She rolled her neck and sucked in a slow breath.

You can do this. Just take it one step at a time.

She found the fetoscope and pressed it on Fabiola's belly. She wanted to shout, "Praise God," when she heard a fetal heartbeat at the expected rate of 160 beats a minute. She moved the scope slightly and her heart jolted. She'd heard a *second* fetal heartbeat. Could it be?

Twins!

CHAPTER 6

The woman had twins. Allison's breath caught, and her knees turned to Jell-O.

When she shared the news with Grant, he wanted to listen for himself. After moving the fetoscope several times, Grant pulled it from his ears, and his lips tightened. "Unfortunately, you're right—twins." He rubbed his chin. "That ups the risk exponentially. Now we have to worry about how stable the babies will be. Fabiola is thin, so they're bound to be low birth weight." He gestured toward the newborn bassinet. "We have oxygen, but it's not like this is a neonatal intensive care unit."

Allison inquired of the husband, Robaire, how many months along he thought his wife was. He guessed eight months, but he wasn't sure.

Allison did a quick mental calculation and estimated the babies would probably weigh at least four pounds each—*if* the mother was at least eight months along. She didn't want to think what they'd weigh if the mother was only seven months along.

Dr. Jones wheeled over an ultrasound machine on a cart and squirted a large blob of KY jelly on the woman's abdomen. He then ran a probe over her abdomen and immediately found the two babies.

One, an obvious boy, he estimated to weigh five pounds, but the other, a girl, was considerably smaller—perhaps only three-and-a-half pounds. At least both babies had healthy, beating hearts and no hydrocephalus or obvious birth defects.

After wiping off the woman's belly with a towel, Dr. Jones informed Grant and Allison, "The boy baby will probably be fine, but the little girl…"

His voice trailed off, and his worry crease deepened. "This isn't a Neonatal ICU. If the baby's lungs are too underdeveloped to breathe, I don't have a baby ventilator, and it's too late and too dangerous to make the trip to Port-au-Prince."

The three doctors reviewed the risks of proceeding with the C-section. Clearly, immediate C-section would best serve the mother and baby boy, but if the girl's lungs weren't developed enough to breathe on her own, she could end up a casualty. But if the mother died, all three would end up a casualty.

"Do you have any infant surfactant?" Allison inquired. "That would help her lungs."

Dr. Jones shook his head. "Sadly, no."

"We could try a slug of steroids," Grant suggested. "That might speed up lung development a little."

Allison shook her head. "But it will also shoot up Fabiola's blood pressure."

Grant pursed his lips in thought. "True, but we can always increase the Nitroprusside drip to get the mother's pressure down again."

Dr. Jones nodded. "What do we have to lose? If it can help the baby's lungs even a little, it's worth a try."

He rushed to the medicine cabinet and pulled out a small vial of Solumedrol. "Here's hoping," he said, as he injected the proper dose intravenously.

"With any luck, all the maternal stress of pre-eclampsia and then eclampsia may have triggered the baby's own emergency systems," Allison said. "Maybe the mother's extra cortisol and adrenalin these last few days will be enough to have signaled the baby to produce her own lung surfactant."

Grant nodded. "Good point. Stress does speed up fetal lung development."

Fabiola began to revive from her post-seizure state, and her eyes grew wild at the site of three doctors staring down at her. She gripped the surgical table and began to sit up.

Her husband rushed to her side, and in a torrent of French Creole, he explained what was happening—and that she was carrying twins.

After eyeing Allison and Grant, panic crossed her face. Clearly, the couple had not discussed the decision to come to a Western medical clinic. The decision had been his alone.

Knowing Fabiola's fear of Western doctors, Allison came forward and grabbed her hand. In her best attempt at French, she made eye contact and told her she would pray to her God on Fabiola's behalf before they operated. With a voice that showed as much confidence as she could muster, Allison bent her head, closed her eyes, and prayed loudly for both Fabiola and her husband to hear.

"Dear God, rescue Fabiola and her two babies. I pray for your intervention on their behalf. Give me wisdom to complete this surgery. We pray for the health and wellbeing of these babies, and we ask this in the name of our Lord and Savior, Jesus Christ."

Her prayer was said in English, but she hoped the couple could tell she was praying by her bent head and closed eyes.

Dr. Jones informed the mother in French that Allison had prayed to the one true God to appease the anger of the spirits.

Allison could tell from Fabiola's wide eyes that she still harbored extreme reservations about foreign doctors.

But despite her fear, she nodded her consent. Since she was illiterate, she could not sign a written consent form, so they just had her mark an "X".

Dr. Jones had Fabiola roll on her side, and while she and Grant scrubbed up with Hibiclens, he performed an epidural. When Fabiola realized she was completely paralyzed from the waist down, she screamed in French Creole, "What have you done to me? I can't feel my legs."

Dr. Jones reassured her the paralysis was only temporary so she wouldn't feel the scalpel during the C-section. "You'll be walking again in under four hours," he insisted. He encouraged her to close her eyes and rest, as she would need all her strength to care for her two new babies.

Fabiola's suspicious eyes did little to calm Allison's already frayed nerves. Would the woman start screaming when she realized they were cutting into her? Would she have another grand mal seizure? Would the baby girl survive?

Don't go there. Just take it one step at a time.

She motioned to Robaire to come to the head of the bed and hold his wife's hand. He squeezed her hand and offered words of reassurance.

Allison hoped Robaire could keep his wife calm, because Fabiola looked convinced they had paralyzed her and were about to murder her babies. The last thing Allison needed was a panicky mother flailing her arms or trying to drag herself off the surgical table in the middle of the operation.

After removing his gloves, Dr. Jones strapped Fabiola's legs into the sleeves of a compression pump. The steady squeezing motion on her legs would reduce the risk of forming a leg clot during the surgery and might help with the massive swelling.

"I'm glad the clinic is stocked with compression pumps," Grant said. "I'm all for preventing leg clots and pulmonary emboli."

Allison sucked in a deep breath to quell her nerves. She hadn't even considered those complication.

She noticed Robaire gazing from Grant to Dr. Jones and then back to her. As he saw them strap the strange contraption on his wife's legs deep worry lines etched his brow. What must it be like for him to put his trust in complete strangers who he'd been warned by the witch doctor would anger the spirits and do his wife harm?

If he did nothing, his wife would die and leave him to raise three children by himself. If he brought her here, he risked angering the Ewa spirits. What an impossible situation to be in.

Allison offered him a reassuring smile. "Robaire, we will do everything possible to save Fabiola and babies," she said using her rusty French.

His nod suggested she'd nailed it, though he began to bite a hangnail.

She glanced down at Fabiola's puffy face. Her blood pressure now registered a whopping 180/100. The steroid infusion had raised her pressure, along with her abject fear they were about to paralyze her—or kill her babies.

Dr. Jones' lips tightened. "She's already on the maximum dose of Nitroprusside. "We need to proceed with the C-section before Fabiola has another grand mal seizure—or stroke from the hypertension. Her blood pressure will come down as soon as the babies are out. I'll give her a slug of IV metoprolol to try to lower the pressure a bit more, but then we need to proceed."

As he infused the dose of metoprolol, Allison recanted her plan of attack as Grant scrubbed the abdomen with Betadine and covered the rest of the abdomen with surgical drapes.

With shaking hands, she approached the lower abdomen with her scalpel.

She made a superficial slice through the skin, subcutaneous fat, then the outer muscles. She sliced through each successive layer until she was at the uterus. Here was where she had to be careful. Too deep and she'd prematurely rupture the amniotic sac, or worse yet, stab one of the babies.

Grant pointed to an artery partially hidden by blood. "Stop! You're getting awfully close to the pudendal artery."

"Thanks," she said, offering a grateful smile. Having extra eyes watching for bleeders was a good thing. Truth be told she *hadn't* seen the blood-covered artery. Envisioning a sudden geyser spurting blood to the ceiling and requiring frantic damage control, let alone causing needless blood loss and wasted time, Allison's hands shook.

What if she botched the surgery? They'd all end up dead.

A wave of dizziness overtook her. She leaned against the table to compose herself. Why had she agreed to do this surgery? She wasn't qualified.

She must have blanched because Grant said, "Allison? Are you okay? You're suddenly whiter than the bed sheets."

Doing her best to feign a level of confidence she did not feel, she shrugged and confessed, "I'm suddenly feeling the weight of what I agreed to do. I nearly severed an important artery."

Her eyes welled with tears, but she quickly blinked them away. "What if I accidentally kill them all?"

There! She'd said it. No point trying to act brave when she hadn't fooled Grant in the slightest.

Thankfully, instead of muttering a snide remark like, "Hey, you're the one who bragged she could do this," Grant nodded with understanding. "I've got your back, Allison."

She must have looked unconvinced because he added, "With both of us working as a team, we aren't going to kill anybody. We're going to get those babies out safe and sound."

His unexpected words of support sent a fresh wave of tears to her eyes. She sniffled them away.

Come on. Get a grip!

Unfortunately, her trembling hands weren't cooperating.

As though sensing her abject terror, Grant said, "If I see you about to do something wrong, trust me, I'll speak up. That's why I mentioned the pudendal artery. I wasn't sure you'd seen it."

"I *didn't* see it. That's why I'm freaking out. What if I'd cut through it?"

"But you didn't. Almost mistakes don't count. Let's focus on our goal—getting those babies out."

He was right, of course. She leaned against the table, rolled her neck, and inhaled in two deep breaths desperate to calm her frazzled nerves.

Grant's eyes bore into hers. "Allison, you're a great surgeon. I've seen you operate before. I know you can do this."

She wanted to hug him for his vote of confidence.

But then he blew it by adding, "Look, if you're feeling overwhelmed, I can take over, and you can be my assistant."

And have him gloat that she wigged out, and he had to rescue her mid surgery? *Forget it!*

"No, I'm fine. I can do it," she insisted straightening and readying herself to operate.

Grant appraised her with concern but said nothing.

People were counting on her. She needed to stay focused on the task at hand and take it one step at a time.

She sucked in another deep breath. "Ok, I'm ready to proceed. Let's get those babies out."

CHAPTER 7

Dr. Jones rechecked Fabiola's blood pressure, and reported it was now hovering at 145/90. "Much better," he said, offering Allison a reassuring smile. "The metoprolol did the trick."

"Great," she said, forcing herself to focus on the pregnant abdomen in front of her.

Just take it one step at a time. You can do this.

With trembling hands, she sliced across the uterus and separated it with gloved fingers until the first baby lay exposed but still inside an intact amniotic sac.

Before she ruptured the sac, she wanted to make sure everything was prepared for the babies. She went through the check list with Dr. Jones: warmed towels to rub the babies and stimulate circulation, suction to clean out the nose and mouth, heat lamp to ensure the bassinets stayed at the proper temperature, baby Ambu bags and an oxygen tent should they need it.

Dr. Jones nodded. "We're as prepared as we'll ever be. Take the bigger one first. We'll get him stabilized before we cut the umbilical cord of the little one."

Allison nodded and plunged the tip of her scalpel into the amniotic sac. She was greeted with a gush of clear fluid. Good. The amniotic fluid was not contaminated with meconium.

She freed the baby boy from the womb and handed him to a waiting Dr. Jones who suctioned the nose and mouth and rubbed the baby vigorously with a heated towel, being careful not to tear the umbilical cord.

They were rewarded with a loud squall. With more loud cries, the baby pinked up and moved all four limbs with a satisfying bicycle pedaling motion.

The three doctors broke into grins. Yes! At least one of the babies had made it out alive and seemed to be strong enough to survive without the medical advances of a Neonatal Intensive Care unit.

Grant clamped and then cut the umbilical cord, and Dr. Jones rubbed the little boy with another warmed towel to stimulate the circulation and remove the thick coating of vernix caseosa covering his skin. He brought the baby to the scale and weighed him and measured his head circumference.

"Five pounds, four ounces, nineteen inches long, and an Apgar score of 9. Not bad for your first C-section, Allison," Dr. Jones said with a grin. He swaddled the baby in a warm blanket and handed him off to Robaire.

He proudly displayed his new son to Fabiola, and her face lit up. She cooed and spoke in a reassuring voice to the baby.

Dr. Jones returned to the surgical table after changing his surgical gloves. "Here's hoping our baby girl comes out as healthy. You ready to bring out baby sister?"

"As ready as I'll ever be," Allison said, a wave of trepidation creeping up her spine. Since this baby was considerably smaller, would she survive in such primitive conditions with no respirator, or surfactant?

Allison reached into the uterus and extracted the baby girl.

Her tiny legs seemed no thicker than a twig, and she didn't respond with a howl of protest like her brother. The dusky, mottled coloring sent adrenaline coursing through Allison's blood. The baby was tiny and cyanotic.

She isn't going to make it.

Until the baby inhaled its first breath, Allison didn't want to cut the umbilical cord or evacuate the placenta and all the internal fluids from the mother.

"Hand her to me. I'll perk her up," Dr. Jones said. He displayed far more confidence than Allison felt.

He immediately suctioned out the baby's nose and mouth and began rubbing the baby vigorously with a fresh, warmed towel. When the baby still didn't respond, he listened for a heartbeat with his stethoscope.

"She's got a bounding pulse, if I can just get her breathing." He pulled out a baby-sized Ambu bag and squeezed two puffs of air into the baby's lungs. No response.

Allison's heart pounded, and she prayed the little one would respond to the interventions. She glanced at the clock. Almost two minutes had now passed, and the baby had yet to take her first breath. Her coloring remained an unhealthy mottled blue. If she didn't respond in the next three minutes, brain damage would begin.

Allison exchanged a worried glance across the table at Grant. Every passing second was an eternity, and she felt helpless to do anything but pray.

Dr. Jones squeezed two more puffs of air into the baby. No luck. "She's still got a strong heartbeat," he said, after palpating over the heart.

Grant piped in, "Hey! Let me try a technique I remember from my OB rotation when a baby wasn't breathing."

Dr. Jones handed the baby to Grant, who turned the baby upside down and gently slapped her on the back, as though trying to dislodge any retained fluid in the lungs or bronchial tubes by using gravity to help dislodge it.

Suddenly, the baby released the slightest cough. This was followed by a whimper and then a piercing guttural cry.

After a minute of high-pitched crying, the baby pinked up. Allison clamped the umbilical cord, and Grant cut it.

Dr. Jones cleaned, measured, and weighed the baby then wrapped her in a warm blanket. Meanwhile, Allison extracted the placenta while Grant suctioned out the blood and debris and rinsed the abdominal cavity with saline. He suctioned out the residual blood and body fluids. In doing so, he discovered a tiny bleeder, which he cauterized. They completed a count to make sure no gauze squares were inadvertently left behind. Grant offered to complete the suturing.

Suddenly drained, Allison nodded her consent, relieved to be through with the harrowing ordeal. Her legs were overcooked linguini, and her hands still shook. She peeled off her disposable surgical gloves and gown while Grant sutured up each successive layer of the pelvic floor with neat, evenly spaced stitches. Once the incision was dressed and covered with a dressing, Grant joined her in admiring the newborns.

"Three pounds and fourteen ounces," Dr. Jones said. He handed the blanket-wrapped baby girl to Fabiola. She beamed with pride. "She's a fighter," he insisted.

"I think the 'Use gravity to your advantage' technique I learned in my OB rotation must have dislodged a mucus plug," Grant said.

Dr. Jones nodded with a smile. "It probably saved her life."

"I'm glad I remembered it. My OB rotation was six years ago."

Allison scowled. You might know Grant would take credit for saving the baby when she had done the C-section.

She reprimanded herself for her petty attitude. They were supposed to be working as a team, and truth be told, had Grant not pointed out the pudendal artery, she might well have sliced through it.

Plus, his technique *had* dislodged whatever fluid or phlegm was obstructing the baby's trachea, thereby saving her life. Still...she crossed her arms not yet ready to let him off the hook. Must he be so quick to point it out?

Grow up, she scolded herself. Both babies and their mother had miraculously survived. She should be thanking God for rescuing Fabiola and her babies, not dwelling on who did what to save them. The three doctors had worked as a team, and that's what had saved them.

Determined to table her churlish attitude, Allison focused on the pure joy shining from Robaire's face. He grinned as the baby girl curled her tiny fist around his pinkie finger. Allison didn't completely grasp what he said, but she plucked out enough French words to know he was amazed at how tiny the baby's fingers were, and how shocked he'd been to find out they had twins.

"No wonder she was as big as a house," he teased, puffing his cheeks, and gesturing with his hands how big he thought his wife had gotten.

Fabiola responded with a dismissive swat to his arm. "Next time, you have baby."

He chuckled. "If only I could do that for you."

Allison busied herself reassessing Fabiola's blood pressure and was delighted to find it had dropped into the normal range. Time to lower the Nitroprusside drip.

Fabiola discreetly offered a breast for the baby boy after draping herself with a blanket. Allison heard suckling sounds, so the latching on must have succeeded.

Allison glanced at her watch and released an internal groan: five in the morning. By the time Fabiola's epidural wore off, it would be time for the clinic to open. She'd have to limp through the day sleep deprived. Again.

Thank goodness she'd gotten that catnap in the truck on the way to the clinic.

A twinge of guilt coursed through her since Grant had not had even the luxury of a nap. She glanced over to see how he was faring after their interrupted night of sleep. As he stood next to Robaire rocking the baby girl and commenting on her winsome features, Allison stifled a groan.

You might know—gorgeous as ever. Sure, he displayed an unshaven morning stubble and hair that looked tousled, but apparently, nothing could mar his handsomeness.

As though sensing her watching him, Grant glanced up, and his eyes bore into hers. He offered a grin and a thumbs-up sign at their success in delivering two healthy babies.

Embarrassed to be caught staring at him, Allison quickly averted her eyes. Hopefully, the thumbs-up sign meant he thought she was only staring at him because he held the baby.

And that's all it was. Nothing more. She was only concerned for his well-being because the surgery today proved she was better off with another pair of skilled eyes watching out for bleeders...or obstructed bronchial tubes.

Fabiola finished nursing the baby boy and asked her husband to take him so she could nurse the baby girl. After exchanging the blue-blanketed baby for a pink-blanketed one, she cradled the baby in the crook of her arm, and soon, the baby girl made quiet suckling sounds.

Allison rechecked Fabiola's blood pressure. Still in the normal range. She reduced the Nitroprusside drip another notch and upped the IV rate. Fabiola would need all the liquids she could get to provide milk for two babies. Now that they were waiting for the anesthesia to wear off, perhaps Allison should fix the exhausted mom and her husband something to eat.

She suggested this to Dr. Jones, but he informed her Judy would bring in a full breakfast tray in a couple of hours.

"Why don't you and Grant go grab another three hours of sleep before breakfast? I can take over now. We'll eat at 8:30 instead of 7. Morning clinic starts at nine."

She and Grant waved goodbye to Robaire and Fabiola and promised to check on them in a couple of hours.

As they wandered back to their cabin, Grant squeezed her shoulder. "You did great with that delivery, Allison. I know you were freaking out at one point, but you pushed past your fear, and now you have two healthy babies and a mother out of eclampsia. Well done!"

She smiled up at him, surprised at how much his words of praise meant to her. "It wouldn't have been nearly as successful if you hadn't spotted that hidden artery and dislodged the phlegm from the baby's lungs."

He shrugged. "We make a good team, don't we?"

She had to admit, they did, even if he did infuriate her at times. Maybe things would become easier the longer they worked together.

Her first case had proven nerve-racking to the extreme. She released a weary sigh. Three hours until morning clinic. What would the morning bring?

CHAPTER 8

Grant flipped over on his lumpy thin mattress in a vain attempt to get comfortable. What he would give for a few hours on his Dream Cloud mattress right now. He had never appreciated his comfy king-sized mattress nearly enough.

Releasing an exasperated sigh, he willed himself to fall asleep, but his eyelids would not cooperate. It didn't help that less than five feet away, separated by a mere partition, he could hear Allison's heavy breathing—the sign that she had conked out without a problem. In two minutes flat. That woman could fall asleep on a bed of nails.

Come on, Grant, fall asleep. You're exhausted.

He rolled, and twisted and plumped his pillow, but it wasn't happening, which only gave him too much time to think. While he was elated Allison had saved Fabiola and her babies' lives, he couldn't help but worry. If word got back to Dr. Morrison that Allison, and not he, had successfully performed the C-section, would it sway Morrison to grant the Chief Surgical Resident position to Allison?

Truthfully, she had shown a remarkable display of courage and confidence to undertake a C-section when the mother was in full-blown eclampsia and carrying twins. Initially, Grant had shied away from the surgery as being too dangerous.

Even in the hands of a skilled obstetrician, the delivery would be high risk, but in the hands of two fledgling general surgeons, it seemed far too risky.

But Allison was willing to face the challenge in a valiant attempt to save Fabiola's and the twins' lives. She had put their needs ahead of her own reputation. If the mother and both babies had died, Allison would bear the guilt and repercussions of her failed surgical attempt. But she had been willing to take the risk.

Truth be told, Allison deserved the Chief Surgical Resident position more than he did. In a crisis, she showed valor and gumption, while he'd exercised caution and a worry about his own reputation. Her willingness to take a risk had saved Fabiola and the twins' lives.

Punching his pillow in a futile attempt to plump the lumpy blob, Grand released a frustrated sigh of surrender.

He chided himself for putting his own reputation ahead of the welfare of a desperate patient. They all would have died without surgery, so what did he have to lose?

You should have been willing to risk it all. Allison did.

Of course, if things had gone horribly wrong and the mother and both babies had died, would he be reprimanding himself now, or would he be criticizing Allison for a foolhardy attempt to perform a surgery she wasn't qualified to tackle? Even worse, that witch doctor would have spread the word that Fabiola and the babies died because those American doctors had angered the spirits. The reputation of the clinic would have been irreparably damaged.

Hard to believe in this day and age people held on to such archaic superstitions as angering the spirits or consulting witch doctors.

In his failing attempt to get comfortable on the puny bed, he rolled onto his side and curled into a fetal position. Sweat poured down his face.

He tugged off his top sheet and used it to mop his face. What had possessed him to spend three months in this primitive hospital with no air conditioning?

Hearing Allison's slow relaxed breathing only fueled his frustration—and irritation. How could she sleep in this inferno? Is there nothing the woman couldn't do?

Admitting defeat on the sleep front, Grant sat up and reached for his book of common French Creole words. He might as well put his time to good use. It would beat stewing about the future. Before tackling his language lesson, he fanned himself with the book in a desperate attempt to cool off.

Since Allison would likely win the Chief Resident position, he was probably putting up with all this heat and misery for nothing. If he had a brain, he'd fly back to Hopkins tomorrow.

Except that would require another jostling trip in a truck that had ninety-to-one odds of falling apart before making it to the airport. And if he wigged out on this Haiti rotation after just one day, he'd lose the Chief Resident position for sure.

He shouldn't make a rash decision when he was exhausted and feeling one-upped by Allison. Surely with time he'd get used to the heat and primitive conditions.

Too tired to focus on the French Creole word for house and chicken, he flopped back down onto his bed.

Without warning, the sweet faces of the newborn twins and their proud parents entered his mind. It *had* been gratifying to assist Allison in saving the lives of the desperate family.

Fabiola and her babies would have died without their assistance. Three other children would have been left motherless.

A deep soul-quenching satisfaction coursed through him, and despite the oppressive heat and primitive conditions, he felt needed—far more than he would have if he'd stayed home and taken the plastic surgery rotation. Breast augmentations?

Facelifts? Nose jobs? How vain and superfluous they seemed compared to a poor woman's struggle to survive.

People in Haiti needed him. Perhaps if he changed his attitude and looked for ways to be a blessing, the three months would pass more quickly.

Peace settled over him, and he offered up a heartfelt prayer:

God, help me change my attitude. Use me to help these people who you created and love.

CHAPTER 9

News of Fabiola's remarkable recovery spread throughout town like a juicy rumor on steroids. Fabiola's glowing endorsement, "They prayed to their God to protect me, and then they delivered my babies, and they didn't even charge me," made townspeople overcome their fears about visiting the American-run medical clinic. Haitians who previously avoided the clinic due to the dire warnings from the witch doctor, now poured in in droves.

A week had passed since Fabiola's harrowing delivery, and by ten a.m., Grant had already drained a festering foot abscess, treated strep throat, and injected cortisone into a shoulder bursitis. Allison had treated a woman who'd hobbled in convinced she'd broken her ankle. After x-raying the swollen ankle, Allison reassured her it was just a nasty sprain and would respond to RICE: Rest, Ice, Compression, and Elevation. After icing the offending ankle and wrapping it snugly in an ACE bandage, Allison taught the woman how to walk with crutches and sent her on her way with a bottle of Tylenol for pain.

Seconds after the woman hobbled out the door, a father rushed in holding his eight-year-old son, a grimacing child bent at the waist whimpering and gripping the right lower quadrant of his abdomen.

After a careful history and physical, the child showed classic signs for acute appendicitis. After convincing the father that the child could die without surgery, the man consented to the operation.

Little Jacques clutched his father's hand. Wide, terrified eyes stared back at her. "Don't let them cut on me, Daddy."

Allison squatted down to eye level and smiled at Jacques. She asked Dr. Jones to act as her interpreter. "I'll bet your tummy really hurts, doesn't it?"

After Dr. Jones repeated the words in Creole, Jacques nodded, his eyes filled with tears.

"I can get rid of that pain for you," she offered with as soothing a voice as she could muster.

"Are you going to stick a knife in me?" His eyes were wide as saucers.

No wonder the poor kid was terrified. He probably thought they were going to operate without anesthesia!

"We have a special medicine that will put you in a deep sleep, so you won't feel a thing when we operate. You'll be sound asleep."

After hearing the interpretation, he looked to his father then back up at Allison with a furrowed brow.

"How you gonna make me fall asleep when I'm in this much pain?"

"Smart kid," Dr. Jones exclaimed with a smile.

"It's a special medication called anesthesia," Allison said. "It goes straight to your brain, and within one minute, you'll be sound asleep."

The poor kid still looked unconvinced and gripped his father's hand. His father nodded encouragingly.

"It's true, son. Your Grandpa broke his leg a few years back and we had to bring him to Port-au-Price to get it fixed. He said they gave him a medication that knocked him out. He didn't feel a thing."

Jacques chewed on his lower lip weighing his father's words. He eyed Allison as though trying to sort out whether to trust her or not.

"You can do it, son. We have no choice," his father said. "We can trust them because they saved Fabiola's life."

"Okay." He offered a tentative smile, though his hand still shook.

"Wonderful!" Allison then explained in detail what would happen before the anesthesia kicked in.

As Dr. Jones interpreted, Jacques nodded with understanding.

Dr. Jones escorted the father to the waiting room and reassured him they would provide an update as soon as the surgery was over. He then wheeled Jacques into the operating room.

Once Grant had Jacques draped and prepped for surgery, Allison started an IV. Jacques's eyes welled with tears as the needle pierced his skin, but he did his best not to cry.

"That's the most pain you'll feel," Dr. Jones reassured him.

After Dr. Jones applied a blood pressure cuff and pulse oximeter to Jacques's finger, Allison busied herself with scrubbing up. Dr. Jones assisted her with gowning up and donning surgical gloves.

As Jacques moaned in pain, Dr Jones said, "You ready to be rid of that pain?"

"Oui," he said, his face in a grimace.

After a quick surgical time-out, Dr. Jones injected the IV anesthesia and intubated him. Jacques's body went limp.

Allison sliced into the abdomen and pared through each layer, while Grant held retractors and suctioned. After locating the inflamed appendix, she cut it off. "Let's get this bad boy out of here."

Once all bleeders were cauterized, she and Grant counted the blood-soaked gauze squares to be sure none had been inadvertently left in the abdomen.

"All squares accounted for," Grant reassured her.

As she sewed up each successive layer of the abdomen, deep satisfaction that she had helped Jacques coursed through her. This financially strapped clinic depended entirely on volunteer surgeons who donated their time. If she and Grant had not been here, would Jacques have died? A sobering thought, indeed.

When Grant offered to put in the staples on the outer surface of the abdomen, Allison nodded, pulled off her surgical gown, gloves, and mask, and disposed of them. She arched her back and stretched the tight muscles that had formed in her shoulder blades.

She glanced up and noticed Grant in intense concentration as he pulled the incision together with a tidy row of staples. She really shouldn't stare, but gosh, that guy was eye candy. And so smart. He'd make some lucky woman a real catch. Too bad he was out of her league.

After reassuring Jacques's father that the surgery went well, she mopped the sweat off her face with a towel.

It's so hot in here I could pass out.

She decided to head to the cabin and wash her face. A splash of cold water would feel great.

As she sauntered toward the cabin, a quick flash of movement behind a tree caught her eye. She could have sworn it was a man's face, but it happened so quickly she wasn't sure if she was just imagining it.

Was someone skulking behind the cabin? If so, why did he hide when he saw her approaching?

A shiver of fear wormed its way down her spine. Should she head back to the clinic?

Heart pounding, she called out, "Is someone there? Do you need a doctor?"

No answer. She tried again, speaking French this time. At least she hoped she'd said it properly.

"Qui est-ce?"

Still no answer.

She entered the cabin slowly and looked around to be sure no one was hiding inside.

Seeing and hearing nothing, she grabbed her washcloth and turned on the water. As she rubbed the cold water on her face and neck, the coolness soothed her, and she began to relax.

It was probably just her imagination. Or the heat.

After cooling down, she dried off her face and headed back to the clinic. That's when she saw a giant iguana emerging from behind the cabin and meandering away.

Fred!

That must be what she'd seen behind the tree earlier, though she could have sworn it was a man's face. Maybe the heat was playing tricks on her.

In the five minutes that she'd been gone, a woman came in with an eight-hour course of severe belly pain and vomiting. While she didn't meet the classic Four-F criteria for gallstone attacks typical for Americans—fat, forty, fertile, and female—Allison still suspected gall stones were the likely culprit. After completing a thorough history and physical, she and Grant concluded that acute cholecystitis was the most likely cause of her pain. Dr. Jones pulled out the ultrasound machine.

"I'm no board-certified radiologist," he informed them, "but I've acquired a few skills at picking up gall stones and ectopic pregnancies over the years."

After squirting gel on the woman's belly, he moved the ultrasound wand around on the woman's abdomen.

"Bingo. Look right there," he said pointing on the screen. "Her gall bladder is loaded with stones. And do you see how thick and irritated the wall looks?"

He scanned the rest of the abdomen and pointed out the normal liver, pancreas, and kidneys.

"A classic case of acute cholecystitis," Grant agreed.

The woman consented to exploratory surgery with the likely probability she'd need her gall bladder excised.

"Since you got the C-section and appendix, this one is mine," Grant said, gesturing toward himself.

Yes, if she had done two surgeries, then, of course, it was his turn to operate. But yeesh? Did he have to be so grabby about it? Did he think she would try to snatch up every surgery and leave him empty-handed? Besides, a cholecystectomy bested a measly appendectomy any day, so Grant had no reason to complain. She knew she was being childish, so she forced herself to nod. "By all means it is your turn."

Grant eyed Dr. Jones. "Do we have a laparoscope?"

Dr. Jones nodded. "Thanks to our generous donor, we do have a laparoscope, though it's getting old, and we don't have the funds to purchase a new one. We also can't do robotic surgery."

As she and Grant scrubbed up for surgery, Allison tried to content herself with her secondary role as a surgical assistant.

You are here to save lives, not to compete with Grant.

Attitude adjusted, she attached telemetry, started an IV, and scrubbed the woman's abdomen with Betadine. She covered the sterile field with drapes and scrubbed up again then pulled on sterile gown and gloves with the assistance of Dr. Jones.

After Dr. Jones administered anesthesia, Grant sliced into the woman's abdomen.

He then advanced the scope to the gall bladder, the woman's telemetry started showing premature ventricular contractions. At first, it was only every fifth or sixth beat, so they weren't concerned. After all, occasional PVCs were harmless enough. Then, before Grant could suggest starting a lidocaine drip, the woman converted into a highly dangerous ventricular tachycardia.

Allison's heart jolted. Yikes! She thumped the woman's chest, a maneuver that thankfully converted the woman back to normal sinus rhythm.

"Inject a lidocaine bolus and start a drip," Grant barked.

Dr. Jones dashed to grab a bottle of lidocaine from the drug cabinet. "I guess we should have gotten a baseline EKG on her, but since she's only in her late thirties, I didn't think it was necessary. Big mistake, that."

"Even if we had, it would have been normal," Allison pointed out. "After all, the telemetry was completely normal when we first started operating."

"True," he agreed, as he hung the lidocaine onto the IV pole. Within a minute, he had the bolus infused and a maintenance dose dripping into her veins.

"I hope that's the last we see of cardiac issues," Grant commented, a worried crease etched across his brow. "Hard to operate in the middle of CPR and defibrilla—"

Before he could finish the word, the woman had converted into full-blown ventricular fibrillation.

Allison stared at the monitor in momentary shock before snapping into autopilot. "You start CPR, and I'll get the defibrillator charged and ready."

Grant put down his surgical tools and began the rapid thrusting motion of CPR on the woman's chest. Allison reached for the crash cart.

After ensuring the paddles were fully charged, she cranked the voltage to 120 volt and placed both paddles on the woman's chest. "Everyone back," she barked.

Grant stepped back, and Allison administered the quick volt of electricity.

Praying the electric shock had converted her back to normal sinus rhythm, they stared at the monitor. No such luck. Still ventricular fibrillation. Grant resumed chest compressions.

This was the first time she'd ever had a patient convert to ventricular fibrillation right in the middle of surgery. Her eyes met Grant's across the surgical table, and his widened eyes suggested he was equally unnerved. He said nothing and continued firm rapid downward compressions.

Calm down. Rely on your training. You can do this.

She charged the defibrillator to 200 joules and applied the paddles on the woman's chest again. "Everybody clear," she barked, and Grant, once again, stopped chest compressions and stepped back.

She pushed the button to release a sudden volt and held her breath. They stared at the monitor, and this time, thankfully, the patient converted to normal rhythm.

"I'll up the lidocaine drip," Dr. Jones said, pushing up the drip rate. "Hopefully, that will keep her in a normal rhythm. I'll also draw some blood. Maybe her potassium is low and that's what caused the arrhythmia. She said she'd been vomiting for two days, so I'll bet her electrolytes are all out of whack."

"How long until the results come back?" Grant inquired, as he and Allison disposed of their now contaminated surgical gloves. Dr. Jones assisted them in pulling on a fresh pair.

Once both surgeons were re-gloved, Dr. Jones pushed a button on the monitor to increase the lidocaine infusion rate again. He chuckled.

"Since I'm your lab technician and anesthesiologist, our blood results will have to wait until we're done with surgery." He raised open palms. "Welcome to the one man show of surgical care in the back woods of Haiti."

Grant nodded. "If this were an American ER, they would have automatically checked her electrolytes, blood counts, and liver panel, along with a CT scan before I'd be consulted. With no STAT lab results to guide us, it feels like we're operating in the dark ages."

Dr. Jones pointed to the crash cart. "Except there were no defibrillators in the dark ages."

"Touché," Grant conceded, glancing up long enough to smile. "We've got the tools, just not the manpower."

Dr. Jones wrapped a tourniquet around the patient's arm, pulled on a pair of gloves, and palpated for a vein. "Okay, now I'm putting on my phlebotomist hat."

"As opposed to your anesthesiologist, radiologist, pediatrician, and internist hat?" Allison said.

"And don't forget my RN hat," he said raising a finger.

"Amazing how all your hats look alike, Allison commented with a grin."

Now garbed up with a fresh gown and sterile gloves, Grant focused on extracting the gall bladder before commenting, "It must get overwhelming, trying to be a one-man show."

"It does, at times," Dr. Jones conceded, "But keep in mind, before I started this clinic, people like Fabiola, the twins, and Jacques would simply have died. They have no transportation to Port-au-Prince, and even if they did, the nearest surgical clinic is four hours away. Plus, in my experience, locals wait until they are in dire straits before coming in. By then, the four-hour drive to Port-au-Prince is too long. We either operate here, or the patient dies."

Guilt coursed through Grant veins. What a lousy attitude he'd displayed when he first arrived in Haiti. All he'd focused on were the primitive living conditions and had given no thought for the people he'd be helping. So what if he didn't have air conditioning or hot showers? He could survive without them. He'd behaved like a rich spoiled brat. Here in Haiti, he could save the lives of some of the most marginalized people on the planet—a desperate group with no one else to take care of their medical needs.

A deep wave of satisfaction settled over him. Dr. Morrison had been right. Grant would not return from Haiti the same man. But right now, he had a desperately ill patient to attend to.

Dr. Jones placed the tubes of blood in a rack to let the blood settle before he centrifuged it, poured it off, and ran it through the automated laboratory machine. "I'll start a potassium drip just in case her level is low. It may stabilize her heart rhythm." He retrieved a bag of potassium chloride from the storage closet and piggybacked it to the lidocaine drip.

"Sounds like a good idea." Grant agreed. "Removing gall bladders in the middle of CPR is not my idea of a good time."

He glanced across the surgical table at Allison and added, "I'll bet you're glad you got the appendectomy instead of this nightmare-of-a-surgery."

She smirked. "Hey, at least I got to practice my skills with the defibrillator paddles. At Hopkins, we have a whole code team that handles everything during cardiac arrests."

Grant nodded. "We really are a bare-bones crew here."

"Unfortunately, we received funding for the clinic and for all the supplies and equipment, but not for the salary of an RN, scrub nurse, anesthesiologist, laboratory tech, or radiologist."

"That must make it difficult," Allison said.

"Even if I had the funding, it's hard to find professionals willing to move to a remote part of Haiti. Consequently, I've had to learn how to do everything myself and trust God to provide volunteers like you two to perform the surgeries. That's why I'm so grateful to you both for coming."

Another stab of guilt. If he hadn't been vying for the Chief Resident position, he would be at Hopkins doing facelifts on rich women with no problems except a vain dissatisfaction with their wrinkles. Instead, he was now in Haiti saving lives.

"Are you able to get surgical residents on a consistent basis?" Allison asked.

Dr. Jones shrugged and adjusted the drip rate on the potassium drip. "Probably eighty percent of the time I can get a surgical resident or practicing surgeon to come for a week or two as a short-term medical missionary. I'm always on my own at Christmas and Thanksgiving, though. No one wants to be here then."

"So what do you do if a surgical emergency comes in during the holidays?" Allison asked, already dreading his answer.

"I do as much as I am trained to do, but the surgical emergencies get driven to Port-au-Prince. Sometimes they make it in time, but unfortunately, usually they don't."

"Especially with no ambulance," Grant added.

Dr. Jones chuckled. "Sadly, Angelina serves as our ambulance."

Grant's scalpel stopped midair. "That rust bucket is your only means of transporting people to the hospital?"

"Grant!" Allison scolded.

He raised his hands, scalpel in tow. "Hey, I'm just calling it the way I see it."

Dr. Jones shrugged. "Unfortunately, Angelina is all we have right now. The financial grant we received did not cover the cost of a new vehicle or the upkeep of an ambulance."

Grant shook his head. How did Dr. Jones stand practicing with such an unreliable vehicle? He hoped none of the patients he saw would need transport to Port-au-Prince.

As he glanced at the heart monitor, he noticed with alarm that the patient was throwing off PVCs again. He'd better focus on operating before he needed defibrillator paddles again. He returned to his laparoscope and had the gall bladder removed within thirty minutes. As expected, it was loaded with stones and the duct was thickened and irritated. After suturing up the incision sites, he released an audible sigh of relief. "Thank God we managed to finish up without another bout of V. fib."

Allison pulled off her surgical gloves and snapped her fingers. "Shucks! I wanted more practice with the defibrillator." She mimed zapping a patient with her paddles.

He rewarded her a glare. "Wicked, wicked woman."

"Just kidding. I'm glad her heart behaved itself."

Dr. Jones returned from the lab waving a printed report. "No wonder she went into ventricular fibrillation."

"What was her potassium level?" Grant inquired.

"You got that right. It was only 1.8."

"Wow! Good thing you gave her that run of potassium mid surgery."

"If we want to get her level over 4.0, she'll need another four or five bags," Allison said.

"Absolutely," Dr. Jones agreed, bee-lining toward the drug closet to pull out another bag of potassium chloride.

Grant dressed the surgical incision site then tugged off his gloves and disposed of them. He stretched his back muscles and rolled his neck.

Once the patient had recovered from anesthesia and was fully awake, the two exhausted surgeons flopped into a chair. Dr. Jones offered to man the recovery room while they took a thirty-minute break and grabbed a bite to eat.

He didn't have to ask twice.

CHAPTER 10

As they trudged into the kitchen, Grant grumbled, "I could hardly stay focused for fear she'd snap back into ventricular fibrillation again."

"I can imagine." Allison opened an upper cabinet, grabbed a can of beef stew, and pulled a can opener from the drawer.

"It's weird, isn't it? On the one hand, we have a state-of-the-art surgical suite but no staff or CT scanners to assist us."

"It's forcing us to rely on our clinical skills." She pried open the soup can, dumped the contents into two bowls, then placed the bowls in the microwave and punched in three minutes. "In some ways, it's forcing us to be better doctors."

"What do you mean?" Grant opened the cabinet, pulled out a box of crackers, and placed a handful on a plate.

"In the States, having the luxury of STAT labs, CT scanners, and Board-certified radiologists to read the films has kept us from having to rely on our history and physical exam skills. It's made us lazy." She opened the refrigerator, retrieved a bottle of mango juice, and filled two glasses.

"I suppose you're right. I mean, it's easy to diagnose acute appendicitis when you have a CT scan telling you exactly what's wrong."

"Here, we have to rely solely on palpating the abdomen—and gut instinct—pardon the pun," Allison said.

"Ha, ha," Grant said, rolling his eyes. The microwave dinged that their soup was hot, so Grant retrieved the bowls and placed them on the table next to the plate of crackers.

"I still prefer the reassurance of a positive CT report before I go plunging a scalpel into someone's abdomen," Grant said, sitting in the chair.

Allison grabbed two spoons from the drawer. "Can you imagine opening someone up thinking they had a hot appendix, and then when you get in there, you find out the patient was just constipated?"

Grant shook his head. "That's a conversation I'd rather not have. 'I'm sorry, Mrs. Smith. I thought your appendix was about to burst, but, you just needed a couple of Ex-lax.'"

Allison giggled. "Thankfully, I've never had to look a patient in the eyes and tell her that before."

Grant's lips thinned. "Here's hoping we remember all of our Physical Exam 101 skills since the nearest CT scanner is four hours away."

Raphael wandered into the kitchen and offered a shy smile. He stared at their soup with obvious longing. Allison waved several crackers in his direction. "Est-ce que tu as faim?"

He nodded.

She handed him the crackers and then reached for another bowl and dumped half of her soup into the bowl. After offering the soup to Raphael, he scarfed it down in two minutes flat as though he feared she might change her mind and take her soup back.

He offered a grateful smile and mumbled "Merci" before dashing out of the kitchen.

"Do you know where he lives? I know he hangs out here at the clinic a lot and likes to help Mrs. Jones with the cooking, but does he have an actual home?"

Grant shoveled in a bite of potato and after swallowing, said, "Dr. Jones tells me he lives in a ramshackle tin house about the size of an outhouse."

"Where is it?" Allison asked.

"Not far from our sleeping quarters. It doesn't have indoor plumbing, so Dr. Jones worries he'll get cholera. He says there is raw sewage running nearby. He's counseled Raphael about washing his hands before he eats, but with no purified water nearby, it's an infection waiting to happen."

"He's an orphan, correct?"

"Yes, but Judy says she keeps him here as much as possible." Grant munched on a cracker.

"That's nice of them."

"They don't have the bedrooms to watch all the orphans in town, and if they let Raphael live with them, it would be hard to say no to the others."

Allison nodded. "So that's why they say Raphael is training to be a cook. If they word it that he is a cooking apprentice, they can justify giving him extra food and attention compared to the others."

"It's pitiful seeing all these homeless children in Haiti."

"I wish I could do something for them," Allison said, spooning in a bite of carrot.

"Dr. Jones says they're trying to raise the funds to start an orphanage and school, but as of right now, he barely gets enough to keep the medical clinical afloat."

Allison frowned. "As can be seen from the lack of RN and medical technologists. He literally runs a one-man show at the mercy of surgeons like us volunteering to come help. Plus, when would he find the time to do fund-raising?"

A wave of guilt coursed through Grant again. If he'd had his way, he'd be obsessing about the size of noses and breast implants right now.

How superfluous it all seemed compared to the dire need for surgeons in Haiti.

"It must be frustrating to never have a steady staff. Dr. Jones can handle all the primary care and pediatrics, but he's at the mercy of volunteers for the life-threatening surgeries."

"No wonder Dr. Morrison was so keen on getting us down here," Grant reflected. "He told me when I signed up that he's done similar rotations, and it changed his life."

"I believe that. Americans have first-rate emergency rooms in nearly every town. Look at what they have in rural Haiti."

Swallowing the last of his soup, Grant said, "Once I'm out of residency and earning a decent income, I'm going to contribute some serious funds to help this clinic."

Allison pursed her lips. "I wonder if we could hold a fund-raiser when we get back."

He scratched his neck. "What kind of fund-raiser?"

"I don't k "A bake sale? A carwash?"

His shoulders dropped. "Seriously? That would raise enough to feed one orphan for a month. If we're lucky."

She folded her arms in protest. "Hey, every little bit helps."

"Maybe so, but we need more than brownies and buckets of soapsuds to do any real good."

She popped a cracker in her mouth and chewed with annoyance. "What's your brilliant idea then?"

Grant's face brightened. "Maybe the Stockdale Foundation could be persuaded to donate."

Her eyebrows furrowed. "The Stockdale Foundation? What's that?"

"It's a charitable foundation my great-grandfather started to advance medical care and the sciences at Johns Hopkins and a few surrounding hospitals. Stockdales have pledged twenty percent of their income to the Foundation since the late 1800s. With careful investing, the Stockdale Foundation's endowment has done really well."

"So that's where the money for the new science building and parking garage came from?"

He smirked. "Lord knows it didn't come from my bank account. The Foundation also has a lot of wealthy benefactors in the D.C area. They're members of my parents' country club."

"I suppose a ritzy country club is a great way to hob-nob with the wealthy."

He leaned forward conspiratorially. "I'll let you in on a secret. My father *hates* golf. He claims it's a total waste of time, but he plays to dig up more donors for the Foundation."

"That's commendable," Allison said, surprised to learn the Stockdales were so committed to giving back.

Grant chuckled. "Either that or it's a lame excuse for his pitiful golf game. I could beat him blindfolded."

Allison laughed. "That bad, huh? It's big of him to keep playing when it makes him look bad."

He wiped his mouth with his napkin before adding, "My mother drummed it into me before I was five that the Bible says, 'Of whom much is given, much is expected.'"

"Your mother is a Christian?" she said, not sure why the news warmed her heart.

He looked across the table at her. "My whole family are committed believers."

She must have looked surprised because he added, "I know I don't say much about my faith around the hospital. I've always believed Christianity is a verb and not just a belief system. We're called to demonstrate tangible love."

"That's true," Allison agreed.

"Up until this rotation, I assumed donating twenty percent of my income to charity was proof of my faith. I see now it's so much more than that. It's committing my time and talent, as well as my money."

She nodded, "Though money could go a long way to support this clinic's need for a new ambulance and nurse."

"When I get back home, I'll write up a proposal and present it at the next Foundation meeting. I'll also write a couple of our reliable donors."

"The worst they can say is 'no'," Allison agreed before munching on another cracker.

They ate in companionable silence until Allison said, "Grant, I need to confess something. I've totally misjudged you these last four years."

His hand holding his soup spoon froze. "How so?"

"Don't take this the wrong way, but you always seemed aloof. Stand-offish. I assumed you were a snob and thought you were better than me. That you looked down on me."

His head pulled back. "Why would I look down on you?"

She shrugged. "My background."

"Didn't you graduate at the top of your medical school class?"

"A-ya, but UVM is hardly Harvard."

"You think dissecting a cadaver at Harvard is any different than dissecting a cadaver at UVM?"

She responded with a wry smile. "Last I knew, dead bodies have 206 bones no matter which school they're dissected at."

He reached for her arm. "Then why would I look down on you?"

She stared down at the table refusing to make eye contact. Remembering Alexander's parents, she felt the familiar wave of shame course over her. "Come on, Grant. I know you've heard the rumors about my hometown."

He shrugged. "I did hear a few jabs about you being born in Mount Trashmore."

She bristled. "The town is called Coventry." She felt her eyes fill with tears. "I love the people of my hometown."

He reached for her hand across the table. "Allison, you have nothing to be ashamed of. The people of Coventry saw an amazing economic opportunity and grabbed the bull by the horns."

She stared back at him with mouth agape. He didn't laugh at her behind her back like so many others had? She'd overheard more digs than she cared to admit. Surely Grant had added his fuel to the fire over the last four years, as well. She crossed her arms. "You honestly believe your parents wouldn't eye me as white trash?"

"Not at all. Northern Vermont is economically depressed. If Coventry found a way to bring good-paying jobs to the town, my parents would commend their ingenuity." He added, "My father always preaches, 'Make the most of every opportunity.' Well, that's what Coventry did."

Perhaps due to sheer exhaustion, her emotional barriers were down. Tears poured down her cheeks. She quickly brushed them away. "For years, I thought you and all the rich Hopkins elite looked down on me because of my humble background."

He squeezed her hand again. "If I ever did anything to make you feel judged by me, I apologize. I've always admired your strong work ethic and surgical skills. Plus, you're always so friendly with the nurses. I'm an introvert, but because of my background, people take it as snobbishness."

She nodded. "A-ya. I thought you were too high and mighty to waste your time on the likes of me."

"Ouch!" His shoulder sagged. "I guess I need to work on my people skills, huh?"

"It may just be that I'm oversensitive due to—" She stopped herself before confessing what happened with Alexander. "Due to some experiences in my past."

He picked up his dirty soup bowl and brought it to the sink then filled the sink with water and added a few drops of Clorox and began to scrub vigorously with a dishcloth. "You know how you think people judge you for being poor? Well, I have the opposite problem. People act like I was born with a silver spoon in my mouth and had everything handed to me on a platter." He rinsed the bowl and slammed it a bit too hard on the dishrack. "I've worked really hard to get where I am, and it bugs me when I hear murmuring that I only got accepted into Hopkins because I'm a Stockdale, or I'm only up for Chief Surgical Resident because of my family name."

Shame coursed through her. Hadn't she harbored those exact same thoughts?

"Grant, you're the hardest worker in our class. I don't think anyone could accuse you of not earning the position on your own merit. It's time you let that go."

He grabbed her soup bowl and plate and scrubbed them as though they were covered with Ebola virus. "It isn't just the silver spoon thing. I mean, how do I know if someone likes me for me, or if she's just impressed with my family's wealth and status?"

She grabbed a dishtowel and dried the soup bowls. "Find someone even richer and more powerful than you. Then you'll know she loves you enough to marry down."

He shook his head and chuckled. "Great advice, Allison. So, I should hold out for Paris Hilton?"

"Or a Kardashian. Then you'll know she isn't in it for your money."

He rolled his eyes.

"Seriously, Grant. When you meet the right person, you'll know. She'll share your vision for life, and she'll believe in you. You'll feel safe sharing who you are, even your weaknesses and insecurities."

He rubbed his chin. "Sounds like a pipe dream to me."

"Well, it's not. She also ought to share your faith, unlike that slutty unit clerk on 5-East who is always flirting with you," she added with a scowl.

He pulled back with wide eyes. "Slutty unit clerk on 5-East? I never noticed. Who are you talking about?"

Arms akimbo she snapped, "Pul-lease! You know perfectly well who I'm talking about. That Brittany What's-Her-Face. She throws herself at you every time you come near. Tee, hee, hee," Allison mocked with an exaggerated giggle. She pointed at him. "Now there's a woman to stay away from. Total gold digger."

His eyes narrowed. "How do you know that?"

"Because she flirts ruthlessly with all the guys who come from money but completely ignores the guys from poor or middle-class families like Jason Long. I can tell he's sweet on her, but she won't give him the time of day."

"Good to know." He grinned before adding, "Maybe I should hire you to be my matchmaker—like Yente in *Fiddler on the Roof*."

"I love that musical. And you don't have to pay me. If you want my input about a woman's interest in you, I'm more than willing to give you my two cents."

He reared up cat claws and hissed. "I'll bet you are."

She whipped his arm with the dishtowel. "Hey! I am not being catty. I'm just telling it like it is. Guys can be notoriously stupid at falling for women who flirt and flatter their ego, but then they completely ignore the solid, salt-of-the-earth types who would make faithful, loving wives."

His lips thinned. "Oh, really! And how many women have you seen *me* fall for? When have I been notoriously stupid?"

She opened her mouth to speak and then abruptly shut it. Hmm. He was right! While the women flirted and stroked his ego with abandon, he never seemed to respond to any of them, other than with professional politeness. She remembered overhearing Catherine sputtering how she'd invited Grant to her house one night, but after he'd brushed off her advances, she'd decided he was gay. Allison had to bite her tongue from snapping that just because a guy wasn't willing to flop into bed with her on the first date hardly made him gay!

"You know what, Grant, you're right. I haven't ever seen you fall for any of the throng who drool over your every word."

He rolled his eyes. "It's hardly a throng, Allison, and they certainly don't drool. But to answer your question, I'm not convinced any of them truly like me for me."

"What do you mean?"

"I mean, stripped of my family's money and my MD degree, if I were a truck driver or grocery store clerk, would any of them give me the time of day?"

She considered his question before responding. "They would, because women think you're easy on the eyes."

He grinned. "Easy on the eyes, huh?"

No way would she tell him he was drop dead gorgeous.

"That's not the whole reason, though," she added. "In fairness to your throng of groupies, part of your appeal is your intelligence—and your ambition. Women find that attractive."

He grinned. "So, you think I'm handsome and brilliant?"

She felt her cheeks flush. "I didn't say *I* found you handsome and brilliant. I said *other* women think that."

He lifted a brow with that infuriatingly playful grin still plastered across his face. "But you don't?"

She swatted him with the dishtowel again. "Quit fishing for compliments. Obviously, you're brilliant, and I'm not blind. A woman would have to have end-stage macular degeneration not to acknowledge that you're handsome."

"So, you *do* find me attractive," he said with a wink.

Flustered, she rose from the table and dunked her juice glass in the dishwater. "I find you vexing! Now quit goading me! If we're working together for the next three months, it would be unprofessional of me to comment on your attractiveness. We're supposed to be colleagues, remember?"

"Colleagues can't acknowledge one another's intelligence and attractiveness?" Grant countered.

Her eyes narrowed. "Not when they're sleeping in beds less than five feet apart. It wouldn't be right." She crossed her arms, and in her most prudish voice added, "Highly unseemly."

He grinned. "So that's what's got you all riled up! It makes you hot and bothered that we're sleeping right next to each other."

"What has me hot and bothered is no air conditioning!"

He roared with laughter. "Touché!" He then sobered and added, "For the record? I find you attractive and intelligent, too, Allison."

Her eyes must have widened in shock because he added, "Relax! You don't need a chastity belt. I'm perfectly capable of behaving like a gentleman and a professional."

At that point, Dr. Jones walked into the kitchen to grab a bite. "Did you remember to add Clorox to the dishwater?"

"Yes," Grant assured him.

"Judy and I have never had cholera, but that's because we are diligent to filter our water and use Clorox or chlorine tablets when washing the dishes. Sadly, many locals don't take the time to do that."

"I thought the Bill and Melinda Gates Foundation offered free purification systems to anyone who wanted one in Haiti," Allison said.

"Yes, but getting the locals to *use* them on a consistent basis is a different matter," Dr. Jones said as he reached for a loaf of bread and pulled out two slices. Smearing peanut butter on the bread he added, "I've treated ten cholera outbreaks since I've been here."

"Ten?" Wow! That's a lot," Allison said.

"After every outbreak, I do my best to educate the locals on the importance of boiling their water, or using a purification system, or adding chlorine tablets. Things get better for a while, and then they get lax with their safety measures again, and we're back to square one."

Grant glanced toward the recovery room. "Who's watching our patient?"

Dr. Jones smiled. "Raphael."

Grant's eyes widened. "You're letting an eight-year-old watch a surgical patient fresh out of ventricular fibrillation?"

"Believe it or not, I've taught Raphael how to read a cardiac monitor, and if he sees anything worrisome, he hollers for me."

Allison's face mirrored his own concern. "Is that even legal? To leave the care of a patient in the hands of a child?"

Dr. Jones met her gaze head-on with steely eyes. "This may surprise you, but Raphael is more skilled at reading EKGs than ninety percent of the surgical residents who rotate through here. I've trained him extensively, and he is always spot on with his EKG interpretations."

Allison's mouth dropped. "Wow! That's impressive for a kid his age." She rose and reached for her lab coat.

As though still defensive, Dr. Jones added, "I only came in here long enough to spread peanut butter on a slice of bread. I haven't had a bite to eat in hours."

Slamming his sandwich on a plate, he added, "I have no nurse, so sometimes I have to run in to grab a bit to eat. Or go to the bathroom. Raphael is well-trained."

Allison patted his shoulder. "I'm sorry. I didn't mean to make you feel defensive. I'm not questioning your judgment, and I should have kept my mouth shut."

Grant added, "We're done eating, so we'll go check on her. You take a well-earned lunch break and enjoy your sandwich."

Calling over her shoulder as she exited the kitchen, Allison teased, "Maybe we can get Raphael to help us brush up on our EKG skills."

Dr. Jones chuckled. "You do that."

Grant followed her to the clinic whispering, "We have got to get him some help. I get that he can't work 24/7 without a chance to grab lunch, but leaving someone fresh out of surgery to the care of a child?"

Allison whispered back, "If this were the States, he'd be shut down in an hour."

"And then, ironically, the locals would be worse off because they'd be left with no care."

As Allison and Grant reached the recovery room, sure enough, Raphael stood at the patient's side watching the monitor attentively. "Normal sinus with a heartrate of eighty."

He continued. "She's had two PVCs but no bigeminy or ventricular tachycardia."

Allison and Grant looked at each other with dropped mouths.

Grant affixed a stethoscope to his ears and listened to her heartbeat, which proved steady. Now somewhat awake, the patient asked in French, "Did my surgery go as planned?"

Raphael acted as the interpreter.

Grant and Allison tried not to laugh. Did her surgery go as planned? Ah, that would be a gigantic "No!" But what were they supposed to tell her?—"Other than needing CPR and defibrillation twice in the middle of your surgery, everything went great!" No, that was probably *not* the way to alleviate the woman's fears about Western doctors!

Grant cleared his throat and responded, "Tell her there were no problems we weren't fully trained to handle."

The woman smiled up at him and attempted to speak in broken English. "You good doctor. Fix pain. Merci beaucoups."

"You're welcome, I mean, Bienvenu." He was amazed he'd managed to pull out one of the French terms he'd attempted to memorize on his flight to Haiti.

She gripped his arm, and her eyes welled with tears. "If you no here, I die."

He blinked back tears. It didn't matter whether he could speak her language, or whether he was rich, and she was poor. Some things were universal, and the desire to live without pain was one.

"Glad to help," Grant said. "That's why we came to Haiti."

His conscience kicked him in the stomach for blatantly lying. He'd come to secure the Chief Residency position.

But no longer.

How self-absorbed he'd been just a week ago when he'd grumbled about the lack of wi-fi and air conditioning when all around him were desperate Haitians needing the services he and Allison could provide.

Dr. Jones dashed back into the recovery room chomping on the last bite of his sandwich. He eyed the cardiac monitor and inquired, "Did she have any ectopy while I was gone, Raphael?"

Raphael shrugged his skinny shoulders. "Not really. Just two isolated PVCs, so I wasn't worried."

Dr. Jones grinned. "Good boy! I'm hard-pressed to tell whether you'll make a better cook or a better doctor."

Raphael grinned impishly. "Can't I be doctor who also cook good?"

Dr. Jones laughed and pointed at him. "That's my boy. Indeed, you can."

Raphael blushed with pride.

"Raphael, Mrs. Jones wants you to meet her in the living room for your English and Science lessons. Damian and Clarisse will be joining you today."

Raphael nodded, waved goodbye, and then he scampered out for his lessons.

After he left, the patient, still groggy from her anesthesia, fell back to sleep and released a snore.

Dr. Jones explained. "Judy has been home-schooling Raphael and two of the neighborhood children for a year now. They're all eager to learn, but Raphael is our star pupil. He's now reading at a sixth-grade level, and as you can see, he's mastered EKGs."

Dr. Jones continued. "Judy and I have applied to adopt him, but since we are not Haitian citizens, so far we've faced nothing but red tape."

Bile boiled up Grant's chest. "So they would rather these poor kids be left parentless than allow them to be adopted into a loving home just because you and Judy aren't Haitian? That makes no sense."

Dr. Jones' lips thinned. "Actually, it makes more sense than you realize."

"Why is that?" Allison inquired.

"After the earthquake, these defenseless and desperate orphans became easy prey for sex traffickers."

Grant shook his head, his lips thinned. "That's terrible."

"Scumbags from all over the world poured into Haiti and convinced officials they wanted to adopt these kids because they felt sorry for them. Months later, it was revealed many became victims of sex trafficking rings."

"How did they find out?" Allison asked.

"Some of the kids escaped and managed to make it to the local police. That's when the truth came out. Now Haitian officials are understandably suspicious of foreigners who wants to adopt a child and whisk them off to another country."

Allison's eyes pooled with tears. "Those poor kids. First, they lose their parents and home, and then they get exploited by sex traffickers."

Grant's jaw clenched. "There's a special place in Hell for anyone who would do that to an orphan. To any child."

"You got that right," Dr. Jones said. "So, I have no problem with the government taking its time to make sure Judy and I are everything we claim to be."

He added, "In the meantime, we treat Raphael and several of the other children as though they were already ours."

"That's commendable of you," Allison said.

He paused, as though hesitant to say more, but he finally confessed, "Judy was unable to have children of her own due to severe endometriosis. She struggled to get pregnant even after surgery and extensive treatment, and then she miscarried three times. After that, we just gave up and decided it wasn't God's will for us to have children."

Allison's eyes misted. "Little did you know, God had Haitian children desperately needing love and attention already picked out for you."

"We didn't understand God's will at the time, but I see now it put us in a perfect position to foster children here in Haiti. If we'd birthed the three or four children we'd envisioned having on our own, Judy wouldn't have had the time or energy or motivation to take in orphans."

"God had a plan all along," Grant said.

Dr. Jones nodded. "His ways are higher than our ways, though at times I don't understand His ways at all."

"I'll bet there's been a lot of healing for Judy in loving these motherless children," Allison commented.

"Judy felt like God had abandoned her or didn't care about her desire to be a mother."

He quickly added, "She never said that, but I could see it in her eyes. A deep resignation and disappointment with life. Like her deepest desire had been squelched."

"So basically, when you sacrificed your life to become a doctor at an indigenous clinic in Haiti, that's when God blessed you and Judy with children who would desperately need you," Grant commented.

Dr. Jones grinned. "God is good, isn't He? Sometimes He gives us the desires of our heart when we give up trying to get them on our own—when we least expect it."

Just then, the bell on the front door of the clinic rang. As the three doctors rushed to the waiting room to see who needed help, a man struggled to carry in a woman whose arms flopped lifelessly. Thankfully, her moans and clutched abdomen let them know she was alive, but she seemed lethargic. Delirious, even.

As they ushered the man, Pierre, back to an exam room and placed the woman, Regina, onto an exam table, Dr. Jones inquired, "What symptoms is she having?"

The man offered a rapid litany of complaints in French Creole which neither Grant nor Allison understood.

After completing his inquiry, Dr. Jones summarized his findings in English for Allison and Grant.

"Four days of incessant diarrhea, severe abdominal cramps, and now she is so weak she fainted on her way to the clinic."

"Cholera," Grant and Allison said simultaneously.

"Afraid so. Put on your roller skates, because if there's one case, there's bound to be a dozen. We're in for a long week."

CHAPTER 11

"Let's find out how they get their drinking water," Dr. Jones said.

After questioning the couple further, Dr. Jones frowned. "He says they normally boil their water before consuming it, but they were out of boiled water, and Regina was so thirsty she drank water straight from the well."

"Has anyone else in the family consumed water that hasn't been boiled?" Grant asked.

Pierre, the husband, admitted that yes, he, too, had consumed "just a few sips" of the contaminated water before he realized his wife hadn't boiled it. He then acknowledged he was now suffering from intestinal cramps and loose stools, as well. "But nothing like Regina."

"Perhaps because he only drank a few sips instead of an entire tumblerful, he got a smaller load of the cholera bacteria," Allison surmised.

"Or, he may be earlier in the course of his disease," Grant countered. "He may deteriorate before this thing is through. Ask him if they own a water purification system."

Dr. Jones raised the question, and the man's shoulders slumped like he'd been asked if he owned a Lexus SUV. "Four children to feed. No money for purification system," he said in broken English. He glared at his wife. "If Regina boil water, this no happen."

Allison gripped the woman's hands and asked in French, "Where are the children?"

"Gabriella watch them," she groaned as an intestinal cramp doubled her over. She clutched her abdomen and moaned.

"How old is Gabriella?" Allison asked.

"Ten, but she good girl. Responsible."

"Do any of the children have diarrhea and cramps," Grant asked, with Dr. Jones interpreting.

"The baby," Regina said, gripping her abdomen as a cramp overtook her again. "Yesterday, he fussy. I change diaper many, many times. This morning all he do is sleep."

"How old is the baby?" Dr Jones asked.

"One," Pierre said. "But he better. No fussy this morning. Just lay in his crib quiet."

Dr. Jones' lips thinned, and he informed Allison and Grant in hushed tones, "If they don't get adequate fluids and electrolytes, babies can die from dehydration and kidney failure in less than two days with cholera. Sounds like he's already going into shock. This is a life-threatening emergency."

"Then we need to get that baby in here now," Allison said.

"If he doesn't get fluids soon, he'll he dead by tomorrow." He turned to Pierre and said, "You need to go get all four children right now. They need IV fluids, especially the baby."

Pierre looked down and shuffled his feet. "I carry wife an hour to get her here. I had to stop and, ah, you know, three times on the side of the road. I no strength left. Plus, I can't carry four children. Except for Gabriella, they are too young to walk this far."

Dr. Jones' eyes bulged. "You carried your wife for an hour to get her here, even though you are sick yourself?"

"Oui." He shrugged. "What choice I have?"

"You have no means of transportation? A car or motorbike?"

"A bicycle, but I can't carry sick wife on bicycle."

Dr. Jones rubbed his chin in thought. "I'd get Jean-Paul to drive you to your house to get the children, but he went with his brother to Port-au-Price to visit his grandbaby."

Pierre sank wearily into a chair. "Plan no good. Road bad." He gestured with his hands it was bumpy and steep. "Car no make it up steep hill to house."

"Is Angelina here, or did Jean-Paul drive her to Port-au-Price? Allison asked.

"She's here," Dr. Jones said. "Since the brother's car is more reliable than Angelina, they drove to Port-au-Prince in Maurice's car."

"Then we'll drive as far as we can and walk the rest of the way to the house to get the children. We can carry the sick kids from the house to the truck," Allison said.

Dr. Jones eyed Pierre slumped in the chair looking one step from death. "Pierre and Regina are dangerously dehydrated, and Pierre must be exhausted after carrying his wife for an hour in this heat. They both need IV fluids immediately—before their kidneys shut down."

"How will I find the house? If a car can't reach it, it sounds like it's not exactly on a main road," Allison pointed out.

"We'll get them to draw a map with detailed instructions," Dr. Jones suggested.

"Okay. So, we get IVs infusing in Regina and Pierre, and then I'll take Angelina and go get the kids," Allison said, thinking out loud.

Grant shook his head. "Absolutely not! You cannot go alone. You could end up lost, or raped, or murdered."

Allison crossed her arms. "Oh, for Pete's sake. No one is going to murder me."

Dr. Jones pursed his lips. "I hate to disagree with you, Allison, but there is a high crime rate in the area. You certainly can't go alone."

"Exactly," Grant said. "It isn't safe for a beautiful woman to be traipsing around in a foreign country by herself, especially when she doesn't speak the language. Might I remind you that you nearly ended up in a Haitian jail because of your deplorable French skills at the airport?"

She would have kicked him in the shins—hard—except he had called her beautiful. But still, his comment was patronizing. Insulting. She glared at him. "My French skills may be deplorable, but they're better than yours," she countered. "And far more useful than your worthless four years of Chinese," she added for good measure.

Grant raked a frustrated hand through his hair. "I'm just saying, it isn't wise to go by yourself. Besides, there's no way you can get that rat-trap-of-a-truck to run."

"Wanna bet?" She stuck out a challenging hand. "I'm a farm girl, remember? My Dad owned a truck just like Angelina, and I drove it regularly."

She eyed him up and down. "I'll bet you've never driven a standard shift pickup in your life. You're too busy parading around in your overpriced BMW."

Grant's eyes narrowed. "What's up with you today? I'm just trying to keep you safe, and you're attacking me for no reason. Are you PMS-ing or something?"

She wanted to clobber him with an IV pole, especially because she *was* PMS-ing! But must he so rudely point it out?

Dr. Jones clapped his hands. "Stop it! Both of you. We have a medical emergency here, and you're behaving like squabbling toddlers. Now stop it!"

Allison stared down at her feet chagrined for her childish outburst. What must Dr. Jones think? Why had she let Grant get under her skin?

True, she'd always hated people treating her like she was helpless just because she was short, but her snarky remarks to Grant were uncalled for.

She mumbled, "Sorry," to Grant, and he mumbled back, "Whatever," clearly still put out with her.

"I have an idea," Grant said, turning to Dr. Jones, as though dismissing her. "What if I infuse a liter of normal saline over the next hour into Pierre to stabilize him, and then he and I can go together and fetch the kids?"

Dr. Jones shook his head. "If that baby is going to survive, every minute is critical. It sounds like he's already going into shock. One hour could be the difference between life and death." He pursed his lips as he mulled over all the variables.

"Here's what we're going to do: I will start IVs on Regina and Pierre. While I tend to the two of them and manage any additional patients who come in, you two will fetch the children in Angelina using the map and directions Pierre and Regina provide."

Go together? With Grant? After their snippy interaction, she'd sooner go with the witch doctor.

Dr. Jones must have seen her displeasure. "Sorry, Allison, but I agree with Grant that people in rural Haiti won't believe you're a doctor. The kids might even refuse to come with you. Because of his height, they will be more likely to believe Grant is a doctor."

When a murderous glare must have crossed her face, he raised a hand. "I'm not saying it's right or politically correct, but this is no time for a feminist manifesto. We need to get those children here ASAP."

Before Allison could respond, he added fuel to the fire. "Besides, Grant is stronger and more able to lift and carry the children from their house to the truck—or change a flat—if it comes to that."

She opened her mouth to point out she knew how to change a flat, but he clapped his hands. "No more arguing. I am the director of this clinic, and what I say goes."

Grant's eyes widened after seeing the normally mild-mannered Dr. Jones transform into a bossy dictator. She couldn't help but smile.

Truthfully, right now they needed a leader to take charge, and Dr. Jones had risen to the challenge. He was right, of course, as much as Allison hated to admit it. If the kids needed to be carried from the house to the truck, Grant would prove helpful. Plus, she'd give Angelina 50:50 odds for completing the trip without some kind of fiasco.

Dr. Jones handed Regina and Pierre bottles of Gatorade and instructed them to swallow them down.

Clearly thirsty, they gulped down the whole bottle within a minute. He then pulled out a piece of paper and a pen and had Pierre draw a detailed map to his house while giving verbal instructions on how to reach it. Dr. Jones then handed the map to Grant and Allison and provided the interpretation of how to find the house.

He handed the truck keys to Allison and pointed toward the door. "Go find those kids and get them back here as soon as possible. I'll get the IVs started."

CHAPTER 12

Grant stared at the hen-scratched-scrawl-of-a-drawing and then back at Dr. Jones. He rubbed the back of his neck and handed the map to Allison. He hoped she could make more out of the scrawls than he could.

The supposed map outlined at least five forks in the road, and Pierre had used vague markers like "large tree," "sharp turn," "wheel barrel," "mango tree," or "big rock," as a part of his directions. If they found those kids it would be a miracle.

What if someone had moved the wheel barrel? What if they turned at the wrong mango tree? What if Pierre had forgotten about one of the sharp turns in the road? He could see it already. A baby's life hung in the balance, and they would end up helplessly lost in the middle of nowhere looking for the proper big rock!

"What, exactly, does your house look like?" Allison had asked, using Dr. Jones as an interpreter.

"Look for chicken coop. Regina and I are the only ones in town to own ten chickens and a rooster."

He explained that he sold the eggs and chicks to feed the family. "The chicken coop is in front of our house. You can't miss it."

Right. He was sure to miss it. He supposed they could ask people where the chicken people lived.

Pierre then gave them the names of their four children and wrote a note for Gabriella explaining that they should come with Grant and Allison to the clinic.

Allison eyed the map and tried to ignore the premonition that finding this house was doomed for disaster. "We better get going. I have a feeling this may take a while," she mumbled to Grant.

"You got that right," he agreed, glancing at the map over her shoulder.

Dr. Jones held up a hand. "Wait." He grabbed a six-pack of Pedialyte. "Give each of the children a bottle and instruct them to drink it on the way here." He pulled out a clean baby bottle from the cabinet and handed it to Grant. "Give that baby a full bottle as soon as you can. Every little bit helps when a baby is this severely dehydrated."

They dashed out the door. "Since I've driven old pick-up trucks with manual transmission on the farm, why don't you let me drive," Allison suggested.

Grant opened his mouth to protest but then closed it. Truth be told, he *didn't* have any experience driving large trucks with manual transmissions. Not wanting to look incompetent in front of Allison, he held up a hand and said, "Be my guest." He hoped he sounded chivalrous rather than chicken-livered.

He opened the passenger door carefully to avoid pulling it off its rusty hinges—correction, hinge. He climbed in and lifted the creaky door carefully. Meanwhile, Allison turned the key in the ignition. The engine sputtered and rumbled but didn't turn over.

"Come on, Angelina. This is no time to conk out. We need you." She turned the ignition key again, and it released a sickly grinding sound. "You can do it, girl."

"Seriously? You're talking to this hunk of junk?"

Allison glared at him and patted the dash. "Don't listen to him, Angelina. I believe in you." She turned the key again.

Angelina whimpered, sputtered, backfired twice, and then, wonder of wonders, roared to life.

A huge grin crossed Allison's face. She thumped the dashboard. "Good girl! I knew I could count on you."

She glanced over and must have seen his skepticism. "Hey, if a little praise and coaxing worked for Jean-Pierre, I figured it couldn't hurt, right?"

He couldn't help but chuckle. "If you say so." He then focused his attention on the hen-scratched-excuse-of-a-map in his lap. If they found those kids, it would be a miracle.

"It looks like we start off going right until we come to the second sharp turn in the road. Then we take a fork to the left."

Allison rumbled out of the driveway, and when she shifted into second gear, the truck lurched forward. They jostled down the rutty dirt road, a plume of dust billowing behind them. They passed a shanty town of dilapidated shacks and dwellings—if you could call them that, as some appeared to be made of cardboard. Grant could now see why Dr. Jones had located the clinic in this town. It was as impoverished as anything he'd seen so far in Haiti. They snaked past the first sharp turn, and Allison slowed down to maneuver the corner. When they reached the second sharp turn in the road, Grant saw a smaller dirt road veering to the left. "Turn left here."

Allison nodded and turned onto the narrow road. They sputtered along until they came to a shack with a wheel barrel in the front yard. Grant pointed.

"There's the wheel barrel, so at least so far, we're going the right way." He eyed the map again. "It says now to make a right turn at a large mango tree."

They thumped along trying to avoid potholes and deep ruts until they came to a large tree on the left.

"Do you suppose that's the mango tree he meant?"

Allison shook her head. "The fruit on that tree doesn't look like any mango I've seen in the grocery store. I think that one is a papaya tree."

They continued to bounce along until Grant pointed to a tree on the right bursting with fresh green mango. "There," he said. "That's got to be a mango tree. It looks just like the one next to Dr. Jones' house."

Allison slowed down enough to examine the tree. "I think you're right."

She shifted into first gear and turned onto an even narrower strip of road that was more the size of a rutty driveway than a road. "What's our next landmark?"

"Turn right two houses after a big rock on the side of the road."

She said nothing as she mashed on the gas pedal to gain the momentum to make it up a steep rutty climb. After tottering over several ruts, they reached a large rock on the side of the road. After two dilapidated shacks, they turned up an even narrower and more treacherous road. They barreled along until the road petered out. Completely.

"What the heck?" Grant sputtered. He glanced over at Allison "Now what? There's no way to turn the truck around."

Allison glanced in her rearview mirror and released a sigh. "We must have turned after the wrong big rock. Or the turn-off was more than two houses after the big rock."

A bead of sweat meandered down his face, and his shirt soaked through with sweat. He rolled down the window to get some air.

"I'll put it in reverse and back down the hill."

He eyed the non-existent shoulder. "There's no room for error. I hope you don't flip us into the ditch."

She turned and glared at him. "You got a better idea?"

He racked his brain to come up with a Plan B. Finding none, he admitted, "Unfortunately no. I see what Pierre meant. These roads aren't meant for vehicles."

"Maybe not, but the only way we're going to get four sick kids transported to the clinic is to drive them there, so we need to make the best of it. Turn around and be my second pair of eyes as I back down this road. Holler if I'm about to land us in the ditch."

He'd been sweating buckets with them driving forward on this ramshackle excuse-of-a-road. Now they had to go backwards. His inner coward wanted to close his eyes and pray for divine intervention, but he needed to suck it up and help her back down the steep rutty path.

Not waiting for his response, she shifted into reverse and began backing down the road.

Within seconds, he bellowed, "Brake. Your back passenger-side wheel is only inches from the ditch."

She turned the steering wheel slightly and inched downward. "Better?"

"Yes, but in ten feet you'll need to turn more sharply."

They jostled their way down the road, punctuated by occasional bursts of Grant shouting, "Stop! Ditch alert."

Her lips thinned each time, as though she thought he was overreacting, but to her credit, she said nothing and adhered to his recommendation of how to proceed.

When they finally reached the turn-off, Allison suggested, "Why don't we inquire at the next house if they know where the guy who owns the chicken coop lives. We can't be more than a mile from his house, so hopefully, they'll know."

"Good idea." He pointed to a shack in the distance. "Let's inquire there. Since you studied French, do you know the word for chicken in French?"

"Poulet. And house is maison. I hope French Creole is close enough to the Parisian French I studied that they'll understand me."

"If you get desperate, try this." He bent his arms at the elbow and flapped them like chicken wings. "Squawk! Squawk!"

She chuckled. "Seriously?"

"Hey! It's the universal language for chickens."

"I'll keep that in mind."

The truck reached a run-down shack with three children chasing each other around the yard. Allison said, "At least we know someone is home."

Grant commented, "Maybe we should leave Angelina's engine running. If you turn her off, she might not start up again."

"Good point."

The road had no shoulder to pull over, so Allison shifted the truck to park but left the engine running. After pulling on the emergency brake, they hopped out and rushed toward the front of the shack. The children took one look at them and ran inside. Had they run to escape, or to fetch a parent? Thankfully, the front door opened, and a disheveled woman toting a toddler on her hip smiled warmly and inquired, "Est-ce que je peux vous aider?"

"Oui. Où est l'homme qui possede une maison de poulet?"

The woman pointed straight ahead and said to turn left at the large rock near a green house.

"Merci," Allison said with a smile. "Passe une bonne journée."

As they meandered back to the car, Grant said, "Have a good day, right?"

She smiled. "Oui."

As they climbed back into the truck, Grant said, "At least this time we know to turn left after a big rock near a green house. Pierre just said a big rock, and the last big rock we turned at didn't have a green house."

They bumped along for a mile or so until a green house popped into view. "There it is," they both said in unison, pointing at the large rock next to the house.

They turned left onto a narrow weather-worn road. "The woman said it would be a house on the right. Let's keep our windows down and maybe we'll hear the chickens."

As they bumped along a road more fit for trench warfare than automobiles, they suddenly heard the cock-a-doodle-do of a rooster.

Grant straightened in his seat and turned to Allison. "That sounds promising."

She shifted into first gear and began the climb up to a house on the right. As they neared the house, they could see the chicken coop out front, but there was a steep curvy driveway with no way to turn around at the top.

"Let's leave the truck here, so we don't have to back down that steep driveway," Grant suggested.

Allison pulled a face. "I could totally back down that driveway."

He decided not to pick a fight. "I'm sure you could, but let's not push our luck when we'll have four kids with us. It might frighten them."

"Good point." She shifted into park and pulled on the emergency brake.

"Think we'll have trouble convincing them to get in the truck with us? I wouldn't have hopped in a truck with complete strangers when I was their age. Plus, the youngest ones have probably never seen a truck, let alone a blond American."

She eyed him up and down. "They'll probably think you're a giant."

"A gentle giant," he retorted.

She wagged a finger at him. "But a giant, none the less." Allison patted Pierre's note which was tucked in her lab coat pocket. "We do have this letter from their father. That should help." She unhooked her seatbelt and jumped down from the truck. "Here's hoping Gabriella can read."

They dashed toward the house carrying the hand-scrawled letter from Pierre.

"Since I'm apparently of the jolly green giant variety, I'll hover in the background until I see you have success getting them to come with you. Motion to me, and I'll help you carry them to the truck."

She nodded. "Sounds like a plan."

She pounded on the front door shouting, "Bonjour. Viens à la porte, s'il vous plâit."

When no one came, she said to Grant, "I hope I'm asking them to come to the door. High school French was a long time ago."

"I'm pretty sure that's what you said. I've been studying French Creole every night."

She turned to stare at him, mouth agape. "When do you have time to do that? I flop into bed exhausted every night."

He shrugged. "I study thirty minutes a night to help me chill out before I fall asleep."

"I'm impressed," she admitted. "I'm asleep before my head hits the pillow."

"So I've noticed. Unfortunately, I can't fall asleep until I do something calming to relax my mind."

When no one came to the door, Grant frowned. "We need to get that baby to the clinic." He came forward and pounded on the door shouting, "Il y a quelqu'un?"

She turned and stared at him. "What does that mean?"

"Anybody home?" He grinned. "At least that's what I *hope* it means. It's entirely possible I called her a homely lizard."

Allison covered her mouth with her hand to keep from laughing. "That'll really help our cause."

She pounded on the door again. With no response, Grant commented, "No doubt they're hiding under their beds in abject terror."

"Let's hope not." She pounded again. "Ouvez la porte," she shouted.

"Open the door?" Grant asked.

"Oui. I'm impressed how quickly you're picking up the language."

He shrugged. "When in Rome, do as the Romans do."

They could hear footfall coming closer to the door. Eventually, a thin, unkempt girl holding a listless baby with sunken eyes opened the door. She stared up at Allison and Grant with fearful yet droopy eyes. The poor thing looked exhausted.

"Gabriella?"

The girl nodded, swaying the baby gently on her hip.

"J'ai besoin que tu viennes avec moi," Allison said.

Gabrielle stared up at her wide-eyed, as though not sure whether to obey the command to come with Allison or not.

Hoping to make herself less intimidating, Allison squatted down to face the girl at eye level.

She introduced herself and then pointed to Grant and introduced him. She then plunged into the reason for their visit. "Je t'amenerai chez ta mere et ton pere."

The girl chewed her bottom lip as though weighing the consequences of her choice. Soon, a toddler with a dirty face and adorable curls waddled up to her sister and grabbed onto her skirt.

"Give her the note from her dad," Grant whispered. "That'll give us credibility."

Allison unfolded the note and handed it to Gabriella. Not knowing how well the girl could read, she hoped she'd recognize her father's writing.

Gabriella scanned the note, and her face visibly relaxed. She nodded her consent. "Je viendrai avec vous." She hollered to her other sibling to come.

While Allison and Grant had expected resistance about getting into a truck with complete strangers, Gabriella seemed only too willing to hand over the burden of caring for her three sick siblings to someone older and more qualified.

Because Gabriella was willing to come with them, the others offered no resistance. Grant scooped up the two younger children and trudged down the steep driveway toward the truck. Allison offered to take the baby. She and Gabriella trailed behind Grant.

They loaded the three older kids into the back seat of the truck, but Grant held the baby since there was no car seat.

He tried to arouse the baby enough to drink the bottle of Pedialyte, but he refused to suck. Instead, he lay in Grant's arms like a floppy ragdoll.

"He won't take it?" Allison asked, glancing over, unable to hide the worry from her voice.

Grant shook his head. "At this point, I don't think he has the energy to suck."

"At least he's still alive, but the sooner we get IV fluids flowing, the better."

"I've never seen such a dehydrated baby. Look how sunken his eyes are. Look at his flaccid skin folds."

Allison turned the truck around by backing up the driveway.

Once she was driving downhill, every attempt to accelerate on the rutty road was met with the truck lurching and jerking like a state fair ride. With each jarring thud, the children gripped their bellies and moaned. Thus, she did her best to brake for ruts and potholes, but that proved impossible on the narrow, weather-beaten dirt road.

When they were within half a mile of the clinic, the truck suddenly sputtered and died.

"What happened?" Allison cried.

She turned the key and patted Angelina's dashboard. "She was driving great and then just died on me."

Grant glanced over at the dashboard and pointed to the gas gauge. "There's your problem. We're out of gas."

"What?" Allison's head dropped. "Seriously? Jean-Pierre told me the gas gauge was persnickety, so I assumed he'd left the truck full of gas before he left for Port-au-Prince."

Grant released a frustrated sigh. "Apparently not."

Allison glanced around at the sickly children and bit a nail. "What now? We can't just leave the truck in the middle of the road, and I don't know if there's a full gas can back at the clinic."

Grant eyed the oldest daughter. "You suppose she could steer the truck if we put it in neutral and you and I push?"

Allison eyed the road ahead of them, which was straight, except for one sharp turn right before the driveway to the clinic.

"How about we get her to steer until we get to the sharp turn-off. By then, we can run to the clinic and get Dr. Jones and Judy to help."

"Or, he might know where the gas can is," Grant commented.

Just then, Raphael, who must have seen their dilemma from his dilapidated shack, ran up to the truck.

"Angelina no run?"

"No gas," Grant explained, miming filling the gas tank with gas. "Do you know where Jean-Pierre keeps the gas can?"

Raphael stared at him with a deer-in-the-headlights gaze, clearly not understanding what Grant was asking. Allison did her best to translate into French.

Raphael rubbed his chin. "Is it not in the back of the truck? That's where he usually keeps it."

Grant thumped his forehead. "Duh." He jumped out of the truck and checked the truck bed. Sure enough, there sat a large plastic gas container. He grinned at Raphael. "You are a lifesaver." He grabbed the gas can from the truck bed and hoisted it out. It weighed almost nothing. Sloshing the can, he concluded, "It's nearly empty."

"Even a few drops may be enough to get us a half-mile down the road," Allison insisted.

Grant dumped the tiniest trickle of gas into the truck's gas tank then screwed on the cap and replaced the gas can to the truck bed. "Here's hoping."

Raphael eyed all the children in the truck. "What's wrong with them?"

"Cholera," Allison said, "They need IV fluids."

"I run to clinic. Let Dr. Jones know," Raphael offered.

"Good," Allison said, turning the key to the truck.

Raphael sprinted down the road.

After several false starts and sputters, Angelina roared to life. Allison grinned. "Thank you, Jesus!"

The truck bumped along over the next quarter of a mile and then sputtered out again.

Allison hung her head in frustration. "Shoot. I guess two thimbles of gas will only get you so far."

Grant scratched his chin. "How about we just grab up the kids and walk them to the clinic. Once we have the kids hooked up to IV fluids, Dr. Jones and I can come back and push the truck the last quarter mile to the clinic."

"Let's see how hard it is for the two of us to push the truck. It's sweltering out here, and we don't need the kids in direct sun when they're already dehydrated. Besides, it may be as quick to leave the kids in the truck and push as it is to walk with four sick kids."

Grant shrugged. "I guess it's worth a try."

After moving Gabriella to the driver's seat and instructing her how to use the steering wheel, Allison shifted the truck into neutral. They peeled off their now sweat-drenched lab coats and left them in the passenger seat. Then, standing side by side behind the truck, they braced themselves to push.

"Ready?" Grant asked.

"A-ya."

At first, the truck didn't budge no matter how hard they pushed, but gradually, the wheels began to turn ever so slowly. Angelina inched along, slowly gaining momentum.

"If we stop, it will be harder to get her going again, so we can't let up, not even for a second," Grant said.

Allison pushed as hard as she could, though she knew Grant was doing the lion's share of the load. She eyed Gabriella in the driver's seat clutching the steering wheel.

Since the road was still straight, there was nothing for her to do yet, but she eyed the road intently, as though ready to do her part.

As the hot sun beat down on them, sweat poured down Allison's face. Huge rings of perspiration formed on Grant's chest and underarms. They had advanced the truck about half the distance they needed to go, but the worst part of the trip, with a sharp turn to the left and a slight uphill before they reached the clinic's short driveway remained ahead of them. Just one step at a time. They could do this.

The children sat in the truck wide-eyed, except for the baby, who lay lifelessly on the seat staring into space, as though doing anything more was too much of an effort.

Allison's arms burned and trembled from the constant effort of pushing. Even worse, the metal of the truck burned her palms.

As the truck inched along, she ordered her weary wrists to keep pushing. She groaned with each exhausting step up the driveway. She tried to drown out the naysayer inside her that shrieked, "No way can you push this behemoth truck loaded down with four kids."

Oh, shut up, she hissed back.

Each foot of distance the truck advanced made her arms scream in agony and tremble with exhaustion. While the driveway to the clinic was only a hundred feet, the distance seemed insurmountable. She finally confessed, "Grant, my arms are trembling so much I can't push any further."

Before Grant could respond, Dr. Jones, Judy, and Raphael ran out of the clinic, down the driveway, and joined in the push.

"I told Jean-Pierre to always keep that gas can full," Dr. Jones grumbled. "I'll have to get on to him for leaving us in this predicament."

"Turn the wheel to the left," Dr. Jones informed Gabriella in French. "We're almost there."

She turned the steering wheel, and with the help of the three new helpers whose muscles weren't shaking with exhaustion, the truck traversed the driveway and worked its way to the parking place in front of the clinic.

Once the truck was parked and the key removed, Allison helped Gabriella out of the driver's seat. "Great job," she praised.

Miraculously, they had managed to find all four children and transport them to the clinic alive.

Now came the real work—saving them from cholera.

Allison eyed the baby lying lifelessly on the seat, and her pulse quickened.

Would he survive?

CHAPTER 13

Grant reached for the baby on the front seat and handed the lethargic bundle to Dr. Jones. Instead of plump baby folds, the baby's skin hung in shriveled sheets. It didn't take a blood test to conclude this baby was severely dehydrated. Dr. Jones' forehead furrowed with concern. He rushed into the clinic and beelined back to a room where the baby's mother lay hooked up to an IV. Despite his dehydration, the baby's face lit up when he saw his mother. He reached out for her, so Dr. Jones placed him in his mother's arms.

"Bonjour, Roberto," she cooed to her baby, as she rubbed soothing circles on his back.

Allison and Grant brought the other three children in to see their parents, and their faces visibly relaxed. Until now, they had no proof Grant and Allison would bring them to see their parents—they'd just had to trust.

Since the clinic was limited in beds, they let baby Roberto stay in his mother's arms. They placed the two younger children next to their father.

"They'll feel more secure when we insert their IVs if they are next to their parents," Dr. Jones explained. Since Gabriella was the healthiest of the bunch, they pulled up a chair near her mother's bed.

They obtained the children's blood pressure, temperature, and pulse, and then Dr. Jones explained to the children in French Creole what was required to get them better.

He pointed to the IVs in their parents' arms and told them he would need them to be very brave when he stuck the needle in their arm. "It will hurt for a second, but then the pain will be over, he insisted.

The eyes of the two younger children widened with fright, and they clutched the arm of their father.

"You can do it," Pierre reassured them. "I did." He pointed to his own IV. "Now lie very still so the doctor can get the needle in. You need the hanging water to get better."

Dr. Jones collected the poles, tubing, needles, arm boards, and other supplies he'd need to start IVs.

"Since his veins will be the most challenging, and I've had the most experience with dehydrated babies, I'll tackle Roberto. You two see if you can feel a vein in the other kids. Make sure you can feel a vein before you stick, though. You can't poke and prod around on children, or you'll lose their trust. They'll give you one chance before they start to fight you."

Swell. The children were dehydrated, so their veins would undoubtedly be totally collapsed. And she was supposed to hit a vein on the first try on a toddler? Fat chance of that!

While Grant tackled the IV in Gabriella, Allison applied a tourniquet to Francisca's arm. Wide eyes stared up at her—eyes reflecting both fear and trust.

Allison offered the girl a smile and attempted to appear confident, though her shaking hands belied her smile. She wiped her perspiring palms onto her lab coat.

Please, God, don't let me screw this up.

She palpated Francisca's elbow crease and located the slightest hint of a vein. It was much smaller than any vein she had ever attempted to stick before. Since she usually worked with adults who weren't dangerously dehydrated, this was not surprising.

Not convinced she could succeed on the first stick, she decided to plump up the vein with a hot compress. While she waited for the heat to do its work, she glanced over to see how Dr. Jones and Grant were faring.

Amazingly, Dr. Jones already had a bag of fluid dripping into the baby, and he was now taping on a cardboard arm board to keep Roberto from pulling out the IV. Once the arm board was securely taped, he released a loud sigh. "Whew! Thank God that went in easier than I feared."

Snuggled in his mother's arms, Roberto extended his arm and stared at the strange contraption taped around the bend of his elbow. When he started to pick at the board with his left hand, his mother grabbed his wrist. "No touch," she scolded.

Dr. Jones poured Pedialyte into a baby bottle and stirred in several teaspoons of sugar. He screwed on the nipple and shook vigorously then dampened the nipple and coated it with sugar. Handing the bottle to the baby, he commanded, "Drink this."

The baby stared up at him, and then, with his mother's encouragement, he began to suck.

The three doctors all let out collective sighs of relief.

Now that Francisca's vein had plumped up slightly with the hot compress, Allison scrubbed up the site with alcohol and offered up a silent prayer that she'd hit the vein on the first try.

Allison ordered her trembling hands to steady themselves then jabbed the IV needle into the little girl's arm. Her eyes filled with tears, and she flinched, but at least she didn't pull back or scream.

"Bonne fille!" Allison said, offering her a smile, as she saw blood rush into the needle. She had successfully penetrated the vein. She pulled off the tourniquet and attached the tubing.

But try as she might, the fluid would not flow into the vein, and soon a large bleb of IV fluid collected under the skin.

Shoot! The vein collapsed, and now, the IV fluid was pooling rather than flowing into the vein. Would Francisca fight her if she tried to start another IV?

Wide eyes stared down at the expanding bleb and then up at Allison with wide, frightened eyes.

Allison quickly tugged out the needle and applied pressure with gauze until the bleeding stopped. "The vein infiltrated."

The little girl's puckered brow suggested she had no idea what Allison meant. She taped a cotton ball to the site of the collapsed vein, procrastinating her next task of finding another vein. A bead of sweat meandered its way down her face. Since she had ruined the one and only decent vein, she wanted to cry—or hit something.

Applying a tourniquet to Francisca's other arm, she applied a shaky finger to the elbow crease, desperately praying a plump, juicy vein would magically appear.

No such luck. She then examined the top of Francisca's hand. Nada. Not knowing what else to do, she went to the cabinet and pulled out a bottle of Pedialyte. "Drink this," she commanded. "It will help plump up your veins."

Right. Like the fluid would go straight from Francisca's mouth to her left arm in thirty-seconds flat.

Francisca obediently sipped and then stared down at her arm as though expecting the vein to magically engorge with blood because she was drinking Pedialyte.

In my dreams!

As luck would have it, Grant had watched her IV fiasco from across the room. He strolled over and offered, "Want me to give it a try?"

Since he had so effortlessly started an IV in Gabriella, she felt a wave of shame at her incompetence. Her pride wanted to tell him to jump off a cliff and that she would have an IV started any minute, thank you very much! But since she couldn't see or feel a thing, for Francisca's sake, she needed to swallow her pride and relinquish the task to Grant. Truthfully, she was relieved. She never claimed to be any good at starting IVs, anyhow. She was a surgeon, not a phlebotomist.

Admitting defeat, she waved her hand toward Francisca. "Have at it. I can't feel a thing."

Grant nodded, and thankfully, had the decency not to grin at her ineptitude. He applied a tourniquet first to one arm and then the other, palpated her elbow creases, forearms, and hands. He snapped off the tourniquet and frowned. "I can see why you couldn't get one started. She doesn't have a thing to work with."

She could have kissed him.

"What are we going to do? Her blood pressure is only 75/50, and her pulse is up to 125. She needs the fluids."

He pursed his lips. "Maybe we can find a vein on the top of her foot. Once we infuse a couple liters of fluid, we should be able to find a vein in her arm."

They laid Francisca down on the table and explained that they needed to stick the needle into the top of her foot. They asked Gabriella to come over and hold her sister's hand. They would reward the girls with candy if Francisca held very still.

Francisca's eyes widened with fear, and she gripped her older sister's hand. Turning toward her father, her eyes begged him to protect her from these villains.

Her father said, "Do what he says, little one. He's trying to help you."

Or at least that's what Allison *thought* he said. She really needed to start studying that French Creole book with Grant at night.

Grant placed a tourniquet above Francisca's ankle and scrubbed the top of her foot with alcohol until no dirt showed on the cotton ball. He pointed to a visible vein. "Here's our best bet." He grimaced slightly before mumbling, "If I don't botch this up. Truthfully, it was a miracle I got Gabriella's IV started."

Allison wanted to hug him for admitting that he, too, lacked confidence in starting IVs in dehydrated children.

He stretched his back and rolled his neck as though needing to psych himself for the task ahead. "Here's hoping," he muttered, before plunging the needle into the vein. He received a satisfying return of blood, so he hooked the IV needle to the tubing, and soon, the IV fluid flowed freely.

He looked up at Allison with a huge grin.

"Praise God." She offered a thumbs-up sign.

"You got that right."

Grant applied a sturdy foot and ankle board so Francisca wouldn't inadvertently dislodge the needle if she tried to flap her foot.

"Well done," Dr. Jones said with a smile. "We've got three down and one to go." They all glanced over at the five-year-old, Eugene. He had apparently watched his siblings get stuck with needles, and his terrified eyes suggested he feared he was about to be thrown into a meat grinder. He clung to his father's arm and shrieked, "No! I won't do it!"

Dr. Jones asked the father how sick Eugene had been. Just as Allison feared, he had suffered from non-stop diarrhea for two days straight. In short, he needed IV fluids.

Eugene pulled on his father's shirt and informed him he needed to go to the bathroom.

Since Pierre was hooked up to an IV, Grant offered to escort the lad to the bathroom, but the boy clung to his father's arm.

Grant squatted down to Eugene's level, and with a few broken words of French Creole, he told him he needed water in his veins to get better. He pointed to the other children. "They all got one. You need one, too."

"You'll feel better once you have water in you," Allison added.

Shaking his head in protest, the boy wrapped his arms around his father's belly in a bear hold.

Dr. Jones said, "Let Pierre bring him to the bathroom. Maybe Eugene will calm down and cooperate after he's done his business and his belly isn't cramping."

Dr. Jones explained the plan to Pierre. Holding Eugene in the arm that didn't have an IV, he said, "Let's go to the bathroom."

As Pierre worked his way to the bathroom holding his son and pushing his IV pole, Dr. Jones followed behind to make sure the IV tubing didn't get caught up in the wheels. They had to stop several times to untangle the tubing and ensure it didn't get run over.

Once they were inside the bathroom, Pierre put down his son and said, "I am right outside the door. You're a big boy now, so you can do this on your own."

Eugene nodded, and Pierre closed the door to give his son privacy.

Pierre stood outside the bathroom leaning on his IV pole.

When several minutes passed and Eugene did not exit the bathroom or flush the toilet, his father knocked on the door and shouted, "Eugene? Are you okay?"

No answer.

He pounded harder. "Eugene? Do you need help?"

Still no answer.

He rattled the doorknob and shouted, "Eugene, open this door."

"Oh, no," Allison whispered to Grant. "I'll bet he passed out on the commode."

"Or died from dehydration," Grant whispered back.

They rushed to the bathroom just as the father opened the door.

The bathroom was empty.

Eugene was gone.

CHAPTER 14

One glance at the open window and they had their answer on how Eugene escaped. He must have stood on the toilet, opened the window, and shimmied his way out.

Pierre's eyes widened with alarm. "Where'd he go?"

Grant patted his shoulder. "He can't have gone far. You stay here at the clinic. Allison and I will find him."

They ran for the front door as Pierre filled in his wife and Dr. Jones about Eugene's escape antics.

As they exited the clinic, Grant yelled, "You go right, and I'll go left. We have to find him. He'll get even more dehydrated out in this afternoon heat."

Thinking he may have wanted to run home, Allison ran down the rutty, dirt road hollering Eugene's name. How far could go before heat stroke and exhaustion overpowered him?

She sprinted as fast as the potholes and ruts allowed. The last thing she needed was a sprained ankle.

The boy only had a two-minute lead on her, so how far could he have gone?

After she'd run a half-mile, she stopped, leaned forward with her hands on her knees, and gasped for breath.

Surely, if he had attempted to go home, she would have caught up to him by now. After all, the kid was sick and only three feet tall.

Was he hiding somewhere? If so, he could be anywhere. Her shoulder sagged with discouragement.

On her jog back to the clinic she peered behind trees, large rocks, and anything else big enough to hide a child.

Still no Eugene.

She glanced ahead and could see the clinic. She could also hear Grant calling the boy's name. So he hadn't any more luck than she had.

Well, shoot! Sweat poured down her face, and her clothes became soaked with sweat. If she didn't find him soon, Eugene would die of dehydration and heatstroke.

As she turned into the clinic's driveway, she noticed a flash of motion behind the mature mango tree next to Dr. Jones' house. Had Eugene been hiding behind the tree all this time?

She dashed to the tree and looked behind it. But instead of a small, frightened child, she saw an elderly man garbed in a colorful robe with white streaks of chalk on his face. He glared at her and brandished a butcher knife.

A wave of terror coursed through her, and she let out a blood-curdling scream. Thankfully, the man didn't grab her. Instead, he dashed away.

Grant must have heard her scream because he was next to her within seconds.

"Allison? Are you okay?" he said, unable to hide the alarm in his voice. He gripped her arms and faced her.

"Did you see that guy?" she asked, pointing in the direction he'd run off to.

"I didn't see his face, but I saw a flash of color as he ran away. He was wearing a colorful robe."

"I'll bet it's that witch doctor that Dr. Jones mentioned. He had white streaks on his face, and he had a butcher knife."

He gripped her shoulders, his eyes penetrating hers. "A butcher knife?"

She nodded, her heart still racing. "He scared the daylights out of me."

"Why would he be hiding in Dr. Jones' yard?"

Allison let out a gasp. "Do you think he kidnapped Eugene? Or killed him and hid the body?"

Grant's eyes widened. He gazed in the direction the man had run off in. "You stay here, and I'll see if I can catch him."

"No way. I'm coming with you. We're safer together," she insisted.

"Have you forgotten I know karate?" He mimed a leg kick and a hand-chopping motion.

"Have you forgotten he's wielding a butcher knife? He'll be less likely to stab you if I'm there as a witness."

"Good point."

They charged down the road together stopping to look behind trees and large rocks. After fifteen minutes, Grant said, "It's no use. We've lost him. Let's return to the clinic and figure out how to find Eugene. He's only five, and it's hotter than blazes out here. He's probably hiding somewhere in the shade."

"Unless that witch doctor snatched him," Angela retorted.

As they ran toward the house, Allison happened to glance inside Angelina. Sure enough, there, crouched in the passenger footwell was Eugene. He'd been hiding in the truck all along.

"Let's get him out of there. He must be roasting," Allison said.

"I'm glad I left my passenger window rolled down, so at least the inside of the truck is not at hot as it could have been."

"Good thing you did, or he'd be dead by now."

"How are we going to convince him to come with us? He's clearly terrified," Grant pointed out.

"Stay here so he doesn't escape again. I'll go get his father."

Allison ran in the house and notified Pierre and Regina they had located Eugene, but they would need Pierre to coax the boy out of the truck. Remembering the bowl of hard candies in the kitchen, she grabbed a handful of strawberry and lemon candies. Bribery couldn't hurt. Meanwhile, Pierre wheeled his IV pole to the door of the clinic.

With Dr. Jones' help, Pierre lifted the IV pole out the door and across the dirt driveway to the truck. "You need to come back inside and get some water in your veins," Pierre admonished. "You will feel better when you do." He pointed to his own IV. "Look. I have one, and so do your Mama and Francisca and Gabriella. Even Roberto has one."

The poor boy refused to budge.

Allison carefully opened the truck door and squatted to Eugene's level. "Look what I have for you." She opened her palm and revealed the candies. "C'est délicieux."

Eugene reached for the candy, but Allison pulled her hand back and informed him, "No candy until you come inside and get an IV."

Dr. Jones interpreted for her and promised lots of candy if he would get out of the truck and let them start an IV.

Eugene chewed on his bottom lip as though weighing if candy was worth getting a needle stuck in his arm. "Will you keep that mean man from coming after me?"

"What mean man?" Dr. Jones gestured toward Grant. "Dr. Stockdale isn't mean."

"Not him. The man with the big knife."

Dr. Jones' brow furrowed. He turned to Grant and Allison. "What the devil is he talking about? What mean man with a knife?"

"The man with white stripes on his face," Eugene insisted.

Allison and Grant eyed each other, and fear gripped her heart. The witch doctor had gone after a child! She filled in Dr. Jones on what she and Grant had seen.

His jaw clenched. "Louis Villemort. That demented old coot is getting worse and worse. He's been badmouthing the clinic for months now, but this is the first time he's ever physically come on the premises and threatened us."

"As word of the lives we're saving spreads, he's getting more desperate," Allison surmised.

Dr. Jones eyed the perimeter of the building as though looking to see if Louis was still lurking around.

Dr. Jones turned to Eugene. "Let's get you inside out of this heat. You don't want to stay out where that mean man could snatch you, do you?"

Eugene's eyes pooled with tears, and he shook his head. Whether it was fear of the witch doctor or the bribe of candy, he climbed out of the truck and went inside with his father.

After scolding him for running away, his mother informed him, "Once they get the needle in, it's not so bad. I am already feeling stronger with the water they dripped into me." She patted the space next to her on the exam table. "Come lie down next to me. You can squeeze my hand when it hurts."

Eugene did as his mother said. Dr. Jones handed him a hard candy and said, "Once you get the IV in, I'll give you more."

The other children glanced up at Dr. Jones expectantly, as though thinking, Hey! I got an IV, too. Do I get candy?

He smiled and gave each child, except the baby, a hard candy. "You all deserve this for your bravery." He informed Allison, "Getting a little sugar and calories into their bloodstream will be a good thing, also."

Eugene unwrapped his candy and popped it in his mouth. Dr. Jones said, "Time to get you hooked up to water."

"Squeeze my hand," his mother coaxed, as Dr. Jones applied a tourniquet then palpated for a viable vein. He sterilized the skin and plunged the needle into Eugene's arm.

He was rewarded with a backsplash of blood confirming success. He hooked it to the tubing and soon, D5NS was flowing. He attached an arm board to secure the site.

Eugene watched with wide eyes, but he held still.

Once the arm board was secure, Dr. Jones patted his back. "I am so proud of you, Eugene! You did great."

He unwrapped another hard candy and waved it near Eugene's mouth. The boy smiled at Dr. Jones' praise and even more at the treat. He opened his mouth and Dr. Jones popped the candy inside.

Not wanting any dissention among the children, Dr. Jones gave each of the other children another candy. He then offered one to Pierre and Regina.

He glanced up at Allison and Grant. "I suppose I need to offer you two some candy, too." He smiled. "Can't have anyone accusing me of playing favorites."

Grant chuckled. "Ha, ha."

"The way this family is going through candy, we better save our candy stash," Allison said. She eyed the children happily sucking on their candies. "Bribery works like a charm with children, and I have a feeling we're going to need this candy in the future."

"Sadly, it's all I've got left. If I'd thought of it, I would have asked Jean-Pierre to pick some up this weekend."

He glanced around at the family, now content and well on their way to full rehydration. "I need to know more about the man with the knife. We can't have someone like that lurking outside our clinic."

Allison recanted what she'd seen, and Grant added the details he remembered, as well. Dr. Jones squatted down to Eugene, now snuggled next to his mother. "Did the mean man with the knife say anything to you?"

Eugene mumbled so softly they had to lean in to hear him. "He said If I went to your clinic, I would die. That's why I hid in the truck."

Dr. Jones patted his shoulder. "You must have been so scared."

"I could hear people calling my name, but with that mean man around, I didn't dare say anything."

"Did he say why he'd kill you?" Dr. Jones inquired.

"He said your clinic makes the Iwa mad. Said I needed to rely on him to deal with the Iwa."

"Did he threaten to kill you with his knife?" Allison probed.

He shook his head. "No, he said Bondye would tell the Iva to make me die, but he held the knife right here." He patted chest.

Grant turned to Dr. Jones. "Who is Bondye, and what the devil is the Iwa?"

So that they could have a discussion in a private location, Dr. Jones gestured for Allison and Grant to follow him into his office.

Once seated in his office and away from the ears of the Bandeau family, Allison said, "Isn't Bondye the name Haitians give to their Creator? Similar to our God?" Allison asked.

"Yes and no. While we believe in a benevolent Creator who loves us, Haitians live in mortal fear of angering the Iwa. They're very superstitious, and in the voodoo religion, people are constantly trying to appease the Iwa spirits."

"I confess, I know practically nothing about voodoo, except for jokes about someone with a vendetta against me sticking pins in a voodoo doll with my name on it," Grant said.

Allison piped in, "Forget pins! It sounds like Louis would prefer to stick knives in our voodoo dolls."

"Or us," Grant offered grimly.

"I'm no expert, but here is what I've learned about the voodoo religion," Dr. Jones said. The word 'voodoo' means 'spirit' or' deity'. Haitians believe the unseen world is populated by angels called zanj, spirits called Iwa, and the spirits of their dead ancestors. They believe Bondye created these spirits to help Him govern our world."

"So that is why they hold their chanting and dancing ceremonies—to convince the Iwa spirits to intercede and change the outcome of things?" Allison asked.

"Bingo," Dr. Jones said, pointing at her. "They offer up prayers, chants, drumming, dances, and devotional rites to a particular spirit in hopes that the spirit will grant them health, protection, or favor with Bondye."

"Similar to Catholics praying to a given Patron Saint, like Saint Jude or Saint Augustine, asking for intercession with God?" Grant asked.

"Since French Roman Catholic missionaries inhabited Haiti in the 16th and 17th centuries, Catholicism is the predominant religion, but some Catholic practices have become twisted and incorporated into the voodoo religion."

"But in voodoo, don't they take it a step further and believe in actual spirit possession?" Allison asked. She smiled sheepishly. "I only know this because I read it in my traveler's guide to Haiti on my flight from America."

"Yes," Dr. Jones said. "In voodoo rites, the witch doctor or priest enters into a trance where he claims a particular spirit indwells him. When he is possessed by an Iwa spirit, that spirit supposedly gives him supernaturally-inspired advice and medical cures. He can also supposedly communicate with dead relatives."

"Which is why this medical clinic angers the local witch doctor so much. We're competing with him on providing care," Allison said.

Dr. Jones nodded. "Louis believes we have angered the Iwa spirits because we have bypassed them in our efforts to help Eugene and his family."

Grant rubbed his chin. "Wow! When you think about it, if they've been brainwashed into believing coming here angers the Iwa spirits, it's a wonder anyone dares to come."

"Not everyone in Haiti practices voodoo. Many are Catholic, so they have no problem with coming to the clinic. But those who do practice voodoo only come when they're desperate, or when the witch doctor's voodoo rites have failed. This means we end up seeing patients far more advanced in their disease, their last-ditch effort to survive when voodoo has failed."

"Which means some will die who could have made it—if they'd gotten here sooner," Grant commented.

"Exactly. This is why I have to not only practice medicine but confront head-on the control that voodoo has over people."

Allison chewed on her bottom lip. "Doesn't it frighten you, knowing so many people here are hostile to modern medical practices? They may be sticking pins in a voodoo doll with your name on it as we speak!"

Dr. Jones patted his heart. "'Greater is He that is in me than He that is in the world.'"

He continued. "Here in Haiti, I cling to that scripture, or I'd be afraid to get out of bed in the morning. I am convinced God called Judy and me to be medical missionaries in Haiti."

"That's commendable," Allison said.

"We will do our part to convince people of God's love and the freedom that can be found in Jesus. But we have to do it one person at a time."

"I can see how it would be very freeing for a Haitian to no longer live in fear that they have somehow angered an Iwa spirit," Grant commented.

"Or, that they need to appease Bondye," Allison added.

"Once I have cured someone medically, they are much more receptive to the gospel. In fact, there is now a sizeable congregation of Christian believers in town. They meet every Sunday, and when I can, I attend their church service."

"I'd love to go some Sunday," Allison said.

"As would I," Grant added. "I'll bet it's a lot different than our church services in the States."

"The smile on their faces says it all."

"I'll bet," Allison agreed.

"When a Haitian who has always believed in voodoo accepts Jesus as their Savior and rids himself of that demonic oppression, he is truly transformed. It's beautiful to see."

"That verse, "He who the Son has set free, is free indeed,' takes on new meaning, doesn't it," Allison said.

He nodded. "The work here is exhausting, but every day, I see the fruit of my labor. People are being set free physically and spiritually, and if I die early because of the work I'm doing here in Haiti, it will still be worth it."

Grant stared at him, mulling over the words. Would *he* be willing to die young to serve these indigent people? If he was honest, the answer was a resounding no.

Besides, wouldn't it benefit Haiti more for him to raise funds for the clinic so they could hire a nurse or start an orphanage? If he died early, he wouldn't be around to contribute and solicit money. Haiti would be better served if he practiced in America and tithed to the cause, wouldn't it?

In his core, he knew he was selling out. Sure, writing checks would make him feel good—like he was doing his part—but if Dr. Jones couldn't find a nurse or surgeon willing to live in such a remote and poverty-stricken town, did the money really help? What Dr. Jones most needed was a permanent surgeon and nurse. And an orphanage. And a reliable vehicle!

As though aware of what Grant was thinking, Dr. Jones said, "It's like that verse in Matthew where Jesus talked about the harvest being plenty, but the workers being few."

"Well, I'm glad Allison and I are here to help, if only for three months," Grant said, surprised by how much he meant it.

Dr. Jones patted Grant's back and smiled. "I thank God for you two every day, and I pray every morning for your safety. You've been such a blessing to Judy and me."

Wow! He wasn't sure his own mother prayed for him every day! The thought warmed him.

Dr. Jones gestured toward the family a short distance away in the clinic. "While they're hooked up to IV fluids, I have a perfect opportunity to toss out a few crumbs of scripture and plant a seed. If they respond, I can share the gospel and invite them to join our church to learn more."

Dr. Jones stood from behind his desk. "We probably ought to go check on our patients again." He smiled. "No doubt one of the children will insist on getting another piece of candy."

They strolled back to the clinic, and after Pierre and Regina insisted they were feeling stronger, he promised to advance their diet to Jell-O and popsicles. Time would tell how their stomachs would handle eating again.

When they smiled and said they were ready to eat, Allison volunteered to get the popsicles from the kitchen.

"I'll go with her," Grant offered. As the two doctors strolled toward the kitchen, Grant confessed, "Having that witch doctor lurking around gives me the creeps."

"He doesn't make my list of favorite people, either."

Grant rubbed his chin. "Too bad there isn't a police station in town. We could report him. Or get a restraining order."

"Except that would likely antagonize him more. Witch doctors are revered in the community, so if we cross him, we will likely do more harm than good."

"How safe do you feel having some guy with a knife who threatens little kids right outside our clinic?"

Allison opened the door to the kitchen and headed for the refrigerator. "Not at all. Maybe we should investigate a little more about this guy. See if he is all bark and only trying to intimidate us, or if he truly poses a threat."

"How do you propose we do that?"

"What if we go to that church service tomorrow and ask the locals about him?"

Grant raised a finger. "Maybe we could bring Raphael with us so he can help translate. Thanks to Judy, he is almost fully bilingual now."

Allison's face brightened. "Good idea. I'll bet the locals know all about him. Or, if there are any more witch doctors or priestess in town that we need to be aware of."

Allison opened the freezer door and pulled out the large box of popsicles. "We better give one to each of the kids, as well as the parents, or we'll have mutiny on the bounty."

"Right. Because I am so threatened by little children with cholera."

"Hey, those puppy dog pleading eyes of theirs wounded me more than any bullet," she said counting out six popsicles.

"I'll take puppy dog eyes over butcher knives. Dr. Jones faces daily threats from a crazy witch doctor, but he feels compelled to stay. I wish I had that level of conviction."

"He feels compelled to stay because he knows this is where God called him to be."

She returned the remaining box of popsicles to the freezer and shut the door. "God has a calling for each of us, and we need to pray earnestly until He makes that calling clear to us."

"I supposed you're right," Grant conceded.

"Of course, I'm right," she said with a cocky grin.

"I guess I'm still waiting to get my marching orders from above."

"Once God gives us a clear calling, He'll also give us the courage and energy to follow through."

"He who began a good work in me will be faithful to complete it," Grant quoted.

Allison's eyes widened. "Philippians 1:6." She stared at him a second before adding, "You know, until this rotation in Haiti, I didn't even know you were a believer."

He shrugged. "I don't make a big production out of it, but I hope to use my skills to serve God in some capacity."

As though still in shock she continued to stare at him. "I had no idea."

His lips tightened. "That's a pitiful commentary about my witness."

She cocked her head several times as though in thought. "Now that I know you're a believer, things do make a lot more sense."

"What do you mean?" He grabbed a dish towel to keep the popsicles from freezing her hands. "Here. Use this to hold them."

"Actually, after pushing that burning hot truck, the cold feels good on my palms."

"What makes more sense?" he pressed.

"Most of the guys in our class curse like sailors and take God's name in vain all the time. Or they brag about their sexual escapades and the parties they've attended."

"Like Thomas and Jeremy?"

"Exactly. But you're not like that. And with all the women who throw themselves at you, I've never once heard rumors about you sleeping around."

He cocked a brow. "Keeping up with my love life, Allison?"

"Of course not! But I'm not clueless. I swear, if you'd let her, that Tiffany What's-Her-Name would have her way with you in a broom closet."

He shook his head in disgust. "There's nothing flattering about sleeping with a woman who will sleep with any Tom, Dick, or Harry she finds attractive." He chewed on his lower lip before adding, "I guess I'm more of a bald eagle or gibbon."

Allison added, "Or black vulture? Word on the street is, they mate for life, also."

"I think I'll align myself with the bald eagle. Far more regal and patriotic."

Since her hands were full of popsicles, she gestured with her head for him to open the door so she could return to the clinic. "I could have named an albatross. Or a termite."

He rolled his eyes. "A termite? Seriously?"

"I'll have you know termites are very industrious—just like you. Did you know more homes are destroyed by termites every year than by tornadoes and fires combined?"

He rolled his eyes and opened the kitchen door. "The point is, I'm not looking for a quick roll in the hay with any willing woman. I'm looking for that one right woman who makes me laugh, who challenges me, and encourages me to be my best. I want a relationship like my parents. Like Dr. Jones and Judy."

"Are you saying looks don't matter? Just compatibility?"

His eyes widened with horror. "Of course not! The right woman will make my pulse race, or it's a total deal breaker."

Allison scowled. "Why do looks come first with men?"

As they strolled toward the clinic Grant responded, "Not first, but a definite third! Otherwise, I may as well just adopt a dog. Golden retrievers make loyal and agreeable companions." He smirked and added, "With a lot less headache and lip."

She harrumphed. "You're impossible."

He grabbed her arm and laughed. "I'm just pulling your chain." When her eyes met his, he said, "Can you honestly say *you* would marry a man you felt little to no physical attraction for, no matter how Godly or nice or smart he was?"

She opened her mouth to insist she most certainly *would* marry such a wonderful, caring, Godly man but then closed it. Her shoulders sagged and she looked down at her feet. "No, if I'm honest, I want my husband to make my pulse race, too. I wish I didn't."

He placed hands on her shoulders. "You make it sound like a bad thing, but it's a gift God gave married couples. The frosting on the cake."

Her eyes pooled with tears. "Sexual attraction is a curse from Hell that only leads to heartache and despair. Take it from me."

A tear dripped from her eye and trickled down her cheek. Grant reached up with his index finger and gently brushed it away. "I don't know what happened to make you jaded, but I'm sorry you were hurt."

She glanced up at him through her tears as though embarrassed to have revealed such vulnerability. Before he could inquire further, Allison insisted, "I need to get these popsicles to the Bandeau family before they melt." She then pulled away from his probing eyes and charged toward the clinic as though being pursued by Bondye himself.

So, she wasn't going to tell him what happened. It did explain why she could be guarded and prickly with him at times. Something had scarred her and made her fearful of ever letting herself be vulnerable.

He knew she was attracted to him. He'd caught her watching him many times over the last four years. When he'd meet her gaze, her eyes would dart away, and her cheeks would flush, as though she was embarrassed he'd caught her staring.

Despite her attraction, something kept her from flirting with him like most women. She maintained a polite and professional veneer—but guarded. Now he knew why. She'd been hurt—damaged, even—in a previous relationship. No way was she willing to risk her heart again to a man she found attractive.

Of course, her groundless hang-up that he thought less of her because of her background didn't boost her confidence.

He released a frustrated breath. Trust couldn't be rushed. When, and if, she ever trusted him enough to share her painful story, he'd be ready to listen. He had barely begun to penetrate the depths of Allison Smith. Knowing someone had trampled on her heart, made him feel protective of her.

As they reached the clinic, Allison pasted on a smile and offered each family member a popsicle. At first, they stared at it with quizzical expressions until Allison ripped off the wrapper and mimed lapping it.

Regina nodded understanding and licked the popsicle then smiled and exclaimed, "Délicieux!" She gestured for the kids to lick. Seeing their mother's delight with the frozen treat, each of the children began to lick theirs, as well.

Dr. Jones smiled. "Well, those went over well. Judy keeps a large batch of Jell-O in the fridge at the house. If the popsicles don't upset their stomachs, we'll give them each a bowl full."

He chuckled. "The locals love red gelatin. Who'd have thunk Jell-O would be an evangelism tool!"

"Speaking of evangelism, Grant and I were wondering if we could go to the church service tomorrow."

Dr. Jones rubbed his chin in thought. "Raphael can take you. I need to stay here at the clinic in case an emergency comes up. Maybe next week, I could go and you two can man the clinic."

"That sounds like a plan," Allison said. "I think it would help us understand the locals better if we went."

"I'll notify Raphael. You'll need to be ready to leave at ten. It's about a two-mile walk to the church. Since Angelina is out of gas, you'll have to go by foot."

"How are you going to get more gas?" Grant inquired.

"Once Jean-Pierre gets back from Port-au-Price, I'll have his brother take our two gas cans and fill them at the nearest gas station. Then Jean-Pierre will have enough gas to drive Angelina to the gas station and fill up."

"How far away is the nearest gas station?"

"Fifteen miles."

Grant shook his head. "You are isolated. Speaking of Angelina, what are you going to do when she conks out for good? That truck seems like it hit its ninth life three lifetimes ago."

Dr. Jones chuckled. "You got that right. We have prayed over that vehicle more times than you can imagine. I live by faith. I know if it conks out for good, God will provide us another vehicle." He raised his hands. "What other choice do I have?"

"Do you have an email list where you could let your donors know exactly what you need?"

Dr. Jones snorted. "Like I have time for that! I barely get five hours of sleep a night as it is. Plus, I don't have internet reception. Even if I had the time. I couldn't send anything.

Grant strolled the clinic rubbing his chin. "You know, my family runs a charitable foundation, so we have people who know all about fund-raising. Get me the addresses and email addresses of all your donors, along with your wish list of what the clinic most needs and how much it will cost, and I will get our PR team to send out notification. With some serious marketing, we should be able to raise enough to get you a reliable vehicle. Preferably one that can hold a stretcher in the back and work as an ambulance to transport the serious cases to Port-au-Prince."

He stared at Grant with a slack jaw. "Wow! You'd do that for me?"

"Absolutely. If more people knew about what goes on in this clinic, they'd be glad to contribute. The Stockdale Foundation has some very wealthy donors, so if I send out an appeal with my name on it, I'm confident I could raise enough to get you everything on your wish list—including a reliable vehicle."

"Angelina seems like one of the family now, but I know it's time for her to retire."

"How about immortalizing her with a commemorative plaque?" Grant suggested. "Because this clinic needs reliable transportation."

"We lost a newborn last year because we couldn't get her to a Port-au-Prince Neonatal unit in a timely manner. She would have made it if Angelina hadn't conked out half-way there. We had to wait until a mechanic could come and fix the truck. By then, the baby died."

Allison's face blanched. "How awful."

"It's times like that when I wish I worked in a modern American medical center with state-of-the-art equipment."

"I'll bet."

"But if I left, there would be no one but that worthless witch doctor to help people. So, I've had to accept that I can't save everyone, and I can only do the best I can." He glanced over at the Badeau family. "Enough jabbering. Time to get back to work and reassess our patients." He pointed at Allison. "You check the vitals on Eugene and Francisca. Grant, you check on Gabriella and Regina. I'll assess Pierre and baby Roberto. By this point, after two bags of IV fluid and several bottles of Pedialyte, their blood pressures should be back to normal."

The three doctors set to work. When it was clear everyone was stable, Allison volunteered to retrieve the Jell-O that Judy had prepared in the house. Grant offered to go with her.

They headed out the clinic door and trudged down the dirt path leading to Dr. and Mrs. Jones' home. They made small talk about how much better the Badeau family looked—anything to avoid their earlier discussion of Allison's broken heart.

As Allison knocked on the front door, a shudder of fear coursed its way down her spine. She instinctively looked around for the witch doctor, half expecting him to jump out from behind the house with a knife.

Not seeing him, she knocked on the door again calling, "Judy? We're here to get Jell-O."

Not hearing a response, Allison surmised Judy must be in the bathroom and thus, unable to come to the door. Since the door was unlocked, they headed inside to retrieve the Jell-O. Grant rummaged through the cabinets until he located six bowls and spoons. Still seeing no signs of Judy, Grant whispered, "I'll bet she's taking a nap. Let's not wake her."

They closed the front door quietly and ambled down the path that ran back to the clinic.

Another uneasy vibe—like she was being watched or was in danger—coursed over her. She whirled around eyeing everything around her.

Grant's brow furrowed. "Allison? What is it?"

Before she could answer, she glimpsed an arm adorned in a colorful ceremonial robe pull back behind the mango tree as though hiding from them.

So the movement she'd seen earlier wasn't Fred. The witch doctor was back.

He'd been spying on them. Not wanting a confrontation when they were armed with nothing more than a bowl of Jell-O and soup spoons, she whispered to Grant, "Witch doctor." She sprinted to the front door of the clinic and charged inside with Grant behind her. She instinctively locked the door behind them.

"I saw him behind the mango tree next to the house."

"I'm glad you didn't go to the house by yourself," Grant said. "No telling what he might have done to you."

They raced into the clinic where Dr. Jones was tending to the Badeau family.

"Louis is outside lurking behind the mango tree," Allison said, her voice shaky. "I saw him when Grant and I were walking from the house to here."

Dr. Jones' forehead wrinkled with concern. "I assumed he left after we came out and rescued Eugene."

"Apparently, he circled back, and he's armed with a butcher knife, so we can't let the Badeau family leave."

"Let me go talk to him," Dr. Jones said, with the same calm tone he might use if needing to alert a waitress about an undercooked piece of chicken.

"What?" Grant said, unable to suppress the alarm in his voice. "You can't go out there. He might stab you."

"Then let's pray for my safety before I go. You can come with me. If there are two of us, I doubt he'll stab me. Besides, you're tall and muscular." He smiled. "I'm counting on you to intimidate him."

Grant's fists balled. "Gladly. I'm sick of this bully scaring everyone."

They offered up a quick prayer for protection, and then the three doctors headed out the front door.

Would they make it through unscathed? The man had a butcher knife and a grudge the size of Mt. Everest.

CHAPTER 15

"Remember, our goal is to befriend the guy, not threaten him," Dr. Jones cautioned, as they exited the clinic.

Grant stopped dead in his tracks. "Befriend him? I'm ready to beat the tar out of him."

Dr. Jones grabbed his arm. "Wrong approach. If we can eventually convert the witch doctor, it will be the most powerful weapon in our evangelism toolbox. Witch doctors carry a lot of clout in the community, and our goal is to get him on our side."

Grant scowled with his hands still balled into fists. "How do you propose we do that?"

Allison pursed her lips. "If we want to befriend him, why don't we offer him some hard candies. That worked like a charm with the Badeau family."

Dr. Jones chuckled. "Not a bad idea. Nothing like a little sugar to sweeten the deal, huh?"

Grant pointed at him. "Exactly. I'll run get some from the kitchen. Wait here."

After dashing back to the house and grabbing a handful of lemon and strawberry hard candies, Grant joined Dr. Jones and Allison.

Allison pointed to the mango tree next to the house. "He was hiding there."

Dr. Jones froze. "Wait. The tree next to the house? You don't suppose he would have hurt Judy, do you?"

Grant's heart stopped. "Even though we called out her name several times when we knocked on the door, Judy didn't answer, so we thought she was taking a nap."

"You mean she left the door unlocked?"

"Yes. We were able to walk right in."

"Oh, dear Jesus." Dr. Jones sprinted toward the house. "I've told that woman a hundred times to keep the door locked, but she never listens to me."

Grant and Allison ran after him. He charged into the house. "Judy? Judy? Where are you?"

They heard a shout from the bathroom. "In here. I just took a shower."

Dr. Jones released a huge sigh of relief. "Thank God you're alive."

Judy emerged from the bathroom in a robe, her hair in a towel turban. "Why wouldn't I be? Is something wrong?"

"Louis Villemort is hiding behind our mango tree. Allison saw him when she came inside to get the Jell-O. Earlier today he came after one of the children with a knife."

"A knife?" Her eyes widened in alarm, and she tied the belt of her bathrobe tighter. "Did he hurt the child?"

"No, but he told him if he went to our clinic he would die because Bondye would kill him."

Her mouth dropped. "That poor child. And now that bully is lurking outside my home wielding a knife?" She glared at her husband and crossed her arms. "And this is the first I've heard of it?"

Dr. Jones stared at his feet shamefaced as she continued her rant. "Thanks for the notice! There I am in the shower, buck naked, and you didn't have the decency to inform me some madman with a knife was skulking around outside? If I'd known, I would have at least locked the front door."

Dr. Jones hung his head. "Judy, I'm sorry. I screwed up. I should have informed you immediately. Or sent Grant to guard you. I was so wrapped up with taking care of a family with cholera and looking for Eugene after he ran away, I didn't think to warn you."

"Since I'm not injured, you're off the hook." She pointed an accusing finger at him. "But don't let it happen again."

Grant stifled a smile. Until this moment, he'd been ready to nominate Dr. Jones for sainthood. He and Judy seemed like the perfect couple with nary a marital spat. Nice to know even they had chinks in their armor.

Dr. Jones wrapped a protective arm around his wife and kissed her cheek. "If anything ever happened to you, I'd be devastated. You know that don't you?"

She rewarded him with a swat. "Now you're just trying to butter me up. I already told you you're forgiven."

He smiled impishly and genuflected to the floor. "The queen has offered me clemency."

She gestured with her hand for him to stand. "Get up, peasant. If this happens again, I'll sharpen my guillotine blade, so you bear that in mind."

"Now that we know you're okay, Grant and I are going to confront him and see if we can begin a friendship."

Judy frowned. "Friendship? With Louis Villemort? You're acting like Chamberlain negotiating with Hitler."

Dr. Jones pointed at the candy. "We're not negotiating, we're bribing. If we can convert the witch doctor, the rest of the town will follow."

Judy sucked in a deep breath. "I don't like the idea of you tangling with someone who carries a knife."

She added, "As far as I'm concerned, the further you stay away from that man, the better."

He patted her shoulder. "Now Judy. You know we're called to love our enemies. He's God's child as much as you and me. Besides, I can hardly stay away from him when he's lurking in our yard and threatening the children who come to the clinic. I have to confront him."

She exhaled. "I suppose you're right, but the whole thing terrifies me."

"Greater is He that is in me than…"

"He that is in the world. Yeah, yeah, I know," she grumbled. She pushed him toward the door. "Go do what you have to do. I'll be praying for you." She pointed a scolding finger at him. "Don't you dare come back in here with a knife dangling from your heart. You do, and you'll be in deep trouble with me."

He smiled but didn't point out the ridiculousness of her statement. "I'll do my best. I promise."

She jabbed a finger at him. "You better."

Grant and Dr. Jones approached Louis slowly with Allison hovering closely behind.

When they were ten feet from the mango tree Dr. Jones yelled, "Bonjour. Nous sommes amis."

"We are friends," Grant said. "I was able to translate that."

A short elderly man garbed in a colorful robe with white chalk streaks on his face stepped out from behind the tree. He greeted them with narrowed eyes and a snarl, but at least his knife was not in his hand. "Qu'est ce que tu veux?" he snapped.

"We want to be your friend," Dr. Jones said in French Creole, offering the man a handful of hard candies. "Vous pas de mal." He translated under his breath what he'd said to Grant: "We mean you no harm."

The witch doctor eyed them with crossed arms and accused them of wanting to poison him with their candies.

Dr. Jones shook his head, unwrapped one of the candies, and popped it into his own mouth. "No poison. See? I'm eating one myself," he said in French.

The witch doctor stared at Dr. Jones, as though waiting to see if he'd drop to the ground dead.

To further prove they had not been poisoned, Grant also unwrapped a candy and tossed it into his mouth. "Délicieux!" he said, trying not to reveal how unnerved he felt to be standing with a witch doctor who likely had a knife tucked in the pocket of his ceremonial gown.

"Why would you want to be my friend?" Louis growled.

"We both want to heal people," Dr. Jones explained. "We just go at it in different ways."

"How so?" Louis inquired.

"You use spiritual powers, and I use modern medicine. They aren't mutually exclusive." Dr. Jones mumbled the interpretation to Grant and Allison.

Louis shifted his weight, as though mulling over his words.

When he didn't respond, Dr. Jones added, "We both worship a god. You worship Bondye, and I worship Jesus. We aren't enemies. We can be friends."

Dr. Jones extended his hand holding the hard candies and nodded to the witch doctor to accept his gift. "My gift of friendship," he said with a smile.

Grant was impressed with how fluently Dr. Jones spoke in French Creole. So far, with his paltry thirty minutes of study per day, Grant had learned to say hello and ask for a bathroom. He clearly needed to up his game and increase his study time. Perhaps he could practice speaking the language with Raphael and Allison. He'd start tomorrow on their way to church.

"Take the candies as a gift from me," Dr. Jones coaxed, a forced smile on his face.

The witch doctor snatched up the candies and heaved them onto the ground. He charged forward but still hadn't pulled out his knife. "Anyone who tells people to believe in your Jesus instead of the Iwa is no friend of mine. We are enemies, you and I, and I have placed a curse on you."

He glared at Grant and hurled, "On you, too." He jabbed a finger toward them. "Bondye will see you dead." He charged off and only turned around to hurl, "Raide mort!"

Grant felt a cold wave of fear shudder through him despite the oppressive heat. He didn't know exactly what the man had said, but judging from his angry voice, threatening gestures, thrown candies, and the word 'mort', and Grant was pretty sure the guy had just told him to drop dead.

When Dr. Jones didn't provide an immediate interpretation, Grant knew it couldn't be good. No doubt Dr. Jones didn't want to frighten them.

Dr. Jones put a hand on Grant and Allison's shoulders. "Well, that didn't go as planned. So much for candy winning him over, huh?" he mumbled with a chuckle.

Grant shook his head, still in shock from the disturbing interaction. How could Dr. Jones be so glib? "He told us to drop dead, didn't he?"

"And worse," Dr. Jones confirmed. "He's put a curse on us."

Grant's breath caught. A voodoo witch doctor had put a curse on him and was likely performing incantations on an hourly basis praying for his demise. Not that Grant believed in such nonsense, but he couldn't deny a truckload of angst had wormed its way into his head.

Just knowing someone was pleading with Satanic forces to see him dead made his palms sweat. Or was it this insufferable heat...

Greater is He that is in me than He who is in the world.

Grant repeated the scripture silently, praying it was true. He now understood why Dr. Jones made this a daily scripture.

The three doctors trudged back to the clinic in silence as the unsavory news sank in. Dr. Jones must have noticed the worried glance that passed between Grant and Allison. "I know this is new to you, but you can't let fear control you. With the Christian congregation in town growing exponentially, Louis is feeling threatened. That's why, every day, I remind myself God is stronger than Satan. Every day, I ask God to put a spiritual cloak of protection around Judy and me so we can continue our work here. And I pray for Louis' salvation."

"Not that I believe in curses, but I sure don't like being the brunt of one," Grant admitted.

"Well, truthfully, it doesn't make my day either," Dr. Jones said with a chuckle. "But never forget, 'Greater is He that is in me, than He who is in the world.' Claim that verse over your life every single day, and no curse from Louis Villemort will have power over you."

"Tell me more about Louis so I'll know what I'm up against, Allison suggested.

"He's been the town's witch doctor for decades, and he's made a bundle from offering up incantations and supposedly channeling the spirits of dead people. He also charges a bundle for his various snake oils and potions."

"Wait! He *charges* for his services?" Allison asked in shock.

"Oh, yes! Church members tell me he is hands down the richest man in the town."

"You're kidding!" Allison said.

"Desperate people hand over what little money they have for him to supposedly sway the Iwa spirits on their behalf. If they don't have money, they give him food or goats or whatever they do have," Dr. Jones explained.

"How would anyone prove he hasn't communicated with their dead relative or a spirit of Iwa?" Grant inquired.

Dr. Jones nodded. "Exactly. He likely tells people what they want to hear, claiming it is the word of their dead mother or one of the spirits."

Allison opened the front door of the clinic. "Except, if he's so all powerful, why is the infant and child mortality rate in this section of Haiti so much worse than in Port au Prince where people receive decent health care?"

"He's all bells and whistles, but before I came to town, who else did they have? Voodoo is all they know."

"It's what they were raised on since birth, just like we were raised to believe in Jesus," Allison added.

"Good point," Grant conceded. "We practice what we were raised with."

"When they're in dire straits, they need something or someone to give them hope. They want to believe Louis has the power to change their circumstances," Dr. Jones said.

"Why haven't the townsfolk figured out he has no power—that he's a croc?" Grant inquired.

As they entered the medical clinic, Dr. Jones said, "A lot of our new church members are people who handed over their last gourde or chicken to Louis to gain his supposed influence with the spirits, only to be left empty handed. After seeing no results with voodoo and feeling ripped off, they are far more receptive to the gospel, especially if I provide free medical care that actually fixes their medical problem."

"I'm looking forward to attending that Haitian church service tomorrow," Allison said.

"Trust me, it will be an experience— nothing like the staid Protestant services you likely attend in the States." He grinned. "These people know how to dance, sing, and praise the Lord."

"Who's the preacher?" Grant asked.

"A local mango farmer, though Judy or I sometimes preach when he is unable to."

As they entered the treatment rooms, the entire Badeau family was asleep. Roberto was snuggled up in his mother's arms, and Pierre had a child on each side. Gabriella was sprawled in a chair with her mouth open and her head leaned against the back of the chair.

"Must be they were exhausted from so many sleepless nights of diarrhea and intestinal cramps," Allison whispered as they tip-toed by.

"Let's get a nap of our own," Dr. Jones whispered. "You have to catch sleep when you can."

"But we can't go off and leave them, can we?" Grant asked.

Dr. Jones smiled. "I've learned to sleep anywhere. I'll catch a few zzzs in the lounge chair in my office. If anyone stirs, I'll hear them and wake up. I've learned to sleep with one ear open." He gestured toward the front door. "Go grab a nap. If anything exciting comes in, I'll come get you."

Grant eyed the zonked-out family and released a yawn. A nap would be nice…If nothing else, it would give him a few extra minutes to study his French Creole. As he strode toward the front door, he whispered to Allison, "You coming?"

"In a bit. I want to retrieve those wrapped hard candies the witch doctor tossed at us. There's only a dozen or so left, so I hate to see them go to waste."

Grant grimaced. "I'm not eating one. He probably uttered a death curse on anyone who eats one." He motioned a hand at them. "I'll bet they'll cause food poisoning."

"Don't be ridiculous. He doesn't have the power to supernaturally put Salmonella in candy."

"Maybe not, but I'm coming with you," Grant insisted as they headed out the door. "No way am I leaving you out there to face Satan Incarnate alone."

She glanced up at him. "He really spooked you out, didn't he?"

"I admit it. The guy got to me. I know I sound paranoid, but aren't you afraid—even a little? He utilized the occult to put a curse on us. The guy means business."

"He means business because we're hurting *his* business."

"Exactly. Which makes him dangerous."

As they strolled toward the strewn candies on the ground, Allison brightened. "I have an idea. Didn't someone once say, 'Keep your friends close and your enemies closer?'"

"Al Pacino in *The Godfather*, though I think the Godfather got the advice from some Chinese military strategist. Why do you ask?"

"What if we found a way to employ Louis to get him on our side?"

Grant's mouth dropped. "You want Dr. Jones to hire a voodoo witch doctor? The guy threatens little kids and skulks around wielding a butcher knife."

"But if we no longer threaten his bottom line, maybe he won't threaten us. He wouldn't want to destroy the hand that feeds him, right?"

Grant rubbed his chin. "What would we hire him to do?"

She shrugged. "I don't know. A janitor, maybe?"

"If Dr. Jones doesn't have the money for a reliable vehicle, how could he possibly afford a new employee?" Grant asked, as he bent over to pick up the pieces of candy.

"Good point."

"Besides, how do you know he won't inject poison in the IV fluids? Or slit our throats when our backs are turned?"

She pursed her lips as she mulled over his comments. "I suppose you raise some legitimate concerns."

"Legitimate concerns? He terrorized Eugene and put a death curse on us!"

Allison bent over to scoop up a handful of candies. "Let's pray about it and see if we can find a way to get him on our side, if only for financial gain. Otherwise, he might burn down the clinic or kill Dr. Jones—or Judy."

"Or us," Grant added glumly. He picked up the remaining hard candies. "I can't believe we're so desperate for candy we're reduced to scraping them off the ground."

"They're still fully wrapped." She pointed a finger at him. "Waste not, want not."

"If I'd known what an asset lemon drops were, I would have stuffed my luggage with bags with them."

She chuckled. "Then wouldn't those thugs at the airport be doubly sorry you knew karate."

He shook his head. "Can you believe we're down here facing thugs, witch doctors, and cholera? These three months can't pass soon enough."

"Well, at least one good thing came out of this experience," Allison said, smiling up at him.

He stopped to stare at her. "Really? I can't think of a thing."

"I can. Before Haiti, you and I never spoke to each other, unless it was about a surgical case. I felt intimidated by you. But now, I feel like we're comrades. Friends, even."

"We are." He stood from collecting the candies and stuffed them in his pockets. "You had no reason to be intimidated by me. You're at the top of our class, too."

"True, but you come from money, and I come from—" She stopped abruptly, as though already regretting her words.

"Mount Trashmore," he said, filling in the blank. When she stared down at her feet, he added, "Allison, you really need to let that go. I don't look down on you."

Trying to ease the intensity she quipped, "Well, technically, you *do* look down on me since I'm a foot shorter than you." She lifted a brow. "In fact, I believe you called me a midget."

Not deterred by her attempt at humor, he put both hands on her shoulders and stepped close.

"Look at me," he whispered, and she forced herself to meet his eyes. "I'm not going to say this again. Ever. I don't think any less of you because of your background."

He squeezed her shoulders. "I've always admired you, Allison, and you're right. Becoming friends is the best thing that has come out of this rotation." His eyes searched hers with such intensity it left her holding her breath.

She stared up into his dark chocolate eyes transfixed—no hypnotized—by the acceptance and kindness radiating back at her. She reveled in that glorious place of intimacy never wanting to leave. His face inched closer, and for a moment, she was convinced he was going to kiss her. The thought both thrilled and terrified her.

Caving into fear, she stepped back. "It's n-not the only good thing that's come out of this rotation."

"What else has been good?" he whispered, stepping closer to caress her cheek.

Standing mere inches apart, her eyes locked with his, and her heart thudded like a bass drum on steroids when she sensed he was about to kiss her. Addled by the magnetic pull between them, she began to babble. "Think of all the lives we've saved. If we hadn't been here, Fabiola and the twins would have died, and that sweet Bandeau baby wouldn't have made it. And don't forget that woman with gall stones."

Shut up! You're ruining the mood.

She tucked a lock of hair behind her ear hoping he hadn't noticed how much her hand shook. Was she ready for this?

A sudden wave of panic overtook her, and desperate to escape the magnetic pull between them before she did something irreversible. Something she might regret. She stepped back and hurried toward the cabin.

Thankfully, he made no comment about her obvious retreat. He followed her to their cabin without a word,

He unlocked the door and gestured for Allison to enter first. "You're right. It has been rewarding to save lives. We're also getting lots of operating experience." He pulled out the hard candies from his pockets and piled them on the dresser. "I'm still unnerved by that witch doctor, though. I fear we haven't seen the last of him."

"I suspect you're right, but I refuse to let him get to me."

"Let's get some sleep before another train wreck crawls into the waiting room."

"Good idea. I'm going to change into something cooler. It's stifling in here."

She opened a dresser drawer, pulled out some shorts and a tank top, then wandered into the bathroom. A minute later she emerged and strolled to her side of the partition.

Grant only caught a flash of Allison's shapely physique in her scanty outfit before she crossed to her side of the partition.

The enticing image burned in his brain. Beneath the baggy scrubs she wore in the OR and clinic lived a woman male dreams were made of.

As he plumped his pillow and tucked up his long legs so they would fit on the scrawny bunk, Grant tried his best to rid his brain of the tantalizing vision of Allison in that tank top. He'd nearly caved into his desire to kiss her earlier, but she'd made it clear she only wanted to remain friends, though for a moment he was positive she'd wanted his kiss. But then she'd pulled back with a look of panic on her face and started babbling. She clearly wasn't ready for a relationship with him.

The image of Allison's alluring physique swirled in his brain refusing to leave, and as the minutes ticked by, he feasted on the beguiling image.

He heard her slow breathing and knew she was asleep. How did she do that? Asleep before he could even make his pillow comfortable.

Four years of residency together—how had he never fully appreciated how pretty she was until now?

He longed to curl up on her bed next to her and hold her close—except it was too darn hot for cuddling. He wiped sweat from his face and commanded himself to fall asleep.

Fifteen minutes later, he released a frustrated sigh. Sleep was not going to happen—not when his fantasies had degenerated from viewing Allison as a colleague and sister in Christ to something far more enticing but far less wholesome. He commanded himself to pull his mind out of the gutter and forced himself to quote his least favorite scripture in the Bible: *Take captive every thought and make it obedient to Christ.*

What a killjoy!

He reluctantly reached on his nightstand for his phrase book of French Creole words. He'd rather fantasize about Allison in her skimpy shorts and tank top, but he sighed in surrender and forced himself to review the words he'd studied last night. He looked up phrases he could use at church tomorrow. *Bel rankontre ou.* Nice to meet you. He tossed the phrase around in his brain until he had it memorized. *Li bel yo dwe isit la.* It's nice to be here. If only he knew how to pronounce the phrases properly. He needed a tutor.

And then it dawned on him. *That's* how he could employ the witch doctor! They could hire Louis to be a French Creole tutor. Grant could offer to pay him extremely well to help him learn to speak the language properly.

They could meet somewhere other than the clinic, so the clinic would not be held accountable for mingling with the local witch doctor.

Allison would love this plan! Hadn't she admonished Grant that they needed to keep Louis close so they could keep an eye on him? Surely Louis wouldn't harm the hands that paid him.

Once Grant formulated his plan, he looked up the French Creole words for 'I am sleepy'. *Mwen fatigue.* He muttered the words like a chant until he was sound asleep.

CHAPTER 16

"You ready to go?" Allison asked, eyeing her watch. "We're supposed to meet Raphael at his house in five minutes."

Grant swallowed the last sip of his coffee and placed the coffee cup into the kitchen sink. "Sure, I guess I can wash these dishes when we get back." He grabbed a bottle of water from the refrigerator and headed toward the door.

As they hoofed the short distance to Raphael's house, Allison spotted the huge iguana lumbering across the road and pointed. "Look, there's Fred!"

Grant grinned. "Hey, there, big guy."

Fred turned his head briefly to stare at them as though aware they were talking about him. He then ambled across the road out of sight.

"Can you believe how big that thing is compared to the iguanas that kids keep as pets in America?" Allison commented.

"He looks prehistoric. Like he has dinosaur genes in him."

"One of the perks of living in Haiti—seeing tropical birds and wildlife in their natural habitat."

Grant suddenly stopped and reached for her arm. "Wait! Before Raphael joins us, I meant to run an idea by you." He then shared his idea of paying Louis Villemort to tutor him in French Creole.

"Do you think it's safe?" her voiced rose with alarm.

"You were the one who said we should keep our friends close and our enemies closer."

She whacked his arm. "Quit using my own words against me. Besides, it wasn't me who said that—it was Al Pacino, and it was in a movie. Fiction, not real life."

"I think it would work, though. If the guy is losing money because of the clinic, we offer to supplement his income by paying him to tutor me."

She crossed her arms. "If you go, I'm going with you. The guy carries a butcher knife. You can't be left alone with him."

"That way, you can be a witness to my brutal stabbing?"

She whacked his arm again. "Don't be morbid. It isn't funny."

"Before I agree to meeting with him, I'm going to get the scoop on him at the church service today. See if he's all bark, or if he has actually hurt someone before."

"Good idea."

They reached Raphael's house—more of a dilapidated shack than a house—and knocked on the door. Raphael exited with a shy smile holding a tattered Bible. "Bonjour."

"Bonjour," Allison and Grant said simultaneously.

"Ready to go?" Grant gestured toward the road.

"Oui. Je suis prête."

Judy exited behind Raphael. "I decided to join you today. I haven't gone to church in a while, and Robert said he was fine with me going today. I just finished eating homemade muffins with Raphael."

"Great," Allison said. "The more the merrier."

The four strode down the pot-holed road while Grant and Allison peppered Raphael and Judy with questions about what to expect at the church service. Raphael's English was surprisingly fluent, though at times he had to resort to pantomime and gestures to get his point across, or Judy interpreted.

When Grant asked about Louis Villemort, Raphael's voice shook. "Il me fait peur."

"Why does he scare you, Raphael?" Allison inquired.

He rattled off several sentences, which Judy interpreted. "He said Louis always looks like he hates Dr. Jones, and Raphael has heard him make threats and chants against him."

"But has he ever actually harmed someone, or is he all bark?" Grant asked.

"He threatened Eugene with a knife. That's enough for me to fear him," Judy said. "I don't think he would actually stab me, but I don't think he's above burning down our clinic or threatening us in hopes of motivating us to leave town."

"Your home and the clinic are made of brick, correct? That wouldn't burn," Grant pointed out.

"True, but he could torch the couch, the kitchen table, our mattress. There's still plenty to burn, and the smoke damage would make the place a total loss."

"True," Grant conceded.

"I'll keep a watch for him," Raphael promised. "If I see him coming, I'll run over and warn you. He has to pass my house before he reaches you."

She patted his head. "You are such a good boy. I don't know what Robert and I would do without you."

He smiled up at her with his dimpled grin.

As the sun beat down with unrelenting force, Allison brushed the sweat from her face and fanned her skirt over her legs in a futile attempt to provide a breeze. How did people stand it down here?

She glanced over at Grant. He wasn't faring much better. His shirt was soaked with perspiration, and it stuck to his chest and back. He undid his top two shirt buttons and fanned his shirt to keep it from sticking.

"How much further 'til we're there?" he asked, clearly drained from a two-mile hike in such sweltering humidity.

"Almost there," Raphael reassured them. He pointed to a bend in the road about a quarter mile away. "The church is right around the corner."

The church proved little more than an outdoor pavilion, but at least it had a roof, which provided protection from the energy-sucking rays of the sun.

When they reached the church, Judy introduced them to a plump woman with a red scarf covering her hair and a gored skirt, each gore in a different vibrant color. She opened her arms wide, face beaming.

Judy hugged her and responded that they were glad to be here. She then introduced the friendly woman as the minister's wife. She handed them each a palm branch and said they would need them for the worship service.

Soon, the pastor, Delense Etienne, clapped his hands together and announced they were about to start. Within seconds, a team of six singers came forward singing a loud chorus of praise songs. Bongo drums and shakers added to the festive worship. The congregation, some fifty to sixty members in size, waved hands and palm branches overhead while swaying and dancing and exclaiming, "Jesus est roi," and "Loue le seigneur." Judy shouted over the singing to Allison, "They're singing, 'Jesus is king,' and 'Praise the Lord.'" Judy waved a palm branch overhead and swayed to the lively drum beat.

Allison joined in and repeated the chorus, which rose both in volume and speed until the congregation danced with abandon. Energized by the infectious enthusiasm of the smiling congregation, all thoughts of the oppressive heat disappeared. Allison did her best to join in. She glanced over at Grant to see how he was faring.

The uninhibited dancing and loud praise tunes were no doubt a shock. Probably Grant attended a more formal Presbyterian or Episcopal church. Just as she suspected, he stood stiffly next to her mumbling the words politely but clearly uncomfortable with the charismatic praise all around him. Definitely more of an observer than a participant.

She had to chomp on the inside of her cheeks to keep from laughing. She could only imagine how Grant's dignified family would react if they were here.

As though sensing she was observing him, Grant leaned over and hollered in her ear, "My church service back home suddenly seems very dry."

She handed him her palm branch and shouted back, "When in Rome..."

Grant chuckled and put forth an effort to wave the palm branch and sing with more enthusiasm. "Je suis libre."

After a full half-hour of singing, Pastor Etienne came forward with a joy-filled countenance and announced, "Dieu est grand, n'est pas?"

"God is great, right?" Grant mumbled to Allison.

She smiled. "Oui. Dieu est grand. God is great."

The congregation all sat on rough-hewn benches. Some of the women began to fan themselves with palm leaves. The pastor asked the congregation to turn in their Bibles to John 8:36. Raphael picked up his tattered French bible from the bench and flipped to the appropriate chapter.

Those who didn't own a Bible followed along with someone who did. Pastor Etienne read chapter eight and launched into a sermon about the freedom found in Christ. Forty minutes later, he offered an alter call, and two congregants came forward. The congregation erupted into praise and shouting as the Pastor laid hands on the men and pronounced them free in Christ."

Singing erupted throughout the room and the drummer thrummed out a beat that drove the congregation into a frenzy. The new converts beamed with happiness.

After the service, two church members, Robaire and Sebastian, offered to drive all four of them back to the clinic on their motorbike. Since it was nearing the pinnacle of noonday heat, Allison quickly consented. As she climbed behind Grant on the beat-up bike with barely enough room on the seat to keep from being pitched off, she regretted her decision immediately. Would she end up headfirst in the ditch?

Robaire revved the engine with a grin, and off he flew, bouncing over the craggy rocks and potholes as though they were nothing.

Allison gripped her arms around Grant's waist praying she wouldn't meet her Maker before the harrowing ten-minute drive was over. Judging from Grant's stiff posture and arms gripped around Robaire's waist, he was equally terrified.

Allison forced herself to inhale after holding her breath far too long. Eyeing the wheel just inches from a sharp drop off, she clenched her eyes shut.

Beseeching the Almighty for divine intervention, she could only hope Judy and Raphael were safe on the motorbike behind her. She opened her eyes to turn around and look when Robaire hit a particularly large rock and the motorbike lurched upward and then the wheels skidded. Amazingly, Robaire somehow managed to keep them all on the vehicle.

"Pardonnez-moi," he shouted as he bumped along rattling her brain until she feared she'd end up with a concussion before she made it back to the clinic. When they finally pulled into the driveway and Robaire turned off the motorcycle, she climbed off still rattled both physically and mentally from the ordeal.

Grant pulled out his wallet and offered Robaire a handful of gourdes.

He stuck up a hand and refused the money, but Grant tucked the bills in his hand insisting. "Merci beaucoups!"

Robaire nodded with a grin, waved a goodbye, and wheeled out of the driveway with a loud Vroom.

Grant and Allison stared at each other as though still in shock at what they had just endured.

"Apparently, we aren't going to die at the hand of Louis Villemort. We'll both die from a motorbike wreck long before we get stabbed."

She held up her tremulous hands. "I'm still shaking. I had to close my eyes and pray the whole way."

Grant's mouth formed a crocodile grin "I have a feeling we're going to wish a competent masseuse lived close by when we're racked with back spasms tomorrow."

As Grant opened the door of the clinic for her, Judy and Raphael's motorbike squealed into the parking lot.

They climbed off and thanked the driver. Judy invited him, along with Grant, Allison, and Raphael, to join them for Sunday lunch. He insisted he couldn't stay, as he was expected home. Raphael agreed and offered to help Judy in the kitchen.

Grant glanced at his watch. "Let's go make sure Dr. Jones doesn't need our help in the clinic, and then, if everything is fine, I'm relishing a nice cold shower."

Allison agreed. "After two hours in that oppressive heat, a shower will feel heavenly. The colder the better."

Dr. Jones told Allison and Grant they'd have time for a quick shower before lunch. "The Badeau family has made a remarkable recovery. I'm going to serve them soup and crackers for lunch, If all goes well, I'll get Jean-Pierre's brother to drive them home this afternoon."

"Jean-Pierre gets back today?"

"He's supposed to. And in the nick of time since we need gas desperately." He rubbed his chin.

"If I know Jean-Pierre, he'll arrive in the next thirty minutes so he can eat with us. He loves Judy's cooking, and she promised to make him griot and accra for lunch."

"What, dare I ask is that? Grant inquired, his stomach already tightening with dread.

Dr. Jones chuckled. "No monkey brain or rooster gizzard if that's what you're thinking. Griot is fried pork, and accra is made with a vegetable grown widely in Haiti called a malanga. It's quite tasty."

After their brief showers, Grant and Allison joined Judy and Raphael for lunch. Sure enough, no sooner had they offered the blessing then Jean-Pierre and his brother, Maurice, strolled in. Judy had been so sure they'd arrive for lunch that she'd already set out plates and forks for them.

As they served the dishes Judy and Raphael had prepared, Jean-Pierre filled them in on their trip to Port-au-Prince. "It was wonderful. We got to see relatives we hadn't seen in ten years."

Halfway through the meal Jean-Pierre asked what was new at the clinic.

Jean-Pierre hung his head after hearing the challenges of transporting the Badeau family to the clinic when the truck was out of gas. "So sorry. I meant to fill Angelina before I leave. I get gas as soon as lunch is over."

"Louis Villemort threatened Eugene Badeau with a butcher knife," Raphael piped in face alive with excitement. "And he put a curse on Dr. Jones."

"And us," Grant added, gesturing at himself and Allison.

Jean-Pierre's eyes bulged. "A butcher knife?" He turned to Dr. Jones and crossed his arms. "Robert, what are you going to do about that trouble-maker?"

Dr. Jones released a sigh and ran troubled hands through his hair. "Truthfully? I don't know what to do. He has so much clout in the community I fear antagonizing him. It's not like there's a police department in town that could put a restraining order on him."

"He no obey it," Jean-Pierre agreed. "How about when we get gas in Saint-Marc, I inquire at police station what to do?"

"It wouldn't hurt to inquire, I suppose," Dr. Jones agreed. "In the meantime, we must all be diligent." He pointed at his wife. "Judy, you must keep the front door locked at all times."

Judy saluted her husband with a smile. "Yes, Sir!"

"Maurice and I leave now to fill gas cans. I drive back to Saint-Marc tomorrow to fill up Angelina."

"I'll go with you tomorrow," Judy said. "I'm in desperate need of some kitchen provisions, shampoo, and dish soap."

Dr. Jones raised an index finger. "Add hard candies to your shopping list. After bribing the Badeau kids, we're down to a handful."

Judy chuckled. "Works like a charm every time, doesn't it? I'll see what I can find."

After everyone shoveled in their last bites, Raphael rose from the table and cleared the dishes.

Dr. Jones smiled as Raphael took his plate. "Raphael, did you help Judy prepare the griot and accra today?"

"That depends... You like it?" he said, with a grin.

Dr. Jones belly laughed. "Is that how it works? If I like it, you helped, but if it's awful, Judy made it?"

Raphael grinned impishly. "Oui."

Judy crossed her arms with mock indignation. "Well, I never! Traitor!"

"I liked it very much," Robert said, appeasing his wife. "Délicieux."

Raphael giggled. "In that case, I help."

Jean-Pierre patted his stomach. "Judy and Raphael, you have outdone yourselves, as always." He kissed his fingers. "C'est magnifique."

Maurice rose from the table. "Jean-Pierre, if we have to go to Saint-Marc for gas and then to the police station, we need to leave."

"Hey, before you go, do either of you know exactly where Louis Villemort lives?" Allison asked.

"He's in the largest, nicest house in town," Jean-Pierre said.

"A big green house a kilometer past the Badeau's house," Maurice said. "There's a sign out front advertising his services."

Jean-Pierre eyed her suspiciously. "Why do you ask?"

She did her best to look nonchalant. "Oh, just curious how far away from the clinic he lives."

"Not far enough," Judy sputtered, as she helped Raphael gather up the remaining dirty dishes.

Dr. Jones rose from the table and turned to Jean-Pierre. "As soon as you and Maurice return, I'll get you to drive the Badeau family home."

"Assuming they tolerate their lunch," Allison amended.

"True, but I'm an optimist. I'm going to go check on them and give the kids some hard candies as a reward for being so good and not pulling out their IVs."

Jean-Pierre slapped his forehead. "Oh, I have a letter for you, Grant. It arrived at our post box in Port-au-Prince."

He pulled out a cheery pink envelope from his pants pocket and handed it to Grant.

A pink envelope. It must be from a girl.

Allison tried to ignore the twinge of jealousy that gripped her. She was dying to ask who the letter was from, especially when he tore it open, skimmed it, and grinned.

How could she ask who it was from without appearing nosy—or worse yet, jealous. She gave herself a mental slap. If Grant had a girlfriend, why should she care?

Except...as much as she hated to admit it, she *did* care. A lot!

"Why don't you two kids take a break. Call it your afternoon off," Dr. Jones said, waving his hand at Allison and Grant. "Go take a nap or a swim in the creek out back or something."

Allison rose from the table, stretched, and tried to sound innocent. "I think I'll go for a walk." She patted her belly and added, "I need to burn off this delicious lunch."

Grant eyed her suspiciously. "A walk? It's like an oven set on broil out there."

She refused to make eye contact as she beelined for the front door mumbling something unintelligible.

Grant charged after her. "I'm coming with you to keep you safe."

"I'm fine," she insisted, upping her pace as she bolted down the driveway.

"If you're going where I think you're going, I absolutely need to come. The guy had a knife, Allison. If you think I'm going to let you go alone, think again!"

She turned to face him. "How did you know where I was going?"

He grinned. "Because I was planning to go there myself this afternoon."

She smirked. "Brilliant minds think alike, huh?"

"We'll be safer if we go together." He raised upturned palms as though saying, "Be reasonable."

She released a sigh. "I suppose your karate skills could come in handy—again."

"Let me grab my wallet so I can bribe Louis with a few gourdes for tutoring us. If I wave some bills in his face, I'm hoping he'll get greedy and agree to the tutoring."

"Unless he pulls out his knife, grabs the bills, and tells us to drop dead again."

"Or slits our throats," Grant added dryly.

She waved a finger at him. "Let's be optimists."

When they reached their cabin, Grant pulled a handful of gourdes from his wallet and stuffed them in his pocket. He then grabbed four bottles of water. "We'll definitely need these."

Allison nodded. "It's hotter than Hades out there."

They exited their cabin and trudged over the rocky road in the direction of Louis Villemort's house.

Grant eyed the sun. "I can't say I'm looking forward to a long hike in this inferno."

"It's probably at least four miles, if you count both ways," Allison agreed.

Grant's shoulders sagged.

They ambled onward, their pace slowed by the never-ending potholes, rocks, and crevices. "Can you believe how awful the roads are in Haiti?" Grant stepped over a large rock in the middle of the road. "Do they even have a Department of Transportation?"

"Since over half the population resides in the Port-au-Price area, I suspect most of the road funds are funneled there."

Stumbling slightly on a loose rock, Grant added, "If we manage to get to Louis' house and back without broken bones, it will be a miracle."

Allison stepped around a deep crevice. "We should ask Louis how to say 'fracture', and 'ankle'."

"Or heatstroke and dehydration," Grant added wiping away the sweat from his brow with his T-shirt.

Allison forced herself to look away from his toned six-pack and instead focused on uncapping her water bottle and swallowing several swigs. She waved the bottle at him. "Better drink up. The sun is unrelenting."

He unscrewed the cap on his water and downed half a bottle. "We should have brought more than two bottles each. I could drink this entire thing right now, and we're not even halfway there yet."

Allison fanned her skirt. "I'm drenched with sweat."

Just then, they heard the rattle of an approaching vehicle groaning over the rutty dirt road. Maurice honked the horn of his truck and rolled down the window. "Need a ride?"

Allison wanted to clap with joy. They would be spared part of the hot, dusty journey.

"Oui! Can you bring us to Louis Villemort's house? We want to befriend him by paying him to tutor us in French Creole."

"We go with you, so we can interpret," Maurice said.

Jean-Pierre scowled. "No like plan. Louis Villemort bad man, but we take you, if you insist."

CHAPTER 17

Allison and Grant climbed into the back of Maurice's truck and jostled down the road until they were in front of a large—for Haiti standards—green house. The sign in the yard advertised guaranteed favor with Iwa and communication with dead relatives. The two-story French colonial home featured inviting picture windows donned with fancy curtains and shutters.

Maurice parked his car off the side of the road, and the four strolled to Louis' front door and knocked.

When Louis opened the door, he eyed the four of them and scowled. "Pourquoi es-vous ici?"

Jean-Pierre tipped his hat and smiled. "Bonjour, Louis." He then informed him Allison and Grant wanted to hire him to tutor them in French Creole for a "very generous salary." When he asked why Dr. Jones didn't coach them, Jean-Pierre claimed Dr. Jones was too busy running the clinic to have the time. He gestured toward Grant, who pulled a wad of gourdes from his pocket.

Louis eyed Grant with narrowed eyes. "Est-ce un truc?"

"No, it's not a trick," Jean-Pierre insisted. "Grant and Allison asked me who could tutor them, and I immediately thought of you since you are the most revered and intelligent person in town."

Maurice continued to mumble the English interpretation of the conversation to Allison and Grant.

Most intelligent person? Allison wanted to roll her eyes. Talk about brown-nosing!

But hey, if bribing Louis with tutoring motivated him to leave the clinic alone, it was worth a try.

Louis looked from Jean-Pierre to Maurice to Grant and then focused on Allison. "You want me to teach you French Creole, too?"

Luckily, Allison could understand his words. "Oui." She whispered to Jean-Pierre, "Tell him we'll pay him extremely well."

After Jean-Pierre interpreted, Louis crossed his arms and glared up at Grant. "How well? I am a busy man."

Busy man? Allison had to force herself from snapping, "Not too busy to waste time spying on our clinic yesterday."

Grant and Louis haggled back and forth until they settled upon a price. Grant counted out the agreed-upon number of gourdes and handed them to Louis.

"We are heading to Saint-Marc to get gas and a few supplies," Maurice said. "We return in two hours to pick up Allison and Grant. You begin Lesson One right now while we are gone."

"Absolument." The eyes of Louis dilated with greed as he counted out the gourdes in his hand. These lessons would undoubtedly provide quicker and easier cash than hours of supposed divine intervention with the spirits of dead relatives from the impoverished locals. He crammed the gourdes into his pocket not bothering to crack a smile.

Jean-Pierre and Maurice headed toward the ornate front door then turned. As though wanting to ensure Louis didn't exploit Grant and Allison, Jean-Pierre added, "I look forward to finding out all they learn from their lesson today. See you in two hours."

As the two brothers exited the house, Allison glanced at Louis, and a wave of trepidation coursed through her.

What had she been thinking when she agreed to meet with a witch doctor who puts curses on people and threatens little children with knives?

Louis ushered them into a large living room of sorts, though it looked like no living room Allison had ever seen before. The walls were painted a gaudy bright red. At the front of the room hung a huge mantle laden with a dozen or more white candles of various sizes.

Bottles of rum, a bowl of crushed white chalk, several foot-tall crosses, pictures in gold frames of ancient saints and the Virgin Mary were propped behind the candles. She remembered Dr. Jones telling her some Catholic rituals had become incorporated into voodoo practices. Hence the crosses, pictures of saints, and photo of the Virgin Mary.

Glass bottles of various sizes and colors—potions and medicinal salves of some kind—were arranged between the candles. Apparently, this was how Louis made his money—by selling bottles of glorified snake oil to treat his client's ailments.

Under the mantle hung strands of rosary beads and necklaces, along with colorful prayer cloths. On the floor—beneath the mantle—lay bongo drums, bells, and a tambourine. Two ceremonial robes—one white and one with colorful stripes—hung over chairs at the front of the room. Here was where Louis performed his voodoo ceremonies of channeling the Ewa spirits or a customer's dead relative.

A shudder of fear coursed through her, and Allison offered up a prayer of protection. She glanced over at Grant. His furrowed brow suggested he was equally unnerved. Thank God he'd come with her.

Before she could dissolve into a panic attack, Louis pointed to a chair. "Chaise."

Allison wanted to tell him she'd studied French for years in high school and already knew that much, but remembering their real goal was to get on Louis' good side and keep him from torching the clinic or knifing someone, she smiled and repeated the word obediently. "Chaise."

She nodded toward Grant, who touched the chair and then repeated the word.

Louis walked around the house room by room pointing at things and providing the French Creole word. Bed was "lit". Bowl was "bol", spoon was "cuiller" and fork was "fourchette". She and Grant dutifully repeated the word until Louis nodded with satisfaction that their pronunciation was acceptable. When they had learned all the items inside the house, they walked outside and wandered around the yard. Tree was "arbre", sky was "ciel", and mango was "mangue".

None of these words would prove useful in diagnosing patients, but Allison had to concede that "vomiting" and "abdominal pain" were hardly found in Lesson One in any French class.

After two hours, Maurice and Jean-Pierre returned. Louis suggested they demonstrate all they had learned during the two hours. His smug expression suggested he expected them to have forgotten half of what he'd taught them.

No doubt he was eager to sputter in disgust when they forgot one of the two-hundred-plus words he'd taught them.

As they wandered room to room and then outside, Grant and Allison remembered every item Louis pointed out. Of course, it helped that Allison already knew most of the words from her years of French class, and Grant had been studying thirty minutes a day. She suspected from his perfect recall of every word they'd learned that Grant had a near-photographic memory.

Louis shook his head in amazement and actually smiled. "Tres bien."

Good. Let him think we're smart. Maybe he'll be less likely to cross us.

Allison suggested they continue their lessons next Sunday afternoon.

"Oui," Louis said with a nod, no doubt salivating at the easy money he'd just made.

After a few more moments of small talk, they climbed into Maurice's truck and headed back to the medical clinic.

"I pray whole time," Jean-Pierre said. "Louis knew we'd find out if he be bad."

"Actually, he was on his best behavior," Grant said, buckling his seatbelt. "Far less creepy than when he's in his robe with white chalk all over his face."

"I no like, but maybe lessons work to turn his heart from hate," Jean-Pierre said.

"Well, if nothing else, Grant and I will learn some French Creole."

"That way, when he's about to plunge a knife into my chest, I can say, 'Wait! I know, the French word for knife is couteau,'" Grant quipped.

"That no funny," Jean-Pierre said, waving a finger at Grant.

"He dangerous man," Maurice agreed. "Don't want to lose his, how you say it... power."

As Maurice's truck thumped its way up the clinic driveway, Jean-Pierre said, "I fill Angelina with gas from gas can, then I drive the Bandeau family home."

"Let me drive them," Maurice insisted waving a dismissive hand at Angelina. "That piece of junk will break down before you get around the corner."

Jean-Pierre smacked his brother on the arm. "Don't you speak ill of my precious Angelina. She good girl—most of the time."

Maurice wagged a finger at his brother. "I insist on driving Bandeau family home."

They strolled into the clinic, and the Bandeau family were sitting comfortably no longer hooked up to IVs.

"Maurice will drive you home," Dr. Jones informed the family as he gestured toward the door. "Remember to boil your water or use the purification system all of the time, so you won't get cholera again."

Regina flailed her hands. "I no want cholera ever again."

He pointed at her. "Then mind my words. Boil your water."

"Merci beaucoups," Pierre said, as the family strolled to the front door with Maurice.

Pierre turned back and smiled. "We no want to come here. Louis Villemort said we die if we came, but his potion no good. I pay him a chicken, but we got worse."

Dr. Jones translated the message for Allison and Grant. Seizing the opportunity, Dr. Jones followed Pierre to the car and handed him a slip of paper. "If you ever want to come learn more about the Jesus we worship, here is the info of where we meet on Sundays at eleven." He smiled. "And unlike Louis Villemort, Jesus doesn't charge a chicken for his services."

Pierre laughed and stared at the paper. "We might go."

"We'd love to see you again," Allison said. "A lot of your neighbors come."

Pierre and the family climbed into the truck and waved as Maurice jostled down the bumpy driveway. Allison had no idea if the family would ever show up for church, but at least they had planted a seed. The rest was up to God.

CHAPTER 18

Dr. Jones had barely flipped the sign on the clinic's front door to "Open" when a mother and her son jingled the doorbell.

No sooner had he examined the boy then he called Grant and Allison over. "I'll bet you've never seen a case of this."

Grant and Allison dutifully exited the kitchen where they were finishing up the dishes to examine the face of an eight-year-old with ulcerating skin lesions all around the nose and mouth. The lesions exuded a honey-colored fluid, and several of the lesions were crusty.

"Any idea what we're looking at?" Dr. Jones probed.

Allison racked her brain for skin conditions common in Haiti. Since she hadn't studied dermatology or tropical infections since her second and third year of medical school, the only tropical skin disease she could think of was filariasis, but she was pretty sure it wasn't that. Impetigo? Leprosy? Unsure of the answer, she said nothing. Grant looked equally perplexed.

Dr. Jones pulled on a pair of Latex gloves and examined the child's arms and legs.

"Just what I suspected. Here is the scar from the original ulcer that probably formed two months ago. See how the scar looks like the skin atrophied? See how the skin lacks black pigment in the middle of the scar?"

They nodded.

"This is classic for the mother lesion." He then asked the mother, "Did Claude have a big oozy, crusty ulcer on his leg a few weeks ago?"

"Oui," Claude's mother confirmed. She then confessed since the ulcer went away on its own after a couple weeks, she didn't think it was anything to worry about.

Dr. Jones nodded knowingly. "The mother lesion heals up, and then a couple of months later, satellite lesions form, usually around the mouth and nose." He glanced from Allison to Grant. "Any idea what it is?"

When they both shrugged, he offered a hint. "A spirochete bacterium? Begins with the letter 'Y'?"

"Yaws?" Grant said, though he didn't sound confident.

Dr Jones grinned. "Exactly. Claude, here, has a classic case of yaws."

He then informed the mother in French Creole what her son was inflicted with and what caused it.

He glanced back at Grant and Allison. "Any idea what the treatment is?"

Now that she knew what she was looking at, she knew the treatment. Maybe she could redeem herself. "Azithromycin."

"Exactly. We'll have Claude healed up in no time."

"Is yaws common in Haiti?" Grant asked.

Dr. Jones nodded. "Fairly common, and since it is spread through skin contact with another infected person, we need to see if anyone else in the family is infected."

He broached the subject of whether other family members had similar lesions. The mother nodded. Yes, two of her other children had oozing skin ulcers, but the lesions had gone away after a week or so, so she had assumed it wasn't anything to worry about.

"You will need to bring in the other children and get them treated, or your children will spread it back and forth, and you'll never be rid of it."

When her eyes widened, he added, "The liquid in the skin ulcers is loaded with highly contagious bacteria. That's how it spreads from person to person."

Claude stared down, as though embarrassed.

Poor kid. He must feel self-conscious with three doctors staring at his ugly oozing ulcers and talking about him in a foreign language he doesn't understand. He was probably scared to death.

Allison tugged on a pair of gloves and then reached for the child's shoulder and gave it a gentle squeeze. With a reassuring smile she said, "Nous pouvons vous aider." She hoped she'd told him they could cure him. She and Grant had been dutifully studying his French Creole book and practicing their French pronunciation every night before bed for the last month, but some nights she was too tired to study more than ten minutes before she couldn't keep her eyes open.

Claude smiled up at her, so she must have said it correctly.

"On peut te guérir," Grant added.

She wasn't sure what he'd said, and it annoyed her. She was the one who had studied French for four years in high school, yet with the few extra minutes he spent studying after she'd fallen asleep at night, he could now speak the language better than she could! He'd even pulled "yaws" from the recesses of his brain.

Gosh, their microbiology professor hadn't spent more than five minutes discussing yaws, and that was years ago!

She stared at Grant in amazement. Did he have to be brilliant at everything? Much as she hated to admit it, she wanted that Chef Residency position, but Grant would get it—and he deserved it! He studied longer and worked harder than anyone she'd ever met.

Wanting to distract herself from her depressing thoughts, she said, "I'll go dig up the azithromycin."

"You'll have to pull out the mortar and pestle. The tablets are huge, and in my experience, eight-year-olds have trouble swallowing horse pills."

She located the mortar and pestle and the large stock bottle of azithromycin 1000mg tablets. After retrieving a pill, Allison returned the stock bottle to the cabinet and began mashing and pulverizing the "horse pill" into powder.

"What do I sprinkle it on?" she asked Dr. Jones.

He tapped his chin in thought. "See if we have any peanut butter in the kitchen." He turned to Claude. "You do like peanut butter, don't you?"

A quizzical face stared back at them. The child had clearly never tried it before.

"Maybe we better have him try a cracker with peanut butter first in case he doesn't like it. If he won't eat it, we don't want to waste the medicine."

Allison scrounged up a jar of peanut butter and a roll of crackers from the kitchen. After smearing some peanut butter on a cracker, she handed it to Claude. He dutifully ate the cracker.

"What do you think? Did you like it?" she inquired.

Claude grinned. "Oui. C'est délicieux."

Allison then stirred the crushed azithromycin into a teaspoon of peanut butter and spread it on another cracker and handed it to Claude.

"Ca te guérira," Grant said.

He'd said it again, and Allison made a mental note to look up guérira in her dictionary—when Grant wasn't looking.

The boy munched down the cracker.

"He should see improvement in the next week or two," Dr. Jones told his mother. "However, unless you get his brothers and sisters in to be treated, he could get reinfected. Yaws is highly contagious." He inspected the mother's arms and inquired, "Have you had any signs of it yourself?"

"No," she insisted.

He looked over at Allison and Grant. "I'm not surprised. For some reason, yaws infects children more than adults."

Claude's mother thanked them for their services, and she promised to bring all the children in for treatment.

After they left, Dr. Jones peeled off his gloves and disposed of them in the toxic waste container. Scrubbing his hands at the sink, he commented, "That's one infection I hope not to catch."

"You got that right," Allison said, peeling off her own gloves and scrubbing up.

"Let's sterilize the exam table where he sat."

"And the doorknob on the front door," Grant added.

The three doctors set about sanitizing the clinic from all traces of the highly infectious yaws bacterium.

No sooner had they sterilized the clinic when the bells on the front door chimed and in staggered a wizened old man bumping into walls and mumbling unintelligibly. He was accompanied by a worried-looking woman, most likely his wife.

This can't be good.

CHAPTER 19

"He had too much to drink, and he fell and hit his head three days ago. It knocked him out for an hour but then he came to," the wife said in rapid French. "The next day he was staggering around talking nonsense. I thought he'd get better when the liquor wore off, but he's gotten worse. Now I can barely wake him up."

Dr. Jones' eyes widened with alarm. He turned to Allison and Grant. "Thoughts?"

"Subdural hematoma?" Grant surmised.

"Most likely," Dr. Jones said. "And we aren't equipped to do brain surgery in this clinic."

"So what's our next step?" Allison inquired.

"Bring him back. We'll see how bad he is," Dr. Jones said.

They quickly grabbed a wheelchair and rushed the man back to an exam table. With the three of them hoisting him, they were able to lift him onto the table.

Shining a light in each eye, Allison noted that while his left pupil constricted normally, the right one was sluggish. He also displayed a slight facial droop on the right.

When shaken awake, he could fully lift his right arm off the table but was unable to lift the left arm up for more than a few seconds.

"He's suffered a right-sided subdural hematoma, don't you think?" Grant surmised. "Or a stroke, although strokes don't usually wait a day to cause symptoms."

Allison nodded. "Strokes also don't worsen gradually over three days."

Dr. Jones rubbed his chin as he paced slowly across the clinic. "If it is a subdural hematoma, he needs surgical drainage immediately, or we're looking at a very high mortality rate."

"Wouldn't a four-hour delay on the bumpy roads to Port-au-Prince lead to permanent brain damage," Grant added.

Allison glanced around the clinic. "We have drills, oxygen, and anesthesia."

Grant's eyes bulged. "You can't seriously be thinking of attempting a craniotomy? Not here in these primitive conditions. We don't have a CT scanner to confirm our diagnosis."

"We don't *need* a CT scanner," Allison countered. "We know what's wrong with him based on history and physical exam. And look at this big knot on the right side of his head," she said pointing at the goose-egg sized bump on his head.

"It doesn't take a CT scanner to know that the bleed occurred underneath that big goose egg," she added.

Grant raked a hand through his hair. "Allison, are you crazy? You've never operated on a subdural hematoma before."

She averted her eyes. "Not by myself, obviously. But I took a three-month neurosurgery rotation last year, and I assisted with three subdural hematoma craniotomies. I can at least do the Burr hole procedure. If that stabilizes him, we can then get him to Port-au-Prince for the full craniotomy, if need be."

Grant shook his head. "It's too risky. What if something goes wrong?"

Arms crossed, she countered, "But if we don't try, he'll die, or have permanent brain damage."

"You're not a Board-certified neurosurgeon. You have no business doing this. You could be sued."

Dr. Jones put up a hand. "Grant, this is not the United States where malpractice attorneys advertise on TV and try to drum up business for the flimsiest of excuses. We know this man will be dead before we can get him to Port-au-Prince. I say, we counsel the wife and patient and let *them* choose whether we operate here or attempt to transfer him to a Port-au-Prince hospital where a neurosurgeon can perform the surgery."

Grant paced the exam room running a hand through his hair as though still in shock that they would even consider operating in such backwoods conditions. "If wife signs a consent that she knows he will die if we don't attempt surgery, and that we are not Board-certified neurosurgeons, and this is not an NICU, we could attempt the procedure."

"Grant, these are not educated people. They won't know what you're talking about if you mention Board-certified neurosurgeons or NICUs. In the simplest of terms, we need to explain that this will be very risky surgery, but without it, he will definitely die. We can then give them the option of attempting to make it to Port-au-Prince instead, Dr. Jones said.

Grant rubbed the back of his neck. "The whole thing makes me nervous, but I get that we have no choice but to try."

Allison said, "Dr. Jones, while you get the consent and explain what we need to do, I'm going to pull out the *Techniques in Neurosurgery* textbook I noticed in your office and review the procedure. Once we get him anesthetized, intubated, and hooked up to oxygen, Grant can shave the scalp and sterilize the site while I'm setting up all the supplies we need."

She raised an index finger. "Actually, let me first make sure we have the proper supplies *before* we talk to the wife. If we don't have a cranial drill, it's a 'no go', and we'll have no choice but to send him to Port-au-Prince and hope for the best."

Allison hurried to the surgical supply cabinet to ensure she had the necessary drill bits and supplies.

One part of her was excited to perform the surgery, but another prayed they would lack some necessary piece of equipment, so she'd have an excuse to get out of attempting such risky surgery.

As she located each of the required surgical supplies, a wave of fear washed over her. Was she seriously going to attempt a Burr hole procedure without an experienced Board-certified neurosurgeon watching every move? What was she thinking?

But a man's life was at stake. She had no choice.

You can do this.

She gathered the required tools and left them to soak in sterilizing solution until they were ready for the operation.

She reread the surgical technique one more time then wrote out a step-by-step cheat sheet on an index card. She taped the card it to the surgical table in case she got flustered during the surgery and needed the guide to redirect her.

After reviewing all the possible things that could go wrong during and after the surgery, she wished she hadn't agreed to operate. Hemorrhage, infection, brain swelling, inflammation, permanent brain damage. Yikes! Should she back out now and admit she wasn't qualified to attempt such a complicated surgery? If she had a brain in her skull, she would!

But an inner voice admonished her. *How can you let him die?*

No way would he make it all the way to Port-au-Prince, especially if Angelina conked out on the way. Could she live with herself if she didn't at least try to save him?

No, she couldn't. She inhaled a deep breath and prayed.

She strode with to the waiting room and introduced herself to the wife and decided to be transparent.

"I have only seen this surgery done three times before, but I feel confident I can do it. Without the surgery, your husband will die. With it, we have fifty-fifty odds of saving him."

Dr. Jones interpreted her words, and when the full impact sank in, the wife crumpled. "You can't let my Charles die. Do what you have to do to save him."

Dr. Jones pulled out a consent form, but the wife had to signed on her husband's behalf since he was incoherent.

Legalities behind them, Allison donned surgical scrubs, masks, and gloves. Meanwhile, Dr. Jones started an IV and applied a cardiac monitor. He administered anesthesia, and Grant intubated him and hooked up the oxygen. After shaving the side of the head where the incision would be made, he scrubbed the site with Betadine three times. He then changed into sterile scrubs, mask, and gloves.

Allison reviewed their plan of attack, and when Grant and Dr. Jones nodded that they were all in agreement, she made the first drill through the skin. She continued until she felt the resistance of bone. She had reached the skull.

Her hands shook. This was where the rubber met the cranium. If she applied too much pressure, she might drill past the collection of blood that needed to be suctioned out and straight into the brain. Having never performed the surgery before, she had nothing to guide her but common sense. Better to be too tentative than too aggressive.

She upped the pressure and speed on the drill slightly. She could feel slight resistance but had no idea how far through the skull she had penetrated. She upped her pressure again.

After several minutes of firm but steady drilling, she felt the pressure of the drill against bone give way, and she was rewarded with the sudden backflash of blood. She had reached the subdural hematoma. Good. She was in the right spot.

Grant offered a thumbs-up sign.

"I need the subperiosteal drain."

Grant handed her the tubing. After removing the drill, she threaded the tubing through the Burr hole and connected the tubing to a suction pump. While some backwash of blood occurred, she knew she had not extracted the whole volume of blood from the hematoma.

"I'll bet the blood is clotted, and that's why it is not coming out," Grant said.

"Let's try irrigation. If I mix the clots with saline, I may be able to break them up and dilute them enough to come out."

"It's worth a try," Grant said.

"Otherwise, he'll need a full bone flap craniotomy, and I definitely don't feel competent to do that."

"Did they use irrigation in any of the brain surgeries you assisted with?" Grant asked.

"Yes, and the textbook said irrigation is often necessary."

Grant raised his glove-covered hands. "Irrigation, it is."

Allison infused a large syringe of saline forcefully through the tubing and then attempted suction again. This time the extracted fluid contained small blood clots. Applying firm suction, she extracted a full tube of bloody fluid.

"Great. It looks like it's working, though we'll need to keep up the irrigation until the fluid coming back is clot-free."

She continued to infuse saline and then pull back with firm suction. By the fifth suction, her hands cramped. She opened and closed her hands, trying to stretch out the pain.

Grant must have noticed because he said, "Why don't you let me take over the suctioning? I have bigger hands, so it might be easier for me."

Her first thought? "Forget it! I'm perfectly capable of doing it myself!"

And she was, though sucking fluid and blood through a large twenty-five-milliliter syringe was hard work. As the ache permeated her fingers, she acknowledged she was being silly. Why not let Grant help? He had larger and stronger hands, and they were a team.

She gratefully handed Grant the syringe, and he took over. He continued the suctioning until the extracted fluid returned with no clots.

"I think we got it all, don't you?" Grant asked.

"Unless he cuts loose with more bleeding."

"Do you think we should leave the drain in, in case we need to extract more fluid and blood?" Grant asked.

"An indwelling catheter poses a risk for infection," Allison countered.

After eyeing the blood pressure and oxygen levels, Dr. Jones suggested, "He's remained stable under anesthesia. How about we let thirty minutes go by without suction? If, after thirty minutes, he has no new bleeding or clots, we'll pull the tubing. If he shows signs of slow oozing, we'll leave the drain in."

Allison and Grant nodded. "That makes sense. Let's do one more irrigation and extraction for good measure then reassess in thirty minutes."

The final syringe contained no clots. They set a timer and anxiously counted the minutes.

"I sure hope this works," Allison said. "We won't really know until he wakes up, and we see if his strength and speech improve."

"The wife said he fell three days ago, so unless he has a clotting disorder, he should have quit bleeding by now."

Allison arched her back and stretched her calves as the thirty minutes ticked by with agonizing slowness.

When the timer dinged, they irrigated and suctioned back clear saline.

Allison grinned. "No bleeding. I say we pull the catheter."

"At this point, we have him stabilized. Even if he needs a full skull flap craniotomy later, we now have time to transport him to Port-au-Prince," Grant said. "I say we pull the catheter."

"Agreed," Dr. Jones said with a nod.

Allison slowly extracted the tubing from the Burr hole and sewed up her incision site. She then applied a dab of Betadine ointment and a dressing.

"His anesthesia will wear off over the next thirty minutes. Then we'll see where we are neurologically," Dr. Jones said.

All they could do was wait. And pray.

CHAPTER 20

"Why don't I go talk to his wife. She was a nervous wreck when we left her in the waiting room," Grant suggested while they waited for the anesthesia to wear off.

"I'll join you," Allison said, peeved that Grant would try to take credit for the surgery she had mostly performed. Initially, he hadn't even wanted her to do it!

Remembering him tackling the arduous, hand-cramping suctioning, she felt guilty for her peevish thoughts. They were a team, so why shouldn't Grant talk to the wife? Since Dr. Jones had to stay in the operating suite to ensure the patient recovered smoothly from his anesthesia, it made sense for the two of them to speak to the wife together, as they could better communicate in French with the two of them.

They tugged off their surgical gloves and masks and discarded them in the waste container and then headed toward the waiting room, where the wife sat rigidly, her hands gripping the arms of the chair.

Upon seeing Grant and Allison, she jumped to her feet and burst into tears. "He's dead, isn't he?"

She wiped her eyes. "Louis Villemort told me he'd die if I took him here, but I had no choice. Nothing he did helped."

The confession poured out of her so quickly, Allison only understood half of it, but hearing Louis Villemort's name and the word 'die' twice, told her all she needed to know.

The couple had first consulted Louis and he had, yet again, failed to deliver any results with his magic potions and incantations, so by default, they came to the clinic.

It was disheartening to know their attempt to bribe Louis into accepting the clinic with tutoring lessons had done little to sweeten his opinion of them. He was still telling people they would die if they came to the clinic.

Mrs. Maison dissolved into tears, already convinced her husband was dead. Grant reached for her hand and squeezed. He then informed her Charles did fine and they expected him to wake up from surgery soon.

Another torrent of tears. "He survived?" Her head jerked up as though still not processing Grant's words.

"Oui. Il a survecu."

Her face lit up and she squeezed Grant's hands. "C'est magnifique!"

"Allison performed the surgery, and she did a masterful job." He gestured toward Allison with a smile.

Guilt stabbed her. She'd assumed Grant would try to take some credit for the positive outcome, but instead, he'd given her all the credit. She'd underestimated him. Again. He wasn't an egotistical snob.

Allison informed the wife it was too early to judge what kind of long-term outcome Charles would have, but they'd have a better idea in a few minutes.

"Charles needs to spend the night here," Grant informed her.

When her brow furrowed with surprise, Allison added, "We need to watch him and make sure he remains stable."

"Je comprends," she said.

"How much does he drink?" Grant inquired, miming a man tipping up a bottle of rum.

She released a frustrated sigh. "Trop. Beaucoup trop."

"That's what I was afraid of."

"Il aime le rhum," she added.

When Grant looked puzzled, Allison interpreted. "He likes his rum."

"No wonder he fell and bashed his head," Grant mumbled to Allison.

Allison and Grant promised to keep her updated, then insisted they needed to go back and tend to Charles. Mrs. Maison agreed to stay in the waiting room.

They hurried back to the recovery room where Dr. Jones was assessing Charles's vitals. "So far, so good. Oxygen saturation at 98%, BP 110/75, and pulse regular at 80."

"Any sign of waking up?" Allison inquired.

He shook his head. "Still out like a light."

"I suspect he was already half-anesthetized with rum when he came in, and that will delay how quickly he comes around," Dr. Jones commented.

As the ventilator methodical inhaled and exhaled, all they could do was wait. Allison scribbled an operative note praying to God when the man woke up he wouldn't be in worse shape than before the surgery.

After another twenty minutes, Charles released the first signs of life: a cough, followed by a spontaneous grab for the endotracheal tube.

"Arrête!" Grant scolded, grabbing Charles's wrist to keep him from pulling out the endotracheal tube bringing oxygen to his lungs.

Dr. Jones handed Grant some wrist restraints. "Put these on him until he wakes up enough to understand."

Grant tied Charles' wrists to the bed to prevent him from tugging out his ET tube.

After another forty minutes, he finally woke up. Eyes wide, he jostled and tugged on the restraints like a grizzly in a bear trap.

Dr. Jones explained who they were and what had just transpired. He promised to release the wrist restraints if Charles promised not to touch the tube running down the back of his mouth.

Charles nodded his consent.

Grant untied the knots and removed the restraints then wagged a finger in his face. "Pas touché!"

Allison tested his strength by asking him to squeeze her fingers and lift each leg off the bed. He passed all of the tests.

She grinned. "Strength is equal on both sides now.

Grant grabbed a penlight and checked pupillary response. Back to normal.

They grinned and slapped hands. "We did it!" Allison danced a celebratory jig, and then Grant pulled her into a bear hug. "Allison Smith, you are one gutsy surgeon."

She knew the hug was just congratulatory, but she lingered there relishing the feel of his arms wrapped around her. When she noted Dr. Jones watching them, she pulled back and grinned up at Grant, trying to make the hug seem like nothing more than an exuberant gesture of two excited colleagues. "We actually pulled it off, Grant! Can you believe it?"

Dr. Jones added, "Honestly? I was worried what we'd find when he woke up."

"We need to remember his love affair with rum. He'll need prophylaxis against delirium tremors, or he'll have seizures," Grant reminded them.

"We'll give him a dose of Librium," Dr. Jones said. "That should prevent alcohol withdrawal."

"Maybe we should tell Charles and his wife to keep this whole thing quiet. We don't need anything else to incite Louis Villemort against us," Allison said.

Dr. Jones' head jerked up. "Wait. He went to Louis Villemort before he came here?"

"Afraid so," Grant said. "Louis told them if they came here, it would anger the Ewa spirits, and Charles would die."

Dr. Jones' lips thinned. "I'm not sure what to do about that man. The needless delay in getting treatment only exacerbated Charles's case."

Allison and Grant made eye contact but said nothing.

They both knew Dr. Jones would not approve their scheme to win Louis over by paying him to tutor them. But it seemed like their best option. She only hoped she wasn't fooling herself.

* * *

Over the next several hours, Charles improved enough they could pull out the endotracheal tube from his throat.

Thankfully, his oxygen levels remained high with just a nasal cannula. After his dose of Librium, he fell back to sleep showing signs of seizures or shaking due to alcohol withdrawal.

Since Raphael had witnessed Charles staggering into the clinic before surgery, he came to visit several times in the days after his surgery to witness the improvement. "I can't believe you drilled a hole through his head. What if you'd accidentally drilled straight through his brain to the other side?" he asked.

She chose not to think about that possibility!

Charles improved quickly back at work and tooting to anyone who would listen how the medical clinic had saved his life when Louis Villemort couldn't.

He promised to quit drinking, though Grant wasn't naïve enough to think once the excitement of the surgery wore off that Charles wouldn't be back imbibing his beloved rum again. Since his wife's years of nagging had failed to keep him sober, Grant could only hope a brush with death would.

Raphael warned Allison and Grant that Louis was seething. Thanks to their impressive brain surgery, Louis' reputation— and bottom line— had taken a serious hit.

Despite their best effort to keep the surgery hush-hush, word had spread throughout town.

Allison and Grant were now deemed as "miracle workers". The clinic buzzed with new cases, and many no longer even bothered with Louis Villemort first.

"Why waste time and money on him when it never works?" one disgruntled townsperson said.

With the increased clientele at the clinic, Grant and Allison hadn't had time for French Creole lessons in three weeks straight.

Louis must have missed his weekly tutoring paycheck because he charged into the clinic one Sunday afternoon demanding to speak with Grant and Allison. They quickly ushered Louis outside so people in the waiting room wouldn't hear his accusations.

"You are stealing my customers."

"We haven't stolen anybody. We both offer a medical service, and if customers prefer our results to yours, that's hardly our fault." Allison forced herself to stand tall and look Louis straight in the eyes. No way would she back down.

Black eyes of hatred glared back at her. "You are taking away my business."

Grant's hand squeezed like a vice grip on her arm, his less than subtle way of telling her to not say anything inflammatory.

"People have trusted you for yours, and you're a great tutor," Grant piped in, clearly trying to assuage the man's rage.

"Perhaps we can increase your pay for tutoring us to make up for your lost income, Louis." How about we come Sunday afternoon?"

He jabbed a finger at Grant. "You better." His eyes narrowed, and he turned to glare at Allison. "Don't cross me, or you'll regret it." He stomped off.

"We need to be sure to go next week and pay him double what I usually do."

"I hope it's safe to go when he's furious with us," Allison said.

Grant smiled. "Wave enough gourdes in his face, and I suspect we'll suddenly become his best friends."

"Maybe, maybe not. We may be deluding ourselves. And what happens when you run out of cash?"

Heading back into the clinic, Grant replied, "We'll cross that bridge when we come to it."

CHAPTER 21

On a Sunday afternoon—their half-day off, Allison and Grant decided to trudge the two miles to Louis Villemort's house for another tutoring lesson.

"We need to keep up the lessons if we're ever going to get him to quit bad-mouthing us," Allison insisted.

About a mile into the hike Grant slapped a mosquito biting him on the back of the knee. "These blasted mosquitos! I must have swatted a dozen of them by now."

Allison jerked to a stop. "Did you forget to douse up with bug spray before we left?"

His eyes widened. "I did this morning before church, but I didn't spray up after my shower." He slapped another mosquito about to bite him. "Shoot! They're eating me alive."

Allison chewed her lower lip. "I should have reminded you when you went to the cabin to get your wallet before we left."

"It's not your fault." He squashed a mosquito buzzing around his face. "I can't believe I forgot to douse up before we left. Here's hoping my malaria prophylaxis works."

She glanced down the road. "Luckily, we've only got another quarter-mile or so before we reach his house."

"Here's hoping Louis is as excited to see me as these mosquitoes are," Grant said, slapping a mosquito biting his neck.

"He won't be happy to see *you*, but he'll be happy to see your money!" Allison quipped.

They rounded the corner to Louis' house, and Grant held his breath as he knocked on the door wondering what kind of reception they would receive.

Opening the door, Louis eyed them with hostility. "Why are you here, again?" he snapped.

Grant opened his palm and revealed a large pile of gourdes. "We'd like another French Creole lesson."

Louis glared at them and then eyed the wad of money again. "I am a very busy man, and I'm in the middle of a séance with Hélène. You will have to wait until I am done." He waved dismissively toward the living room.

Grant and Allison sat as discreetly as they could in the back of the room. Grant noticed the woman had a black eye and large bruises on both arms—like someone had beaten her up. Domestic abuse, most likely. From what Grant could make out, the young woman wanted Louis to channel up her dead mother and ask if she should leave her husband.

For an hour, Louis danced and chanted in his ceremonial robe, all the while calling out the name of the dead mother. Soon, he had himself worked into a frenzy. He repeated words he claimed came directly from the dead mother.

"Your mother says you should stay with your husband and be a good wife. She says you must never disobey him or talk back to him. This is why he beats you."

Grant gritted his teeth. "He's telling a battered woman to stay with her abuser. That the abuse is her fault for being mouthy?" Grant whispered to Allison. "Unbelievable."

"What mother would tell her daughter to stay with a man who beat her up?" Allison fumed.

What a charade! These poor, desperate people came to Louis believing he had divine power with the spirits—or with their dead relatives.

Then again, maybe demonic spirits would want a battered woman to stay with her abuser!

Grant had to force herself not to intervene. He wanted to tell Hélène, "Don't listen to him! Domestic abuse only gets worse with time. Leave your husband now before he kills you."

Could they alert the woman to come to the clinic for help?

Allison whispered to Grant that when Louis finished with the woman, Grant should distract Louis by bartering with him about the price of tutoring. Meanwhile, Allison would hand the woman a note with the clinic's address begging her to seek help.

"Sounds like a plan," Grant said.

She flipped over one of Louis' advertisements and wrote a note in French with the clinic's address.

Hélène handed Louis a dozen eggs and a few coins before heading out the door convinced her dead mother had told her to stay with her abusive husband.

As she exited, Grant bartered with Louis on a price for their tutoring, turning in a way that kept Louis from seeing Allison following the battered woman out of the living room. She slipped Hélène the note and whispered in French, "We are doctors. We will help you at our medical clinic for free. Don't stay with a man who beats you up. It will only get worse."

The woman nodded and tucked the note into her pocket.

Allison then dashed to the bathroom, closed the door, and flushed the toilet to make it look like she'd gone to the bathroom. She wandered back to Louis' living room where Louis scowled at Grant with crossed arms.

"For one-hundred gourdes, you only get one hour today. What you want to know how to say?"

Allison suggested they learn verbs and body parts. Over the next hour, Allison and Grant mimed eating, sleeping, and walking, and Louis named the body part in French Creole.

They repeated each word several times after Louis pronounced it until they could say it correctly. Truth be told, with their recent weeks of intensive study at bedtime, they already knew most of the words Louis taught them, but they pretended Louis was the greatest of tutors.

"We learn so much from you," Allison enthused.

Behind Louis' back, Grant rolled his eyes and whispered, "How do you say, 'suck up' in French Creole?"

On their hike back to the clinic, Raphael saw them walk by his shack and decided to join them. "Did you notice we had over a hundred people in church today? The church is growing every week, thanks to you two and Dr. Jones."

"Well, that's great news," Allison said, stepping over a rut in the road. "Good to hear God's spirit is moving amongst us."

"They say Louis is furious with you for swiping his business."

"Have you heard any rumors he's planning revenge on us?" Grant asked.

When Raphael didn't understand the word revenge, Allison simplified. "Is he planning to punish us—or the clinic—in some way?"

"He's placed a curse on Grant because he assumed Grant did the brain surgery, not Allison."

Sexist jerk, Allison fumed. You might know Louis would assume a male performed the brain surgery.

"He says Grant is going to die," Raphael continued.

"That's comforting," Grant said, kicking a rock off the road.

"I know Dr. Jones says I'm supposed to put all my trust in God, but it makes me scared when I hear things like that." Raphael's eyes filled with tears.

Allison wrapped an arm around his shoulder. "Our lives are in God's hands. We are here to do His work."

Raphael brushed tears from his cheeks and nodded.

"We must pray every day for His protection over us. Living in fear will only rob us of joy, and it won't change the outcome. We have to trust God to look out for us."

"But I already lost my mother and father. I don't want to lose Dr. Jones and Judy, too."

Allison squeezed his shoulders. "I'll bet that was so hard losing your parents, wasn't it?"

He nodded vigorously blinking back a fresh wave of tears.

"But God didn't abandon you, did He? He provided you with Dr. Jones and Judy. If we commit ourselves to Him, trust Him, and pray continuously, He promises to take care of us."

"After losing my parents, trust is hard for me," he admitted.

Allison wrapped him in a hug. "It's hard for all of us. I find quoting favorite scripture verses helps me when I'm afraid."

"Like, *'I will never leave you or forsake you'*?"

"Exactly. Or *'Nothing can separate us from the love of God,'*" Allison said.

"That's one of my favorite scriptures," Grant said.

As they reached the medical clinic, they invited Raphael to join them for supper. They didn't have to ask twice, especially when he found out Judy was serving one of his favorite dinners: lambi guisado and his favorite dessert, banan peze.

"You'll love it," he enthused. "Judy makes the best fried plantains." He grinned and added, "Especially when I help."

After a delicious dinner, Raphael helped Grant and Allison with the dishes and then headed back to his shack.

As they wandered back to their cabin, Grant said, "It's another hour until dark. What do you say we reward ourselves for our four-mile trudge to Louis' house by checking out that cold creek Judy told us about our first night here? I could sure use a refreshing dip right now."

"Sounds great."

She dreaded Grant seeing her in a bikini. If she'd known he would be doing the rotation with her, she would have packed her more modest one-piece. Not that she had a bad figure, but surely the woman who'd mailed him that pink scented envelope could pass for a model. Not that it mattered. He only viewed her as a colleague and likely wouldn't take a second glance.

She changed in the bathroom and grabbed a towel and wrapped it snuggly around her waist before emerging.

Grant then took his turn in the bathroom to change, and they headed out the door wearing flip-flops.

"Judy said to follow this path for about a quarter of a mile, and we'll come across a creek with a swimming hole," Grant said, pointing to a narrow path to the left.

"I can't wait to not feel hot and clammy."

They meandered along the narrow trail with Grant following Allison until a they could hear the babble of running water and soon, a swimming hole. What they didn't expect was a fifteen-foot waterfall at the base of the swimming hole. They both stopped and stared.

"Wow! Beautiful!"

Grant's eyes locked with hers. "Very beautiful."

She got the distinct impression he was talking about her, rather than the waterfall, but not wanting to be presumptuous, she dropped her towel on the water's edge and meandered into the swimming hole letting out a squeal when her toes first encountered the icy water. She strolled forward allowing her knees and then her waist to adjust to the cold water.

As Allison tip-toed into the water clad only in a bikini, Grant couldn't take his eyes off her. She was buxom enough to grab a man's attention.

Her shapely legs and curves showed she exercised regularly. He hitched in a deep breath and forced himself to drag his eyes away.

She's a colleague. Stop ogling, he scolded himself.

"Brrr," Allison said with a grin. "Jump in. It's invigorating."

Frigid water—just what he needed to get his mind and body in a safer place.

With that thought, Grant dropped his towel and charged into the water. Once waist high, he leaped forward to submerge himself completely. His teeth chattered as he rose out of the water covered with goose bumps.

Allison laughed, "Bet you're not hot now!"

I am for you.

The uninvited thought swirled through his mind. He leaped forward and swam several fast laps to warm up his muscles and distract himself from his inappropriate thoughts about Allison in that enticing bikini.

"Want to jump through the waterfall?" Allison asked, and before he could answer, she'd leapt from behind the waterfall underneath the crashing water then came up on the other side laughing. She jumped up and rubbed the water from her eyes. "What a blast! Try it."

Grant swam up behind the waterfall then dove underneath as the crashing water pulled him down and then forward. He came up next to Allison grinning.

They dove under the waterfall several more times before Grant suggested, "Let's go through it together. Climb on my back and wrap your arms around my waist."

"Why not?" They stroked their way to behind the falls. He bent down, and she crawled onto his back and wrapped her arms snuggly around his chest and her legs around his waist.

Grant sprung forward, and they plunged under the falls with Allison gripping hard to stay on.

They emerged from the water laughing with Allison's arms still wrapped around his chest.

He swam until her feet could touch the ground, and then she slid off him, their bodies mere inches apart. He turned to face her and when she wavered, he gripped her shoulders to stabilize her in the rushing stream. Their eyes locked, and in that instant, all laughter ceased. He couldn't drag his eyes away from hers, and as his eyes searched deep into her soul, he saw longing and joy and hope and... was that desire staring back at him?

As their hearts melded into one, he drank in her unchecked yearning for him, and when her lower lip quivered, he could resist no longer. He lowered his head already savoring the feel of those quivering lips pressed against his.

Their mouths merged, and he kissed her gently. Tenderly. Lovingly. But it was not enough. Nowhere near enough. He explored her soft eager lips with increasing firmness and hunger, and when she parted her lips and wrapped her arms around his neck to pull his head closer, his heart hammered in his chest. He nibbled and explored her willing lips soaking in the passion she so freely offered.

But then, abruptly, she pulled away and dove underwater. She swam toward the shore like a contender for Olympic gold.

What the heck? She'd *wanted* her kiss—he knew she did. He read it in her eyes. How could she *not* feel the chemistry between them?

Was she afraid? Not willing to get involved with a colleague? Fearful he would push her to go too far?

He dove in after her and met her at the shoreline. She grabbed her towel and crammed her feet into her flip-flops.

With a shaky voice she said, "We should probably head back before it gets dark."

"Allison, wait! You can't dash off like nothing happened between us. What's going on?"

She charged down the trail as though being pursued by Bondye himself. "I don't want to talk about it."

He tore after her. "I don't understand. Why did you freeze up on me like that?"

She pulled her towel around her waist and wrapped it into a skirt. "I shouldn't have caved into my attraction for you. I need to nip it in the bud before we get too involved." Her walking speed now rivaled Usain Bolt.

He reached for her arm. "Why?"

She barreled down the path refusing to stop. "Getting involved with you will only lead to pain and rejection."

"Why would you say that?"

She stopped suddenly, and he nearly toppled her over.

She turned and faced him with arms crossed. "Look, I know you would never *intentionally* hurt me, but when we get back to the real world, and you get around your high society friends and family, I'll feel like I don't belong. *They'll* feel like I don't belong. I need to stop whatever is happening between us before I have feelings for you."

He cupped her face with his hands and kissed her gently. Probing her eyes he whispered, "It's too late. You already have feelings for me. And I have feelings for you."

Her shoulders sagged, and she released a frustrated sigh.

He caressed her cheek. "I've seen you watching me for years, but you acted so stand-offish with me, I never dared to pursue you—until we got to know each other here in Haiti."

She frowned. "Grant, it could never work. In six weeks, we won't even be living in the same state. You'll be Chief Resident, and I'll be working in Seattle, Denver, or Ann Arbor. I haven't made up my mind which offer to accept yet."

"First of all, *you* may be Chief Resident, not me. But that's not what's really troubling you. If you truly believed we belong together, one year apart wouldn't make one bit of difference, and we both know it."

When she didn't deny this, he continued. "You were hurt in the past, so you're afraid to trust with your whole heart again. You're afraid I'll hurt you the way the other guy did."

She opened her mouth to protest then closed it. "I suppose I am. Once burned, twice cautious."

So, it *was* the Ghost of Boyfriend Past. He'd surmised as much but hadn't been certain until now.

He caressed her cheek. "That's okay, Allison. I hope someday you'll trust me enough to give me your heart. Your whole heart."

She chewed on her bottom lip staring at the ground until her eyes pooled with tears. "Are you saying you'll give me *your* whole heart, even if we aren't living in the same state for over a year?"

He pulled her into a warm embrace. "Of course! Lucky for you, in matters of the heart, I am a very patient man. A year apart won't make an iota of difference."

She leaned her head on his chest and clung to him.

He wrapped comforting arms around her. "Allison, will you tell me what happened with the other guy? Whatever happened traumatized you. It would help me understand you better if you let me in."

He heard her breath catch and then a long silence as though she were weighing the consequences of revealing the details of her broken relationship.

Her hands slid down his arms until she was holding both his hands. "I suppose you deserve to know the truth. If it makes you think less of me, so be it."

"It won't make me think less of you." He eyed the gorgeous sunset painting up the sky. "We better hoof it back to the cabin before we get caught out here in the dark. Once we're in dry duds, you can fill me in, okay?"

She stared down at her feet. "You really want to hear the pathetic details of my broken engagement?"

Engagement? She'd been engaged? Grant's breath hitched. No wonder she was hesitant to trust again.

Now clad in jeans and a T-shirt, Allison patted her bed. "Sit down, and I'll tell you about my relationship with Alexander."

Grant sat on the bed and offered a reassuring smile.

She sucked in a deep breath and then plunged in. They'd met in medical school when they'd been assigned to the same cadaver table in anatomy class. Soon they were study partners, and then he'd asked her out for dinner and a movie. Since Alexander was smart, handsome, and affable, she hadn't thought twice before saying, "Yes".

They dated for over a year before Alexander popped the question with a two-carat diamond at a romantic French restaurant. While she had fears of how well she'd fit in with his filthy-rich socialite New York City family, she squashed her qualms and accepted his proposal with glee. Alexander loved her, and she loved him. Wasn't that all that mattered?

His parents had been polite—though not exactly warm and fuzzy—on the one visit six months earlier they'd made to his family's gated estate in Scarsdale, New York.

But everything changed when Alexander announced to his parents he planned to marry Allison.

She'd never forget that horrible weekend they went to share the news with his parents. While she'd been in the library studying for finals, she overheard the scathing comments and heated argument between Alexander and his parents.

"Alexander, what were you thinking proposing to someone from a town known for landfills and trash? You'll make us the laughingstock of the entire country club," his father bellowed.

His mother was more patronizing. "Allison is a lovely girl but take pity on her. She won't know how to behave in our social circles. She won't know how to dress, which fork to use, or how to order a quality wine. She'll have no experience overseeing maids, cooks, and gardeners. She'll feel so overwhelmed, she'll leave before your first anniversary."

His father piped in, "And unless you have a prenup, there goes half your money." He snapped his fingers.

"Yes, you simply must have a prenup," his mother insisted.

Because she'd been eavesdropping, Allison didn't feel she could confront Alexander or his parents with what she'd heard.

To his credit, Alexander did not immediately call off their engagement, but after that weekend, his eyes were suddenly opened to the differences between them. Her clothes were not stylish enough. He took her to Neiman-Marcus and insisted on the clerk selecting a whole new wardrobe for her—which he'd paid for.

He prodded her to sit with upright posture—her back as stiff as a board—when she ate. Every date turned into a coaching session. Even her beloved Vermont "A-ya" had to go.

In short, Alexander could no longer accept her the way she was. He wanted her to become a socialite. He'd even mentioned after they had children she would, of course, give up her medical practice to raise their kids—with the help of a nanny! Seriously? If she were going to give up her practice to raise the kids, she sure wouldn't need—or want— some nanny raising them for her! Besides, she hadn't put forth all this effort to become a doctor to throw in the towel the minute she had kids! "But I can support us," he insisted, not understanding that she might actually want a career of her own. How they'd fought over that one!

Within two months of that fateful weekend at the Scarsdale estate, Allison knew things with Alexander would never work out. He no longer viewed her through the eyes of love, but through the eyes of his parents, and she would never measure up.

Even if she could pass a crash course in Socialite 101, she'd never be able to be herself. The final straw was the four-page prenuptial agreement he flopped in front of her insisting she sign it. She tore up the prenup and called off the engagement.

Ironically, his mother called the next day all kindness. "We're so sorry things didn't work out between you and Alex. You're a lovely girl. William and I wish you the best."

Just not with *her* son!

While Allison knew it was unfair to assume Grant's parents would be as unaccepting as Alexander's, the thought of facing humiliation and rejection and heartache all over again made her instinctively recoil from Grant's kiss.

Grant shifted on the bed and nodded as though he now understood why she withdrew from his kiss. He reached for her hand and laced his fingers with hers.

"I can see how an experience like that would make you leery to get involved with another guy from a rich family."

"Exactly," she said with a sigh of relief. "Plus, I don't want to ruin the friendship we have."

"I don't know if I ever told you this, but my mother wasn't from a wealthy family. Her father was a high school science teacher, and her mother was a nurse at their local hospital. Mom was the SICU charge nurse at Hopkins when Dad met her. Very middle class."

"Your grandfather was okay with your father marrying her?"

He smiled. "Grandpa Stockdale was on the Surgical Board that approved her to become the youngest SICU charge nurse in the history of the hospital, so he was already impressed with her intelligence and work ethic. It also didn't hurt that she was beautiful," he added with a wink.

"But what if she'd been average looking, or not a charge nurse, or from a town known for garbage?"

"Grandpa would have accepted her anyway because by then Dad was head-over-heels in love with her. More than anything else, Stockdales want their family to be happy."

She stared down at their intertwined fingers then looked up with tears in her eyes. "Alexander told me the exact same thing when he proposed. His parents would only want him to be happy. What a laugh!"

"I can see how that would be very disillusioning." He squeezed her hands.

"It makes no sense, Grant. I've had daydreams about you for four years now, but when something actually happens between us, I run like a scared rabbit." She reached for a tissue next to her bed and daubed her eyes and blew her nose.

"Trust can't be rushed or forced. It has to be earned."

She pursed her lips as though contemplating his words. When she didn't respond, Grant said, "Look, why don't I turn things down a notch? We'll go back to just being friends and colleagues. When you're ready for something deeper, let me know." He caressed her cheek then tipped up her chin with his fingers. "I won't pressure you, Allison. I promise." He gently leaned in to kiss her and whispered, "I'll be waiting."

CHAPTER 22

True to his word, for two weeks straight, Grant treated her as he had before their fateful kiss at the waterfall. He consulted with her on surgical cases, chatted amiably while they ate, studied French with her at night, attended church with her, and trudged the four miles roundtrip to Louis Villemort's house with her every Sunday afternoon. He also never missed an opportunity to make her laugh.

With no gestures of affection or further talk of a future together, she reminded herself she should be glad. After all, they would soon be living in different states. This way, she wouldn't be setting herself up for rejection. This way, she was safe.

But she was miserable.

How she longed for him to pull her into his arms and kiss her senseless, to hold her close until she no longer worried about the future or what his parents would think of her. She no longer wanted to live controlled by fear. It was time to move forward and embrace the wonderful future she could have with Grant.

If only she could jump feet first into the waterfall of trust the way she'd jumped through the waterfall with Grant.

More times than she could count, she was one step from swallowing her fear—and pride—and telling Grant she wanted to give their budding relationship another chance. That she would welcome his kiss. But something made her cave in to the "but what if..." demon.

In her most fragile moments, she convinced herself Grant was secretly glad she'd put the reins on their budding romance. Now he had a tidy excuse for why things ended without looking like a cad. After all, Grant was a red-blooded male who had been deprived of all the flirty women who usually stroked his ego. She'd been dressed in a bikini. And talk about a romantic location—a waterfall at sunset! Perhaps Grant had merely caved into a weak moment, but once he was away from her and had time to analyze how poorly she'd fit into the Stockdale dynasty, he'd thank his lucky stars she'd ended their impulsive kiss.

While she hated to think of Grant as a two-timer, every time he received one of those frilly, scented, pink envelopes her confidence plummeted. The envelope revealed a Chevy Chase zip code, and the letter was signed by a woman named Elizabeth Poston. (Yes, she'd hastily checked out the letter when he was taking a shower.) Did he have a girlfriend back home? If not, who *was* this Elizabeth Poston?

How she longed to ask him, but wouldn't that only confirm she didn't trust him? And then they'd be back to square one... Did she trust Grant with her heart? If she was honest with herself, the answer was no.

Sometimes, she could feel him watching her, as though trying to uncover if her feelings for him had changed. But true to his word, he never touched her or broached the subject again. The ball was in her court, but she felt too paralyzed to make a decision. She prayed and begged God to give her a sign, to let her know unequivocally if Grant was the one.

She'd even shared her tale of woe with Judy and asked her to pray. But so far, she had more fear than peace, more worry than assurance, so she just kept praying. And praying.

God, I need a sign.

* * *

Two weeks later, as Allison hopped out of bed and headed for the bathroom, loud moaning assailed her ears. She rushed to Grant's side where he grimaced and groaned louder.

"Grant? You sound like you were hit by a bus."

"More like a train," he moaned. "Every joint and muscle in my body aches." He pushed on his temples with the palms of his hand. "And my head is killing me."

She reached over and felt his forehead. "Good Lord! You're burning up."

"It even hurts to open my eyes." He looked up at her with frightened eyes. "Something is seriously wrong with me."

"Have you been taking your malaria prophylaxis?"

"Never miss a dose."

"But wasn't there that one day we walked to Louis' house when you forgot to use insecticide. Two weeks ago? You got eaten alive with mosquitoes, remember?"

His shoulders sagged. "You're right. But shouldn't my malaria drug have kept me safe?"

"Not against Dengue fever and Chikungunya virus."

His brow puckered. "Chikawhata virus??'

"Chikungunya virus."

He groaned. "I don't remember that one, but it sounds bad. What's the treatment?"

She sucked in a breath. Grant would not like her answer. "There's no antibiotic for Dengue fever or Chikungunya virus."

"No treatment?" He mumbled under his breath.

"Afraid not. But I could be wrong about your diagnosis."

She hoped it wasn't Dengue fever or Chikungunya virus. If he had one of those two mosquito-spread viruses, he was in for a long two weeks: headaches, muscle pain, eye pain, joint pain, and high fevers.

After she had not recognized yaws in the little boy several weeks ago, Allison used any down time during the day to study up on tropical infections common in Haiti. Little had she known she might need this information to diagnose Grant!

"Let me change into scrubs, and I'll help you limp to the clinic. Let's see what Dr. Jones thinks."

Grant closed his eyes. "Let me lie here a few minutes. Can't walk right now."

Allison dashed into the bathroom and tugged on her scrubs. "I'll run get the wheelchair then. I suspect with your high fever you're going to need IV fluids."

She bolted from their cabin to the clinic, but the door was locked, as Dr. Jones had not yet arrived. After running to his house, she pounded on the front door. "Dr. Jones? Judy?" She kept pounding until she heard footfall coming toward the door.

Judy answered the door in her bathrobe. "Allison? What's the matter?"

Dr. Jones followed closely behind chewing on a piece of toast and still clad in his pajamas. His hair stuck up every which way, and he had a morning stubble. "This can't be good. What's wrong?"

The words rushed out in a torrent. "It's Grant."

"What about him?"

"He's really sick. He's moaning and burning up with fever. He says every joint in his body aches, and it hurts to open his eyes, and he's got a bad headache and he—"

Dr. Jones raised a hand. "Whoa, Nellie! Slow down. I just woke up, and my brain still needs coffee."

Allison smiled. "Sorry. I'm worried about him. I've been studying all the tropical infections of Haiti, and I think from his history, he either has Dengue fever or Chikungunya virus."

He ran a hand through his rumpled hair. "That's not good."

"Can I have the keys to the clinic so I can get a wheelchair?"

"A wheelchair?" His eyes widened with concern. "Is he so bad he can't walk?"

"He says he didn't think he could make it. Every bone in his body hurts."

"Oh dear." Judy turned to her husband. "What's wrong with him?"

Dr. Jones rubbed his chin. "Break-bone fever, most likely. That's what Dengue fever is nicknamed."

"I'll get the keys." Judy rushed to the kitchen and returned with the keyring.

"Wheel him to the clinic. I'll throw on some clothes, shave, and down a cup of coffee. I'll meet you there in five minutes." Allison snatched the keys out of Judy's hand and ran back to the clinic.

Her hands shook as she struggled to get the door unlocked. After locating the wheelchair, she pushed it over the quarter-mile rocky trail from the clinic to their cabin where Grant lay in bed moaning, his hair and face drenched with sweat.

"Here. Let me help you into the wheelchair. Dr. Jones is meeting us at the clinic in five minutes." She reached under his arms to help pull him into a sitting position and he screamed in agony. "Stop! It feels like you're pulling my arms off."

"Sorry. I'll try to be more gentle."

He forced himself to sit on the edge of the bed. "I feel like an old man with arthritis in every joint of my body." He released a loud sigh. "I'm sorry to be such a baby, but you have no idea how much this hurt."

"I can only imagine." She reached under both his arms. "Okay, on the count of three, you're going to stand."

"Or die," he muttered.

She frowned. "I've always heard doctors made the worst patients." She gestured at him. "Exhibit A."

He offered a half smile. "It appears I far prefer to inflict pain than endure it." He inhaled a deep breath bracing himself for the task ahead. "Okay, I'm ready."

"One, two, three." She pulled him into a standing position as he released a howl of pain.

"Great! you're standing," she encouraged. "Now just turned around and sit in the wheelchair."

He slowly turned around. "Just shoot me. Put me out of my agony. That's what vets do to horses with broken legs."

"Stop that crazy talk! You are going to survive this, and in fourteen days, you'll be better."

"Fourteen days?" His face deflated and his shoulders sagged. "Put me in a coma and wake me up in two weeks."

With hands on her hips she snapped, "Grant Stockdale III, I never would have taken you for a wuss. You with your karate moves and bulging muscles. Now cut it out and sit down in this wheelchair." She pointed to the seat.

He glared at her. "Compassion is not your strong suit, Dr. Ratchet."

"It *is* my strong suit, but compassion isn't getting you to the clinic." She pointed to the wheelchair and commanded, "Sit."

"Yes, Ma'am," he muttered before flopping into the wheelchair with a loud groan.

"Alright. We're making progress," she trilled with forced cheerfulness. "I'm going to wheel you over to the clinic and get an IV started. With this high fever, you're probably dehydrated. I'll also give you some Tylenol for the headache, fever, and pain."

"I need a truckload of morphine for this pain."

She ignored his ridiculous request. "Dr. Jones will help me figure out what else we need to get you better."

He gazed up at her with his best attempt to look pathetic. "I wasn't kidding about the coma. Or the morphine. Can't you knock me out with a hefty dose of propofol and keep me comatose until this thing is over?"

Hands on her hips, she snapped, "Forget it! You'll end up dead—like Michael Jackson."

Honestly! Who would have suspected the great and powerful Grant Stockdale III would be such a baby when he was sick?

She pushed the wheelchair over the door ledge and locked the door to their cabin. "I have no intention of turning you a junkie."

"Ow!" he howled. "Take is easy!"

"Sorry," she said, pushing the wheelchair over the rocky trail as carefully as she could.

"Slow down! I feel every one of those bumps." he scolded.

She scowled. "If I push any slower, I'll be going in reverse. Let's just get you there as quickly as possible." She pushed with increasing speed, ignoring his howls of pain and commands to slow down. "We're half-way there."

He gripped the armrest of the wheelchair. "Watch out for that rut."

She pushed onward ignoring his protest. When they reached the clinic, she maneuvered the wheelchair over the door ledge and wheeled him to an exam room. "I need you to stand up and transfer to the bed."

Surprisingly, he cooperated with no snide remarks, though he grunted as he climbed onto the bed. Once he was lying on the bed, she offered him a pillow.

He shook violently with chills. "I'm f-f-freezing."

Rigors. Must be his fever was peaking.

"I n-need a b-b-blanket," he stuttered through chattering teeth.

She fetched several blankets and wrapped him in a cocoon.

She took his temperature and her breath hitched—104.9 degrees. No wonder he felt so wretched. "Let me get you some Tylenol. We need to bring that fever down."

She fetched two extra-strength Tylenol and a glass of water. "Swallow this."

He sat up with a moan, pulled his arms out of the blankets, and took the glass with trembling hands.

Fearing he would drop the pills because he was shaking so badly, she popped the two Tylenol into his mouth. He quickly swallowed them, downed the rest of the water, then handed her the glass back. He flopped back down on the bed with a howl of pain. "I feel t-terrible."

"Really? I never would have known," she said with a wink.

He offered a smile. "You may be good with a s-scalpel, but you need to work on your b-bedside m-manner."

She patted his arm. "I am sorry you feel so bad, Grant. I wish there was a quick slug of antibiotic I could infuse to make this all go away."

"You and me, b-b-both."

"Hopefully, the Tylenol and IV fluids will kick the headache and fever and joint pains, and you'll feel better in no time. Let me get your IV started."

"You better nail it on the first s-stick. No p-poking around."

She wagged a finger at him. "You better talk nice to me. I'm the one with the needle, and you're too arthritic to punch me."

He smirked. "Nothing like hitting a man when he's already d-d-down."

"Cheer up, with all the weightlifting you do, finding a vein won't be a problem."

"I d-don't lift weights. Just do p-push-ups every morning."

"You have the body of a Greek god with no effort?" She scowled. "Figures."

As soon as the words exited her mouth she felt her cheeks flush. So much for sticking with their "just friends" pact.

"I don't feel like a Greek g-god. Except maybe S-S-Sisyphus after he pushed a b-boulder up a mountain."

Allison rounded up supplies for the IV, and after scrubbing up his elbow crease, she located a bulging vein. "Okay, this one looks promising. Now hold still."

She inserted the needle and an immediate backflash of blood told her she'd hit the spot. She hooked him up to a liter of normal saline. After taping down the IV site, she cranked up the flow rate to the maximum it would allow.

He smiled. "Good j-job. You get an 'A' in IVs."

"And don't you forget it."

They heard the ring of the front door as Dr. Jones rushed in.

Allison filled him in on what she'd already done to treat Grant. "His temp is 104.9."

Dr. Jones yanked off the blankets. "Then get rid of these! Even though he's shivering and thinks he's cold, until that fever comes down, he needs cooling blankets, and he needs to drink ice water. Fevers that high cause delirium and seizures. Hopefully, the Tylenol will help."

He ran for the cooling blanket, wrapped it underneath and around Grant's torso and then plugged it in.

"But I'm f-f-freezing," Grant complained. His shivering intensified until it almost resembled a seizure.

"Sorry, Grant, but until you're below 103, we'll need to keep the cooling blanket on."

He retrieved a bottle of cold water from the refrigerator and handed it to Grant. "Drink this. It'll cool you internally."

In full rigors, Grant could barely hold the bottle without sloshing it all over the bed, but he dutifully drank it down.

Dr. Jones reviewed all of Grant's symptoms and briefly examined him. Eyeing the fine red rash splotched across his body he frowned. "They look like petechiae."

Grant's eyes widened. "Petechiae! Are my platelets low?"

"Probably. I'll get a blood sample, and we'll know how low in a few minutes."

"Dengue fever causes a low platelet count?" Allison said.

He nodded. "Also, a low white blood count and elevated liver function tests."

Grant moaned. "I'm going to d-d-die."

Dr. Jones patted his shoulder. "With good supportive care, hopefully not."

Grant's eyes bulged. "But I could die? Do I need to write a w-w-will?"

Dr. Jones averted his eyes. "Don't borrow trouble, Grant. Yes, there are isolated reports of Dengue shock syndrome and abdominal hemorrhage, but those cases are rare."

"Have you ever had a p-p-patient with Dengue fever d-d-die?" Grant pressed.

Again no eye contact. "Once, but the patient waited far too long before coming to the clinic. He went to Louis Villemort instead. By the time he got here, he was already in septic shock."

"But he d-d-died?" Grant eyes widened with fear.

"Yes," Dr. Jones admitted. "He died."

Grant pounded the mattress. "So help me, if I die from this, I'm going to s-s-sue Dr. Morrison. He made me come here. Said it would be g-good for me. Said I'd be s-s-safe. Safe, my eye," he growled.

When Allison and Dr. Jones didn't respond to his rant, he banged his head on the pillow. "I'm sorry. I know I'm being a j-j-jerk, but you have no idea how much this hurts. I don't like being a p-p-patient. It feels like every b-b-bone in my body is b-b-broken."

Allison crossed her arms. "If you don't stop whining, I'll break every bone in your body—then you'll really have something to whine about. Now man up!"

His eyes widened at her rebuke.

She pointed a finger at him. "You are going to fight this thing, and you will be better in two weeks."

He grabbed her arm, and his eyes penetrating hers with surprising vulnerability. "You p-p-promise I'll get better?"

She knew she had no business making promises she couldn't keep, but he stared up at her with such terrified eyes, she found herself saying, "Yes, Grant. I'll stay by your side and take care of you night and day until you're better. I promise."

His eyes pooled with tears. Clearly embarrassed at his display of weakness, he quickly brushed them away. "I'm s-s-sorry. It's this f-fever. It's making me act weird."

"A-ya," Allison agreed, suspecting the usually confident Grant Stockdale hated looking weak and vulnerable. Or feeling out of control.

"That witch doctor put a c-c-curse on me, remember? That's why I'm sick." His eyes went wild with fright. "He's s-s-sticking pins in a doll with my name on it. He's got clout with the d-d-devil. I'm going to d-d-die."

Dr. Jones leaned over and whispered to Allison, "I think he's getting delirious, don't you?"

"With a temp of 104.9, it wouldn't be surprising," Allison whispered back. "I've never seen him like this before. Never. He's usually so controlled."

"We've got to get that fever down," Dr. Jones said. He pulled the cooling blanket up over Grant's shoulders and tucked it in then turned down the temperature on the blanket another notch.

Grant thrashed and flailed under the blanket, his eyes wild and crazed. "There's a c-c-curse on me. I'm going to d-d-die."

Allison gripped his face and ordered, "You stop that crazy talk, Grant Stockdale! You are not going to die."

Just the mention of Grant dying sent daggers through her heart, and she blinked back tears. She wanted to run into the bathroom and weep. But right now, he needed a doctor. He needed her to hold it together.

Compartmentalize. You are Grant's doctor and nothing more. Stay focused.

When Grant made eye contact, she forced herself to say as calmly as she could, "Look, maybe Louis has connections with the dark side, but we have clout with the big guy upstairs." She pointed heavenward. "Remember our verse, "Greater is He that is in me..." She gestured for him to finish the verse.

"Than He that is in the w-w-world," he completed.

"Exactly. When you get scared, repeat that verse. Claim it over yourself."

"I'm so c-c-cold," he said through chattering teeth. "Can't I have a real blanket?"

"Afraid not, but between the Tylenol, ice water, and cooling blanket, your fever will be down soon," Dr. Jones said.

Grant glanced up at Dr. Jones and then looked downward, as though embarrassed at his pitiful display of whining. "My p-p-pity party is over. What do I need to do to f-f-fight this thing?"

Dr. Jones smiled and pointed at him. "That's the spirit. We'll keep you hydrated, give you pain meds, keep your fever down, and wait for your immune system to conquer this thing."

"I guess there's nothing more we can do," Grand conceded.

"I'm going to draw some blood so I can assess your blood counts and liver function."

After extracting several tubes of blood, Dr. Jones inquired, "Has that Tylenol kicked in for your pain yet? It's been an hour since you took it."

"P-p-pain is still a hundred on a ten-p-p-point scale."

Dr. Jones pursed his lips. "We can't use Ibuprofen because of the low platelets, as it could up the risk of hemorrhage. He's already taken 1,000mg of Tylenol."

"Do you have any m-m-morphine?" Grant begged.

Dr. Jones rubbed his chin. "I suppose we can use narcotics for a day or two, though it will aggravate the delirium. Be right back." He wandered to the drug closet, unlocked a safe, and returned with two pills. "You're not allergic to oxycodone, are you?"

Grant shrugged. "Never n-n-needed it before, so I don't know."

He handed Grant two pills with a glass of water. "Swallow these, and your pain should improve in a few minutes."

Grant dutifully swallowed the pills. "Narcotics do weird things to p-p-people. I hope I'm not talking to my IV p-p-pole in an hour."

Allison rubbed her hands together in glee. "Goody! Maybe you'll reveal your deepest, darkest secrets to me."

He glared at her. "Nothing I say under the influence of n-n-narcotics can be taken s-s-seriously, and you know it!"

She raised a brow. "I'll be sure to reveal everything you tell me to Dr. Morrison the minute we return to Hopkins."

"Allison S-S-Smith, you are an evil w-w-woman."

She chuckled and patted his cheek. "I promise to keep anything you say in confidence."

"G-g-good."

"That way, I have ammunition to extort and manipulate you in the future," she added with a grin.

When his head pulled back with alarm, she laughed. "Just kidding, Grant. I'm trying to distract you from your misery."

"Here I thought you were a n-n-nice Christian woman, and you threaten me with extortion."

"And manipulation." She smiled and pointed at him. "But I got you to focus on something other than death and voodoo curses, right? Now let me recheck your temperature."

She thrust the thermometer in his mouth and nodded with satisfaction at the reading. "Good. You're down to 102.4 with the Tylenol, ice water, and cooling blanket. It may not have knocked your pain, but it has lowered your fever."

Dr. Jones returned from the lab, and when Allison filled him in on the drop in temperature, he pulled off the cooling blanket.

"Thank God," Grant exclaimed. "It's weird how a high fever can make you feel cold instead of hot." He looked over at Dr. Jones. "What did my blood work show?"

"Just as expected, your white blood count and platelet count are low which is consistent with Dengue fever."

"How low?" Grant asked.

"Not dangerously so. Platelets are 50,000, so you won't be hemorrhaging. Not unless they drop below 20,000."

"And my liver function tests?"

"Elevated."

"How elevated?"

"SGPT of 140. SGOT 135."

Grant pursed his lips as though contemplating his results.

"In other words, they're bad, but not horrible," Allison said, patting his shoulder.

Grant rolled his head on the pillow. "I can't believe how quickly this thing hit me. I was fine last night and then this morning, BAM!"

"Dengue fever does that," Dr. Jones said. "You can expect wide fluctuations in temperature from 96 to 105 degrees. Unfortunately, you'll get rigors and worsening pain with every fever spike."

Grant scowled. "Swell. And there's no antibiotic to kill it?"

"Afraid not," Dr. Jones said.

"Why hasn't somebody developed a decent treatment for Dengue fever? They have one for malaria."

Dr. Jones shrugged. "I suppose because it is less common and tends to be in poor countries. Pharmaceuticals aren't interested in creating drugs without a decent profit margin."

"I'm getting the Stockdale Foundation to fund research on Dengue fever, if I recover from this thing, that is."

Allison gripped his hand in both of hers. "Not if, Grant, when. You will get better. Dr. Jones and I are here 24/7 to take care of you."

He offered up a devilish grin. "In that case, I'd like some truffles and beef bourguignon. And a glass of you finest Chardonnay, please."

She wagged a scolding finger at him. "With your elevated liver tests? Wine is taboo. So, it's beef broth and Jell-O for you."

"Jell-O?" He crossed his arms in mock disgust. "I am so giving this dive a 1-star review on Yelp."

She pointed at him. "You do that, and I'll give you something to yelp about—like a rectal thermometer, or a botched IV attempt."

He laughed and then gripped his abdomen. "Ow! Don't make me laugh. It hurts too much. Every muscle and bone feels like it trudged through a Bataan death march. Twice."

"Hey, you're not stuttering and chattering anymore," Allison said

"That's because you got rid of that abominable cooling blanket. That thing belongs in a torture chamber."

She glanced at her watch. "It's time for your pain pills. Hopefully, they'll kick in soon, and your pain will lessen. I'll run get them and some beef broth so you can eat before the pain pills put you to sleep."

He scowled. "Beef broth? Don't bother. But I could use some lip balm and ice water. With this fever, my lips are really parched."

She saluted. "At your service."

After rounding up cold water from the frig and a tube of lip balm, she handed them to him.

His hands shook so badly he struggled to unscrew the cap off the water bottle. He gave up trying and his arms flopped on the bed as though exhausted.

"I'll open it for you," she volunteered.

He released a yawn "Actually, I'm suddenly exhausted. I just want to sleep."

Good. Must be the pain medication had kicked in.

Within a minute he was sound asleep. At least now he'd have an hour or two of respite from the intense pain.

She heard the front doorbell jingle, so they must have a new patient.

This is going to be one exhausting week.

CHAPTER 23

"We have someone in the waiting room who says he did something to his shoulder," Dr. Jones informed her. "I examined him, and I think he dislocated it. Have you been trained in relocating shoulders?"

"A few years back—during my orthopedic rotation. Bring him back, and I'll take a look. Maybe I can get it back in place with a joint manipulation."

Dr. Jones winced. "Aren't manipulations painful?

"Shh," she whispered, fingers to her lips. "You don't want him to hear you, or he'll be out the door before I can get it in place."

The thin boy looked to be around thirteen and was carrying a soccer ball with his left arm. His right arm hung limply with the ball of the shoulder joint clearly out of socket. He'd fallen playing soccer with a couple of friends and dislocated the shoulder trying to break his fall.

As Allison palpated the joint the boy grimaced but said nothing. It was definitely out of joint.

She'd observed an orthopod manipulate a shoulder joint back into place twice during her orthopedics rotation, but she had never personally done one by herself.

"If you'll excuse me a minute, I'll be right back," she said.

She then disappeared to the back of the clinic and yanked out an orthopedic textbook. After skimming the section on dislocated shoulders, she mentally pictured the maneuver.

If she could perform neurosurgery, surely she could manipulate a dislocated shoulder.

She had Dr. Jones explain to the boy exactly what she would have to do to get his shoulder back in the socket. She drew a picture of a normal shoulder joint and then one showing what his shoulder joint currently looked like. She mimed the maneuver she'd need to perform to get it back in the socket. "Ça va faire mal," she informed him.

He grimaced at being informed the maneuver would hurt, but he nodded his consent.

With a quick firm tug, she heard the satisfying sound of the shoulder snapping back into its socket.

She asked the boy to move his arm, and he was now able to fully raise and move the joint in a full circle

He grinned and hopped up from the exam table. "Merci beaucoup."

Dr. Jones nodded his approval. "Good as new! Great job, Allison."

She beamed. This rotation had certainly expanded her doctoring skills.

She glanced into the waiting room and seeing no patients, she wandered back to check on Grant. He was still sleeping, though he moaned with every roll or movement.

Seizing the free time, she pulled out her textbook on tropical infections and flipped to the section about Dengue fever.

If she was going to care for him for the next two weeks, she'd better know what she was up against.

She skimmed the chapter making mental notes. Bad headache, eye pain, muscle and joint pain, rash in most patients. Temperature spikes to 106 degrees. Seizures and permanent brain damage develop if the patient can't keep the fever down.

Her heart momentarily stopped. Permanent brain damage? Dear God, no!

She read on: Abdominal pain and protracted vomiting signal the patient has spiraled into the deadly hemorrhagic form that causes internal bleeding. Septic shock and death were then inevitable.

The reality hit her like a bludgeon. Someone as brilliant and gifted and healthy as Grant could die from this? Or end up with permanent brain damage?

She sank into the chair her legs now too weak and trembly to stand. Until this moment the seriousness of Grant's condition had escaped her. She'd even teased him to lighten his mood. Perhaps she hadn't been ready to face the reality that Grant could die from this!

Louis Villemort had uttered a death curse on him. A wave of fear coursed down her spine as the verse about Satan being a roaring lion looking for whom he could devour flashed through her mind. She repeated her now favorite scripture verse: "Greater is He...

She snapped the textbook shut too stunned to move. She sucked in a deep breath, returned the textbook to the shelf, and rushed to Grant's side.

You are not dying, Grant Stockdale! Not on my watch!

Placing her hand on his forehead, she could tell he still had a fever, though not as high as it had been in the cabin.

She reached for the thermometer and hoping not to waken him, slithered it into his mouth. 102.8 degrees. It had gone up a bit, probably because he hadn't been drinking ice water or using the cooling blanket. Glancing at her watch, she calculated when his next dose of Tylenol was due. Another ten minutes. She gently tucked the cooling blanket around his torso and legs and turned it on.

No seizures or brain damage under my care!

She pulled up a stool and sat next to his bed then grabbed his hand in both of hers. "You cannot die on me, Grant." Before she could stop herself, she blurted, "Because I love you."

The confession jarred her. Until this moment, she would not admit to anyone, let alone herself, that she had allowed herself to fall in love with Grant. In fact, despite her four-year physical attraction to him, she'd done everything in her power not to fall in love with him. She'd kept her distance. But as they'd been forced to work together in Haiti, she'd seen the real Grant Stockdale. A smart, hardworking, decent human being who challenged her and made her pulse race. Someone who encouraged her when her confidence was low. Someone who believed in her and was patient with her. Someone who teased her and made her laugh.

She'd kept her feelings under wraps because she hadn't wanted to be hurt by another rich Alexander. Plus, she'd wanted—no, needed—to prove to all her classmates that she was as competent a surgeon as they were despite being from a poor background. Dating a classmate might have interfered with that laser focus. She and Grant would finish residency in four short weeks—if Grant survived. They would no longer be classmates, and if she didn't let him know how she felt, she might never see him again.

Despair coursed through her. Just the thought of not seeing Grant again dug a hole—no, a crater—deep in her soul. She loved him, whether she wanted to or not. If didn't matter if she fully trusted him yet. She loved him.

How had he wormed his way into her heart so thoroughly? So irrevocably?

She laced her fingers with his and offered up an earnest plea to the Almighty to heal him. Knowing Louis Villemort had placed a curse on him to die did little to calm her rattled nerves. Perhaps she should go visit Louis and bribe him into lifting the curse. Had their weekly French Creole lessons done anything to soften his heart? But seeing Louis without Grant there for protection sent a shiver up her spine. Would he attack her or chant a death curse over her, as well?

Greater is He that is in Grant than he who is in the world.

She bowed her head and closed her eyes. "God, I beg you to protect Grant from the plans of the enemy."

She squeezed Grant's hand and continued to beseech the Almighty.

God, please don't let him die. I love him. I need him. He's perfect for me. I know that now.

Tears poured down her cheeks as she poured out her heart to God. When she opened her eyes, she found Grant staring at her.

Embarrassed to be caught holding his hand and crying, she pulled her hand away and brushed away her tears. "You're awake!"

He nodded and offered a weak smile. "Thanks for praying for me, Allison. I can use all the prayers I can get."

"You're welcome." She chewed on her bottom lip, wishing she could tell him how she felt, but this was no time for a heart-to-heart discussion about their future. Not when he was spiking a high fever.

"Could I have some ice water? I'm really thirsty."

"How about some nice cold ginger ale instead? The calories will do you good. It's also time for your next Tylenol dose."

She retrieved the Tylenol, a can of ginger ale from the refrigerator, and a washcloth soaked in ice water.

After he swallowed the Tylenol with several swigs of ginger ale, he put down the can, and she wiped his brow and neck with the icy compress.

She handed him a can. "Drink this. You need the calories."

He complied by finishing the can then handed it back to her. "Pitiful, isn't it? A week ago, we walked four miles to Louis Villemort's house and back, and now I can't even walk from the cabin to the clinic."

"You'll get better, Grant," she insisted, stroking his brow again with the damp cloth.

Worry lines creased his forehead. "What if my faith isn't as strong as Louis' curse?"

She offered a shrug. "Then I guess you'll die and go to Heaven."

When his eyes widened at her glib response, she winked. "Cheer up, I promise to cry at your funeral."

He scowled. "Gee, thanks, Allison."

Seeing the fear in his eyes, she reached for his hand and squeezed it between both of hers. "I'm just teasing. You are not going to die because I won't let you."

"Oh, really! And who made you the great and powerful Oz?"

"I did, because you and I make a great team. I won't let you die because... I need you, Grant." Her traitorous eye pooled with tears.

He squeezed her hand and smiled. "Need me, huh?" His eyes penetrated hers, as though desperate to know if her heart had softened. "Anything more than just need, Allison?"

Before she could answer, Dr. Jones strolled to the bedside. "How's our patient?"

"Temp is 102.8, but I just gave him another two Tylenol and some iced ginger ale to cool his core."

"Good."

"I've also used the cooling blanket and a cold compress on his forehead and neck."

Dr. Jones nodded then turned to Grant. "How's the pain?"

Grant cleared his throat. "You know, with Allison here distracting me, it's not too bad. Down from a ten to a four."

"Must be the Tylenol and oxycodone are working," Allison commented, swallowing the lump in her throat.

"Must be," Grant concurred, though his eyes never left hers.

Noting that Dr. Jones was watching their interaction, Allison said, "I'll run and get more ginger ale." She sure didn't want Dr. Jones knowing how she felt about Grant.

"Sounds like you've got things in good control. I'll be in my office paying bills. Come get me if a patient comes in, or if you and Grant need me."

Allison returned with a dishpan of ice water and another can of cold ginger ale. She popped the top on the ginger ale can, handed it to him, and then dipped the washcloth in the ice water and stroked his neck. "If we want to keep that brilliant brain of yours from broiling, we've got to keep your fever down."

He sipped the ginger ale. "I could really use some lip balm."

She reached for the tube and uncapped it. "I'll apply it for you."

She leaned in and applied a coating to his lips while his eyes studied her face.

Could he sense her feelings for him had deepened? Did he know she loved him?

He rubbed his lips together and gripped her hand and squeezed. "Thanks for taking such good care of me, Allison. It means a lot."

"You're welcome. Just doing my job."

His gaze remained glued on her face. "Is that all it is to you? A job?"

An awkward pause ensued. Allison focused her eyes on the floor and chewed on her bottom lip.

Should she tell him how she felt? What if that moment in the creek was a momentary lapse in judgment for him? What if he was now glad she'd rebuffed him? And who was Elizabeth?

"Do you have any other patients right now?" he inquired, letting her off the hook.

"No, the clinic is quiet."

Awkward silence. She stared at her nails.

"Since you're free, how would you like to distract me from my misery by studying French Creole together?"

She shrugged. "Why not? Let me run back to the cabin and get your book. Is it still next to your bed on the nightstand?"

"It should be."

After retrieving the book from the cabin, she returned and flipped to the section on verbs. "Okay, since you're sick and probably not at your sharpest, I'll just review some words we should already know." She cleared her throat. How do you say, "I walk?"

"Je marche."

She nodded. "You walk quickly."

"Tu marches vite."

"They walk very slowly."

"Do they have Dengue fever?" he quipped.

She rolled her eyes. "Ha, ha, wise guy. Now quit procrastinating. How do you say, 'They walk very slowly'?"

"Ils marchent très lentement."

"Very good. I see the Dengue fever hasn't cooked your brain." She smiled and added, "At least not yet."

They continued studying French until Grant's eyelids drooped and his head bobbed.

She closed the book. "You look exhausted. I'll let you sleep for a while."

He reached for her hand. "Allison, wait. How do you say, 'I love you' in French?"

Her heart jolted.

Why was he asking that? Surely he knew that phrase. Even people who didn't speak French knew how to say that.

Pretending he'd asked her any other phrase in the book, she said in her most schoolmarmish tone, "Je t'aime."

"What was that, again?" he said with a smile.

"Je t'aime," she said louder, trying desperately to keep her voice from quivering.

His eyes bore into hers. "Je t'aime aussi, ma chéri," he whispered. Then the infuriating man closed his eyes, rolled over onto his side, and promptly fell asleep!

What just happened? Had he just told her he loved her, or was he merely repeating the phrase? But why add the ma chéri? And why ask for that phrase in the first place? He would hardly need, "I love you," to practice medicine in rural Haiti.

She tried not to get her hopes up. Grant was sick and no doubt grateful she was taking care of him. Didn't the same thing happen to soldiers injured during World War II? They became infatuated with their nurses and convinced themselves they were in love. No, she ought not read too much into this.

Even if he had said he loved her, what did it mean? He could just be delirious from his high fever. Plus, he was doped up on oxycodone. Heck, he might not even remember saying the words when he woke up. Besides, some people flippantly tossed out, "I love you," every time they ended a phone call, much like she said, "Goodbye," or, "See ya later."

No, until he said the words in a setting where he didn't have a fever or a brain doped up with pain pills, she shouldn't read anything into his words. Hadn't he said not to take anything he said under the influence of narcotics seriously?

But if he was delirious or merely drugged up with pain pills, shouldn't it have affected his ability to conjugate French verbs? He'd nailed every phrase. On the other hand, Grant was so smart maybe even delirium and narcotics couldn't inhibit his frontal lobe.

She released a sigh. She was talking herself into circles!

If Grant were going to say those words to her for the first time, why couldn't it have been in a romantic setting when he was healthy and fully lucid? When she knew he meant it—not when he could merely be loopy from narcotics and fever?

She decided to return the French Creole book to the cabin while Grant slept. As she reached the cabin and placed the book on his nightstand, she noticed the latest pink scented envelope Jean-Pierre had retrieved from the post office. If he did have a girlfriend, she needed to know so she wouldn't take his kiss at the creek or his recent, "I love you," seriously.

She had no business reading his mail. If she trusted him, she wouldn't *need* to read his mail. She forced herself to exit the cabin, but then curiosity—no, a desperate need to know the truth—got the better of her.

If Grant had a girlfriend, she needed to guard her heart and give up any crazy notion of a future with him.

With trembling hands, she pulled the envelope off his nightstand and carefully tugged the letter from the envelope. Unfolding it, she read the first line, and her heart sank.

My darling Grant,

She skimmed on as the woman described the fundraising she'd done for the Stockdale Foundation.

Hmm. The woman had raised over fifteen-thousand dollars so far and had another fundraiser set up for two weeks from now.

Allison lowered the letter and frowned. You might know Grant would fall for someone who worked for the Stockdale Foundation. No doubt she had an MBA from Wharton Business school and was as brilliant in the field of finance as Grant was in medicine.

She forced herself to read on. When she reached the last paragraph, her worst fears slapped her in the face:

I will count the days until your return, and I am praying for your safety every day. With all my love, Elizabeth.

Why hadn't Grant mentioned a girlfriend in all their conversations? More importantly, why had he kissed her at the waterfall and told her he loved her just now?

She folded the letter and carefully tucked it back in its envelope. She placed it on Grant's bed exactly where she'd found it.

A crushing ache stabbed her heart as thoroughly as if Louis' butcher knife had impaled her. Grant had a girlfriend, and apparently Allison was merely a pleasant distraction while he was stuck in Haiti. How could she have been so stupid as to let herself fall in love with him? She *knew* better than to fall for a rich guy from an entitled family. But she'd done it anyhow.

Stupid, stupid, stupid. Why had she let her guard down?

With tears pouring down her cheeks, she reprimanded herself on the way back to the clinic. Since she'd snooped through his mail, she unfortunately couldn't confront him with what she'd discovered. She'd need to stay focused on remaining strictly professional. She'd inform Grant she only wanted to be his colleague.

Thankfully, when she returned to the clinic, Grant was still asleep, and a family with what sounded like strep throat was being worked up by Dr. Jones.

"There you are. You want to help me perform some rapid strep tests on the Bernard family?"

Grateful to have something to focus on other than Grant, she busied herself swabbing their throats and taking their temperatures. All three kids had strep throat. Dr. Jones mixed up a slurry of amoxicillin and explained to the parents how to measure and administer the antibiotic.

Next came a man who had strained his back. Then a woman with an infected foot. Once Allison extracted the embedded thorn and debrided the infection, she dressed the wound and taught the woman to walk on her heel to avoid putting weight on the healing sore.

By suppertime, she knew she'd have to face Grant again. She strolled to his room and checked his IV fluids, emptied the urinal, and focused on checking his temperature and blood pressure.

She reminded herself she was his doctor and nothing more.

She could feel his eyes watching her.

Avoid eye contact at all costs, she admonished herself.

"You okay?" Grant inquired, as though sensing something was off with her. "You seem upset."

Since his temperature was down, she busied herself with removing the cooling blanket as a distraction from answering his question. She responded with forced cheerfulness. "Good news! Your temp is down to 99 degrees."

"I'll bet it means I'm getting better."

"More likely, it just means your Tylenol has kicked in. Unfortunately, your temperature will probably spike again before this thing is through."

She forced herself to make brief eye contact. "You hungry for something more exciting than Jell-O?

"Filet mignon and pomme de terre?" he suggested with a wink.

She rolled her eyes hoping to appear glib. "Nice try, Stockdale. I was thinking more along the chicken noodle soup and crackers line. The textbook says you can develop vomiting and abdominal pain, so we don't want to push eating too fast."

"Chicken noodle soup, it is. Truthfully, I'm not the least bit hungry, but I figure I need nutrition to fight this thing."

She warmed up a can of soup and pulled out a few crackers then brought the tray to Grant's bedside. "Bon appetit."

He lifted the soup spoon to his mouth but the furrows in his brow told her every lift of the arm hurt.

"Here, let me feed you. I can tell it hurts to lift your arm."

He shook his head. "Pitiful! I feel like such an invalid. I can't even feed myself!"

"You can," she corrected, "but when I'm here to help, why hurt for nothing?" She spooned the soup into his mouth one bite at a time until it was gone. She then fed him crackers. Their faces were mere inches apart, and the gesture of feeding him felt intimate. She resisted a desire to kiss him—despite knowing his kisses were apparently nothing more than a pleasant diversion until he reunited with his precious Elizabeth. If you can't be near the one you love, love the one you're near. Was that Grant's philosophy?

She didn't want to believe that. She wanted to believe she meant something to him. But he had a girlfriend back home. She had to make herself remember that.

Anxious to put an end to her tumultuous thoughts, she jumped to her feet. "Let me bring this tray back to the kitchen."

She grabbed the tray and charged toward the kitchen. "I'll go pick a fresh mango for your dessert. The vitamin C will do you good."

She dashed off to pick a mango from the tree outside the house. Anything to get away from Grant's probing eyes. She took her time peeling and slicing the mango.

Get a grip. Treat him like you would any other patient.

She carried the slices back to Grant and spoon-fed him.

"Yum! That tastes surprisingly good. Thank you."

His eyes probed hers, and he frowned. Reaching for her hand he said, "What's wrong, Allison? I can tell you're upset about something. Did I say something wrong?"

Apparently, her acting skills were on par with her French at the airport. She turned her back and sniffed back tears. Maybe it was time to get this charade over with. She turned around and crossed her arms ready to have it out with him. No more games.

"Oh, I'm sure you'll be better and home to your precious girlfriend, Elizabeth, very soon."

His eyes widened in surprise. "Elizabeth? How do you know about Elizabeth? I've never mentioned her before."

She feigned picking lint off her lab coat. "You must have mentioned her the day Jean-Pierre handed you her letter."

He eyed her suspiciously and shook his head. "No, I didn't. I'm sure of it."

Refusing to admit she'd breached his privacy, she said, "Maybe you blurted it when you were doped up on oxycodone."

His eyes scanned hers then narrowed as though figuring out she was bluffing. "I don't think so. You read the letter on my nightstand, didn't you?"

Refusing to confess, she instead asked, "Why didn't you tell me about Elizabeth? Was I just some temporary dalliance?"

He raised a brow. "Jealous, are we?"

She pounded his bedside table. "Of course, I'm jealous! You're getting love letters from another woman! Why didn't you tell me about Elizabeth, you two-timing bucket of pig slop?"

His eyes widened at her sudden attack and his tone went sharp. "For your information, Elizabeth is nothing more than a charming, well-educated, wealthy woman who happens to works for the Stockdale Foundation."

She crossed her arms and glared at him. "Right! I'll bet she's pretty, too."

He had the nerve to laugh. "Yes, her recent facelift did do wonders for her appearance."

Allison's head jerked up. Facelift? In a woman their age? Talk about vain!

"Your girlfriend has had a facelift?" Barely able to contain her contempt, Allison snapped, "How old is she, anyhow?"

He shrugged, sporting an infuriating grin. "I don't know—eighty-four, eighty-five."

She stared at him in disbelief. "You're dating an eighty-five-year-old?"

He snorted and a graced her with a "you-are-such-a-moron" roll of the eyes.

"Of course I'm not dating an eighty-five-year-old! Elizabeth is the Stockdale Foundation's biggest benefactress. I've known her my whole life, and because she couldn't have children of her own, she's always treated me like a surrogate son. I've been corresponding with her about raising money for the clinic here in Haiti. I was keeping it a secret until I'd raised enough for a new vehicle."

"Oh," she said, too shocked to utter anything intelligent.

He shook his head. "You seriously thought she was my girlfriend?" The maddening man then had the nerve to laugh. "That's hilarious."

He pointed a finger at her. "Serves you right for snooping through my stuff. Mail tampering is a felony, you know."

"Oh, shut up!" she snapped, mortified to be caught.

She wanted to clobber him with the IV pole and give him another reason to whine about sore muscles, but she was also thrilled to find out he wasn't two-timing her.

Since she *was* guilty of nosing through his mail, she said nothing and went back to fiddling with the IV fluids. With any luck, he'd let it go.

"Why would you think she was my girlfriend?"

Must he pester her like some irksome extended warranty car insurance salesman?

Careful to avoid eye contact, she adjusted the rate of IV fluids and attempted a nonchalant shrug.

"Allison, look at me," he said gently.

She forced herself to meet his eyes.

"If I had a girlfriend, do you think I would have told you I loved you?"

Her breath caught. "I-I wasn't sure you *were* telling me you loved me. I thought maybe you were just boning up on your French skills."

Another eyeroll. "Because I so need to know how to say, 'I love you' to practice medicine in Haiti?" He shook his head. "Honestly, Allison! For a brilliant woman, you can be awfully dense in matters of the heart."

How dare he! She spat out, "Why wouldn't I be? I trusted Alexander with my heart and look where that got me—feeling like trailer trash."

His eyes bore into hers, and he reached for her hand. "Then Alexander was a moron, and he didn't deserve you. In fact, if I had the strength to crawl out of this bed, I'd go kick him in the nuts for hurting the woman I love."

She giggled. "Grant!"

He stroked her hand with his thumbs. "Surely you know me enough by now to know I'm not like him. I would never have kissed you and told you I loved you if I had a girlfriend back home." He scowled. "In fact, I'm insulted you'd think me capable of such deceit."

Her eyes pooled. "I'm sorry, Grant. It's not you, it's me."

He released a sigh. "Looks like we still have a ways to go in the trust department, huh?" He squeezed her hand. "That's okay. I told you I'd be patient with you. Someday I hope you'll trust me enough to know you don't have to sneak around reading my mail."

She brushed tears from her eyes. If only she could let go of her crippling fear. If only she could embrace a future with him. "I hope so, Grant. I *want* to trust you," she whispered.

He reached for her hand and laced his fingers through hers. "Je t'adore, ma chéri."

Her eyes pooled with tears. "I love you too, Grant."

"Trust will come with time as I prove I can be trusted." He pulled her hand to his mouth and kissed it. "Wo ai ni."

When her brow furrowed, he translated. "I love you, in Chinese."

She swatted his arm. "You and your worthless Chinese! Quit being a show-off!"

He chuckled. "Alright, how about I say it in English? I love you, Allison Smith, with my whole heart. Is that better?"

Joy flooded through her. He'd just told her he loved her— in English— and he wasn't delirious with fever. But... he *was* doped with oxycodone

"You told me earlier not to believe anything you said under the influence of narcotics."

He waved a finger at her. "This is not the pain med talking. We belong together, Allison. Surely you know that by now."

As much as she wanted to believe him, it seemed too good to be true. When they got back to the real word, would his feelings change?

"Are you sure it isn't just that we've had to work together so intently here in Haiti? What about when we get back home, and you're around your wealthy friends with their facelifts and yachts? Am I going to be an embarrassment? What will your parents think of you dating a girl from Mount Trashmore?"

He reached up and cupped her face with his hands then tugged her face down to kiss her gently. "They'll be happy I've found my perfect life companion—my soulmate. Just like my father did when he fell for my mother."

Her heart skipped a beat. He'd kissed her and called her his soulmate.

She caressed his cheek with her fingertips, and he leaned his head into her hand. "I can't believe this is happening. It seems like a Cinderella story."

He grinned up at her. "I don't suppose Cinderella would give me a sponge bath? I feel sticky and gross."

She arched a brow. "Is that some lame attempt to make me ogle your handsome six-pack?"

He touched her nose. "You read my mind, you little minx. But honestly? I do feel disgusting from this fever. And before I kiss you again, I really need to brush my teeth."

She pinched her nose. "Your breath is pretty fetid."

He shook his head. "What a killjoy for my first declaration of love to be on my death bed with me all sticky and gross-breathed and hooked up to an IV."

"Exactly! Where are my long-stemmed roses? The Belgium chocolates? The two-carat diamond?"

He chuckled and raised upturned palms. "Do bedpans and sweaty sheets count?"

She crossed her arms in feigned disgust. "Even the guys in Mount Trashmore do better than that! You need to up your game, buster!"

He reached for her hand. "You have been gypped, my darling. When I get healthy, I'll show you how we Stockdale men impress our ladies."

"Let me guess—mouthwash and Dial soap?"

He laughed. "Touché!"

CHAPTER 24

Grant jerked awake. His head pounded with a thousand jackhammers, and every cell in his body ached. His sheets were drenched in sweat, and just opening his eyes to glance at the clock sent daggers of pain through each eyeball. Five a.m. He groaned and flung off his sweat-soaked sheet. Just lifting his arm to rip off the damp sheet made him cry out in agony. Shoot! His fever was back. He needed Tylenol.

He tugged up his hospital gown to cool off, and glancing down, he noticed a huge new rash all over his chest and abdomen. He shouldn't scratch, or it would only intensify the itch, but he couldn't stop himself. So intense was his need to scratch, he would go insane if he didn't. He scrubbed and scratched and clawed until he let out a temporary sigh of relief. Angry red claw marks now lined his chest and abdomen, but he didn't care. Anything to relieve his misery.

He glanced at the chair next to his bed. Where was Allison?

She hadn't left his side for the four days—or was it five now—that he'd been sick. Must be she'd finally dragged herself to the cabin to get some much-deserved sleep.

He remembered now. Last night he'd told her he was feeling better, and she should go get a decent night of sleep.

He desperately needed to go to the bathroom, but his urinal was full due to all the IV fluids pumping through his veins. The bathroom was only a short distance away, but it may as well have been a mile. He stared at the hallway trying to psych himself up for the arduous trudge to the bathroom.

He forced himself to sit on the edge of the bed, but the wallop of pain made him want to collapse back down on the bed. When had he last taken a pain pill? It felt like an eternity.

After a short pep talk, he stumbled to his feet and hung onto his IV pole until his wooziness passed. He'd have to unplug the IV and push his clumsy dancing partner with him to the bathroom. After tugging the plug from the wall, he hobbled toward the bathroom, careful not to trip over his IV tubing.

Each step made him want to howl in pain. Muscle cramps like he'd run a Boston Marathon with no previous training coursed through his calves and thighs.

This was torture! Why had no one come up with a cure for Dengue fever?

He lumbered one excruciating step at a time until he reached the bathroom. Collapsing onto the commode, he heaved in giant breaths, exhausted from his ridiculously short jaunt from the bed to the bathroom.

After relieving himself, he sat on the commode unable to motivate himself for the return trip back to his bed. And that's when he heard it. A soft but terrified-sounding scream from a distance away. It sounded like Allison! He listened more intently.

It was Allison!

With no further thought about muscle pain, itchy rash, headache, or aching eyeballs, he yanked out his IV needle and applied pressure to the site with a wad of toilet paper. He bolted off the commode and dashed toward the front door barefoot.

Adrenaline surged through his veins like rocket fuel, and he raced over the craggy trail ignoring the jabs to his feet and the searing pain in his legs. The woman he loved was in jeopardy. Keep running, he ordered his tremulous legs.

Allison's screams intensified. Would he make it to the cabin in time? He goaded himself to run even faster.

Dear God, don't let me be too late.

"Leave her alone," he shouted, hoping if the intruder knew someone was coming, he would stop.

Grant flung open the cabin door and charged toward Allison's bed. Louis Villemort straddled Allison with a knife held at her throat. His first instinct was to leap at the man and grab the knife, but with the weapon only inches from Allison's carotid artery, Louis could slit her throat before Grant could stop him.

"Arret!" he demanded, hoping the word was more than a stop sign on the roadside.

Eyes of hatred glared back him as Louis tightened his grip on Allison's throat. Her eyes were the size of moon pies.

"I'm not going to let him hurt you, Allison," he insisted, though he had no business reassuring her of that when his muscles were now trembling and cramping from exhaustion.

Just then, Raphael charged in. "Allison, are you okay?"

Seeing Louis with a knife at her throat, he let out an audible gasp. "Monsieur Villemort, mais no!"

Louis' eyes narrowed, and he screamed at Raphael, "Sortez!" Raphael turned to Grant unsure whether to obey the command or not.

"Go get Dr. Jones and Judy," Grant commanded. "Hurry."

Thank God Raphael's English had improved enough to understand what Grant said. He sprinted out the door hollering for Dr. Jones and Judy.

"Vous me fais mal aux affaires avec Hélène," Louis hissed gripping the knife tighter and touching the tip into Allison's neck. "Elle a besoin de mourir."

Grant didn't know exactly what Louis said, but he could piece together that mal and affaires meant he didn't like them hurting his business. Mourir meant death. Must be he'd found out about Allison slipping a note to Hélène after her séance.

So Louis wasn't here to rape Allison but to kill her.

Grant's calf muscles balled into full-blown charley horses, and his thighs burned from his run from the clinic. He wanted to scream in agony. No way would he be able to grab Louis off Allison and hold him down when the guy held a butcher knife at her neck. He raked a hand through his hair.

Think, think. You've got to outsmart him.

If he could stall Louis until Dr. Jones and Judy arrived, there would be safety in numbers—and witnesses. "Louis, how many gourdes would you need to leave Allison alone?" He hoped he'd asked his question correctly in French Creole, but Louis looked puzzled.

Allison repeated his question but with the proper wording. Apparently, he should have said "combien" not "quel".

"Fifty thousand gourdes," Louis demanded, glaring at Grant as he maintained his chokehold around Allison's neck.

If Grant remembered correctly, 10,000 gourdes equaled around $125 US dollars. So, the greedy SOB was demanding over $600 to let Allison go. Of course, as ransoms went, that was a pittance, and he'd gladly pay a hundred times that, but he needed to stall until Dr. Jones arrived.

He needed to capitalize on Louis' greed, so Grant rubbed his chin as though weighing Louis' offer. He shook his head. "Too much. Trop. Thirty thousand."

He made eye contact with Louis as though they were bartering for a goat.

"Forty-five thousand," Louis demanded. "No less."

"Thirty-five thousand. Not a gourde more."

Louis shook his head. "Forty-thousand."

Grant could hear the footfall of Judy and Dr. Jones on the path. "Alright, you have a deal." Grant stuck out his hand. "Forty-thousand it is. Let her go, and let's shake on it."

Before Louis could comply, Dr. Jones, Judy, and Raphael charged in. Judy held a cast iron skillet. Before Louis could think about escaping, Raphael blocked the door, Dr. Jones grabbed the arm holding the knife, and Judy slammed her cast iron skillet on his head.

Momentarily dazed from the blow, Grant and Dr. Jones were then able to grab the knife from his hands, pull him off Allison, and yank his hands behind his back.

"We need something to hold him until we can get him to the police," Dr. Jones said.

"In my suitcase," Allison said bolting from the bed. "I have two scarfs that will work. One for his hands and one for his feet." She pawed through her suitcase and found two decorative scarves. As they tied up Louis' wrists and ankles with the scarves, Louis struggled to pull away.

Eventually, as though accepting he was now outnumbered, Louis gave up fighting and glared at them.

"Louis, you don't have to be filled with hatred and greed anymore. Jesus can set you free and give you a new life. God has more in store for you than being a witch doctor. He has a plan for your life," Dr. Jones said in rapid French Creole. At least that's what Grant could piece together.

In no mood for proselytizing, Louis made no response.

Smiling at Grant and Allison, Dr. Jones said, "Just planting the first seeds."

"Let's hope they germinate better than our candy and tutoring sessions," Allison mumbled under her breath to Grant.

Allison went up to Louis and said in halting French, "What you did was wrong, but I forgive you. Holding on to hate will only ruin your life. It robs you of happiness."

Louis listened but made no response.

"I'll run get the wheelchair," Judy said. "Since Louis is bound up, we'll need it to get him from the cabin to Angelina."

"Good point," Dr. Jones said. "You get the wheelchair, and we'll guard him."

Grant pulled Allison into his arms momentarily forgetting his burning muscles and weak legs. "Thank God you're okay."

She hugged him back with tears in her eyes. "You came in the nick of time. He was about to slit my throat."

Eying Dr. Jones watching them, Grant pulled away as though it had been nothing more than a hug from a concerned co-worker. Hoping to distract him from conjecturing further about the hug he asked, "How did that truck ever get named Angelina?"

Dr. Jones chuckled. "Jean-Pierre says he needs angels every time he drives it from point A to point B."

"Let's hope angels make her run properly tonight," Allison said. "I'm ready for Louis to spend some serious time in the slammer."

Judy arrived with the wheelchair, and they forced Louis into it. Dr. Jones wheeled him over the craggy trail to the parking lot while Grant put on some shoes and with frequent stops to rest along the way, he hobbled back to the clinic leaning on Allison's arm. They loaded Louis, still bound at the hands and feet, into the truck and buckled him in.

"I'll stop by Jean-Pierre's house and get him to come to the police station with me. You should stay and tend to Grant," Dr. Jones said to Allison. "They'll probably need a statement from you tomorrow about what happened tonight."

He pointed at Grant and grinned. "Aren't you supposed to be in a hospital bed asleep and hooked up to an IV?"

Grant chuckled. "Allison screaming like a banshee put a damper on that plan."

"I didn't even hear her," Dr. Jones confessed. "I must have been in a mighty deep sleep."

"It's lucky I woke up when I did. The rash woke me up with an intense need to scratch, and then I was hurting all over."

"Thank God for rashes and joint pain, huh?" Dr. Jones teased. "It saved Allison's life."

"I went to the bathroom, and since the bathroom window was open to let in the night air, I could just barely make out her screaming. She sounded terrified, so I yanked out my IV and sprinted to the cabin."

Allison crossed her arms in mock disgust. "The guy who supposedly needed me to spoon feed him soup yesterday suddenly has the strength to sprint clear to the cabin?"

"He does when the woman he loves is in danger."

All eyes turned and stared at Grant. An audible gasp permeated the night air. Judy's mouth dropped, and Raphael giggled. Dr. Jones' eyes widened.

Swell! Had he just pronounced he loved Allison in front of everyone? The first time he'd told Allison he loved her, he'd had terrible breath and no bath in three days. Now he'd blurted it out in front of an audience. He seriously needed to up his game in the romance department.

"Right," Allison said with feigned outrage. "You were bartering to get my ransom price down because you didn't want to pay more than 30,000 gourdes for me. Thanks a lot!"

Dr. Jones chuckled. "I need to get Louis to the police station." He pointed at Grant. "Good luck talking your way out of that one."

Clearly sensing that Allison and Grant needed some time alone, Judy wrapped an arm around Raphael's shoulders. "Let's head back to the house, and I'll fix you pancakes with mango."

"Yum!" Raphael said rubbing his stomach.

"I know it's early, but I don't think either one of us is going to sleep after all this excitement," Judy said.

"I love pancakes, and I'm glad Monsieur Villemort is going to jail. He's a bad man."

As they strolled away, Judy said, "God is not through with him. We need to keep praying for him, Raphael."

"Oui," he agreed.

"So," Allison said, eyeing Grant with a smirk. "You weren't willing to buy my safety for a measly 50,000 gourdes? I'm so flattered."

"I was stalling until Dr. Jones could help me out, and you know it!"

"Uh-huh. A likely story," she sputtered.

"I'd used up my adrenaline surge getting to the cabin, and I was afraid I might not have the strength to hold Louis down until Dr. Jones arrived. I didn't want him to escape."

"Plus, he *did* have a knife jabbed an inch from my spinal cord," Allison conceded.

"And carotid," Grant added. "That was one surgery I didn't want to tackle!"

She raised a brow. "What? You didn't want to operate on a sliced carotid artery and severed spinal cord? What a wimp." She blew on her knuckles in a feigned show of confidence. "If the roles were reversed, I totally would have operated on you."

"I'm sure you would have, scary thought that! I'd probably end up a quadriplegic vegetable!"

She whacked his arm. "Hey!"

He chuckled. "Speaking of wimps, I need to sit down. My legs are shaking so much they're about to collapse. I'm afraid my get-up-and-go has gone up and went."

"Let me wheel you inside." She obtained the wheelchair in the driveway where Dr. Jones had left it and rolled it toward Grant. "I've had enough excitement for one day, so I don't need you falling and bashing your head."

"What? You're not in the mood to perform another Burr hole subdural hematoma procedure? Word on the street is, you're pretty good at those."

"Considering our anesthesiologist just left to take Louis to the police station, I doubt you want me drilling holes in your skull without anesthesia."

He winced. "Good point."

She gestured toward the wheelchair and commanded, "Get in."

He collapsed into the chair with a groan. "Bossy little thing, aren't you! Are you going to be this controlling after we're married?"

She cocked a brow as she jerked the wheelchair toward the clinic. "Unless I get a proper, romantic proposal, there won't *be* a wedding. Grant Stockdale III, you may have aced Surgical Techniques, but you get an F-minus in Romance."

He hung his head. "Point taken. How about when we get back to America, I'll take you to a fancy restaurant, and I'll put a beautiful engagement ring in your chocolate soufflé? Then I'll get down on one knee and propose properly."

She swatted his arm playfully. "No, you dunce. You can't *tell* me your plans. You're supposed to surprise me." She wheeled him inside the clinic and back to his bed.

"Now I see why I only offered 30,000 gourdes for you. You're awfully demanding," he teased.

"I am, and right now, I demand you get on this bed so I can take your vital signs and examine you."

He waggled his eyebrows suggestively. "Ooo! Are we going to play doctor?"

She whacked his arm, though she was unable to suppress a half-smile. "That was a totally inappropriate remark to make to your physician. Now stick this thermometer in your mouth and shut up long enough for me to get an accurate reading."

He complied, keeping his eyes fixed on her face.

She pulled out the thermometer, read it, and groaned. "You're back up to 102.8. No wonder you didn't have the strength to tackle Louis. Looks like you get two Tylenol and cold ginger ale for breakfast again."

"And you get another one-star review on Yelp."

"Plus, I get to restart the IV you ripped out." She wiggled her fingers and released an evil laugh. "Where's that dull rusty needle Dr. Jones wanted me to unload?"

"No IV. I can drink enough fluids to stay hydrated."

She lifted a brow. "What's the matter? You afraid to let me stick you after you bartered my ransom down to the price of a used toilet?"

Ignoring the toilet dig, he responded, "Seriously, I can drink enough fluids to avoid another IV."

She crossed her arms. "Prove it."

She retrieved a can of ginger ale and gestured for him to drink. "Glug, glug. And here's your gourmet breakfast." She handed him two Tylenol.

He gulped down half of the ginger ale in a few swigs then swallowed the pills and finished the rest of the ginger ale. "See?" He handed her the empty can.

"Fine, you win. Now pull up your hospital gown so I can examine that itchy rash on your chest."

He smirked. "You just want to check out these strong, virile muscles of mine." He stuck out his chest and flexed his biceps in a mock Mr. Universe gesture.

She rolled her eyes. "Behave yourself! I'm trying to act like a professional here, but you're making it very difficult."

He reached out his arms for her. "How can I behave like a professional when that villainous Villemort threatened to kill my lady love? I'm so rattled, you need to give me a comforting hug."

She frowned at him. "*I'm* the one who nearly got stabbed, and *you* need the comforting hug?"

He patted the bed next to him with an inviting smile. "We *both* need a hug. Plus, we need to celebrate Louis' capture."

She smiled. "I capitulate." She lay on the bed next to him and curled her arms around his abdomen.

"I was terrified, Grant. I can't tell you how relieved I was to hear your voice shouting at him to leave me alone."

He pulled her into a tight embrace and didn't want to let go, despite his total exhaustion and the burning in his arms. Thank God he'd heard her screaming or—no, he couldn't finish that thought. "If he'd killed you, my heart would have splintered into a thousand pieces."

She pulled back from his embrace. "Wow! You just upped your Romance grade from an 'F' to a 'B-' with that line."

"A 'B-'?" His shoulders sagged. "What's a guy got to do to earn an 'A' with you?"

"If you kiss me properly, I might just up your grade to an 'A-plus'," she cooed.

He tugged her into his arms and kissed her gently before caressing her cheek. He raked his hands through her hair then pulled her close so he could inhale her tropical shampoo.

"Ever since our first trip from Port-au-Prince, I've loved the smell of your hair."

She smirked. "You mean when you said I smelled better than the raw sewage and dead dogs in the ditch?"

"Yeah, that day." He chuckled. "That was one of my better lines, don't you think?" He kissed the top of her head and whispered, "I forbid you to ever change shampoos."

"Now who's being bossy," she retorted. "I may buy a bottle of lavender shampoo just to be ornery."

He touched her nose. "I can see I'll have to keep my wits about me with you around."

"A-ya, but that's what you like about me—I challenge you."

He caressed her cheek. "Correction. That's what I love about you."

"I love you, too, Grant," she whispered, then kissed him.

She forced herself to sit on the edge of the bed. "Let me take a look at that rash on your chest before you get me so flustered I lose all my doctoring skills."

He pulled up his hospital gown. "What do you think?"

She pursed her lips as she examined the inflamed rash. "It looks just like the picture in the textbook for Dengue fever."

He patted his pillow. "Why don't you lay down next to me. I'm so exhausted I don't have the strength to do anything more than lay here like a beached whale. Fever sure sucks the life out of me."

She lay next to him and wrapped an arm around his waist. "That and rescuing your damsel in distress." She kissed his cheek and added, "It was clever of you to distract Louis from stabbing me by bartering with him."

"My muscles had cramped up so much, I didn't trust myself to tackle him and hold him down, so I had to come up with a plan B."

He could see love radiating from her eyes, and it brought tears to his own. "You'll always be my one and only, Allison."

"And you, mine," she said caressing his cheek. "I know that now."

"Do you trust me with your whole heart now?"

She smiled. "You ran over jagged rocks barefoot with a temp of 102.8 to rescue me from a man with a butcher knife, so I think you've demonstrated I can trust you."

He kissed her head. "I'm glad."

They lay together eyes closed enjoying their newfound closeness until Allison asked, "Grant, if only one of us can be Chief Resident, how will we keep our relationship going?"

He stroked her arm before responding. "I've thought about that, and I've come up with a solution."

"I'm all ears."

"What if we jointly share the role of Chief Resident? We'll alternate every three months. When one of us is Chief Resident, the other will be in Haiti helping Dr. Jones. We'll plan some overlap weeks, so we get to see each other, and at the end of the year, we'll get married."

"If that's your idea of a decent proposal, think again, buster. That was a definite D-minus."

"Hey, if I try to get down on one knee right now, I won't be able to get back up."

"Alright, point taken," she conceded with a chuckle.

"Any way, after the wedding and honeymoon, we'll set up a surgical practice together somewhere that we both agree upon."

She mulled over his idea. "You think Dr. Morrison will go along with having two Chief Surgical Residents?"

"Yes, because it promotes Johns Hopkins goal of helping the disadvantaged. It will also encourage other residents to come down here."

She scratched the angriest looking part of his rash, and he moaned with relief.

"You have no idea how good that feels. Keep scratching."

She scrubbed and scratched until he moaned in relief. "Ah, much better."

They snuggled together until Grant said, "You know that Elizabeth, whose letter you so rudely and illegally read?"

She took a sudden interest in examining her nails. "I'm pleading the Fifth."

"She wrote me that she's already raised fifty thousand in pledges for the clinic."

"Wow! That would be enough for a decent ambulance or a new truck at least. He could even train someone to assist." She smiled up at him. "And to think you didn't even want to come to Haiti. Look at you now."

He shrugged. "I admit it. Haiti changed me. For the better."

"This rotation changed me, too."

He rolled onto his side and leaned on an elbow so he could read her face better. "How so?"

"I no longer feel ashamed because I grew up poor or because Alexander dumped me."

"His loss was my gain."

"Plus, I'm now willing to do whatever it takes to make your parents accept me. It wouldn't kill me to wear a fancy dress and heels every now and then or learn which fork to use at a formal dinner. I wasn't willing to change myself at all for Alexander, but I am for you."

"Speaking of forks, how about you get a fork and scratch my left shoulder blade. I can't reach it, and this rash is driving me insane."

She chuckled. "No forks handy, but these will do."

She curled her fingers into claws and mimed scratching. "Roll over onto your stomach, and I'll give it a shot."

He complied, and Allison scratched his upper back. "Here?"

"No, a little more to the right. Down an inch. Ooo, right there." He moaned with pleasure. "I knew I fell in love with you for a reason. You make a fantastic back scratcher."

She swatted his arm. "Watch it, Stockdale! Your Romance grade just dropped again."

"That's okay. I have a lifetime to bring it up."

EPILOGUE
Fifteen months later

"Congratulations," Dr. Jones said, pulling Grant and Allison in for a bear hug. "I can't believe you'd take a day out of your honeymoon to come visit us."

"We wanted to see all the changes in the clinic since we were last here four months ago," Grant said, as they strolled from the driveway toward the front door of the clinic."

"Thanks to the Stockdale Foundation, we now have a functioning ambulance, and a full-time medical assistant."

"That's wonderful news," Allison said, following Dr. Jones into the clinic.

"Just last week we used our new ambulance to transport a man to Port-au-Prince after he fell off a roof and needed extensive orthopedic surgeries."

"I'm glad it's been useful," Grant said, as Dr. Jones led them into the newly expanded clinic now equipped with ten beds.

"Of course, Jean-Pierre won't hear of junking Angelina. He still drives her around, and she's still surprisingly functional most of the time."

"How's the new assistant working out?" Grant asked.

"Maria is a fast learner. She now runs all the lab tests, checks vital signs, and dresses wounds. She's also getting better and better at starting IVs and drawing blood."

"What ever happened to Louis Villemort?" Allison asked.

Dr. Jones thumped his head. "Did we not tell you? He's been released from prison, but he's completely changed."

"You're kidding! What happened?" Grant asked.

"Jean-Pierre and I visited him regularly in prison, and he converted a few months ago. He now goes to church regularly."

Grant and Allison turned and stared at each other, mouths agape.

"If he's not a witch doctor anymore, how is he making a living?" Allison asked.

Judy smiled. "You won't believe it, but he's renovated that big old house of his into an orphanage. We pay him rent, and he gets paid for doing janitorial and grounds work. Thanks to the Stockdale Foundation, we now have ten orphans in the home. Two local women oversee the home and teach the children. So far, we have funding for the next five years."

"Elizabeth is an amazing fundraiser, isn't she? I hope I'm half as spry when I'm eighty-six," Grant commented.

"What about Raphael? Where do things stand with his adoption?" Allison asked.

Judy beamed. "We finally got a hearing before the Judge, and the papers were signed a month ago. He is now officially our son."

Allison clapped her hands in glee. "That's wonderful news! We were hoping we'd get to see him before we headed off for the rest of our honeymoon."

"You won't have to go far. He's inside cooking up a tasty lunch for you. Since we knew you were coming this morning, we prepared a special meal to celebrate your recent nuptials and Raphael's adoption. Jean-Pierre and Maurice are coming, as well."

"Fabulous!" Allison exclaimed. "I can't wait to see them."

Judy pulled Allison away from Grant and Dr. Jones. "Are things going okay with Grant's parents? I remember you were anxious that they wouldn't accept you," she whispered.

"They've been wonderful," Allison said beaming. "Grant's father is proud that I matched his son academically, and Grant's mother told me she's never seen Grant so happy. She said she'd been praying he would meet a nice Christian girl like me, so all my worries were for nothing."

Judy clapped her hands. "That's wonderful."

Allison raised a finger. "The Grandfather intimidates the socks off me, but luckily, I don't have to see him much."

"I knew they'd love you," Judy insisted. She grabbed Allison's hand and squeezed it. "How could they not?"

"Grant's mother even asked me to help her select a mother-of-the-groom dress, so we went shopping together. Can you imagine? I don't know the first thing about fashion, but we had a great time together."

"Where are you going for your honeymoon?"

Allison looked askance to see if Grant could hear them talking then whispered, "Grant thinks he's surprising me, but I snooped through his mail and found out it's a fancy place in Haiti called the Abaka Bay Resort. It looked fabulous online. She giggled. "I think he's still trying to earn that A+ in Romance 101 after he tried to barter my ransom price down to 30,000 gourdes with Louis."

Judy giggled. "The Abaka Bay Resort? Wow! I've heard it's a really swank place."

"I'm just looking forward to two weeks alone with Grant with nothing to do but relax together."

Won't that be nice after all the hard work you two have done combining Chief Residency with working in the clinic last year?"

Allison turned and waved at Grant. "It will be wonderful. I can't wait!"

Grant smiled back, and he and Dr. Jones strolled over to join them. "What are you two gossiping about?"

"I was telling her how much we were looking forward to a relaxing two weeks together before starting at our new practice in Burlington."

"Burlington? As in Burlington, Vermont?" Judy asked.

"Yes. We had to find a place that needed two general surgeons, and this hospital offered us both a slot," Allison explained. "Plus, it *is* my alma mater."

"It's also less than two hours from delightful Mount Trashmore. We'll get to tour the landfill regularly." Grant rubbed his hands together with mock glee.

She swatted his arm "Behave yourself, Stockdale, or you'll be sleeping on the beach. Alone!"

He chuckled and wrapped an arm around her. "Sorry, I couldn't resist." He kissed the top of her head. "You know I'm just teasing, right?"

"A-ya, but no more Mount Trashmore jokes. I mean it!"

He grabbed her hand and kissed it. "I wouldn't dream of it. Besides, I'm thrilled with our plans. Vermont is gorgeous, and your parents are great. Plus, we negotiated a fabulous contract with the hospital."

"How so?" Dr. Jones inquired.

"We're each entitled to four weeks a year to do missionary medicine in Haiti, and we'll be starting a Medical Missions program at the local Residency program. That way, between Dr. Morrison's surgical residents, and ours, you'll always have at least one general surgeon available," Grant said.

"We're also hoping to recruit some RNs, as well," Allison added.

"Judy and I can't thank you enough. You've both been an answer to prayer."

"Well, you don't know it, but that rotation in Haiti was an answer to prayer for me, too," Allison said.

"How so?" Judy asked.

"I'd been praying to find a man who was just right for me, but it never happened." She smiled up at Grant. "I'd been attracted to Grant for years but had written him off as out of my league."

Grant reached for her hand. "If we hadn't been forced to work together in Haiti, she never would have given me a chance."

Dr. Jones wiped a tear from his cheek. "God is amazing, isn't He?"

Allison smiled up at her new husband. "He is, indeed."

QUESTIONS:

1. Women make up only a small percent of CEOs, college presidents, and U.S. Senators and Governors. Why is that? How do we get more women in positions of leadership?

2. Allison was shunned by her first fiancé's family because of her background. What challenges face a couple with divergent financial, racial, or religious backgrounds?

3. Haiti is the poorest nation in the Western Hemisphere, despite billions of dollars of financial aid and grants. Due to corruption, the funds get misappropriated, and the poor receive little benefit. Unemployment and crime are also rampant. What can be done to help countries like Haiti?

4. Jesus commanded us help the poor. What ministries do you support? Are there others you would like to support?

5. Allison had difficulty trusting Grant because of scars from her past. Do you have any emotional scars that affect how you interact with others? What have you done to overcome these obstacles?

6. Voodoo is a national religion in Haiti. How did Dr. Jones, Grant, and Allison reach out to those who were indoctrinated in voodoo practices? How should we share about the love of Christ to people who are atheists or who practice other religions without being obnoxious?

ABOUT THE AUTHOR:

Sally Burbank is a practicing primary care internist by day and a writer by night. She lives in Nashville, Tennessee, with her musician husband, Nathan. She has two grown children, Eliza, a veterinarian in Knoxville, and Steven, an engineer in Denver.

When she isn't busy treating hypertension diabetes, and asthma, she enjoys bicycling, hiking, cooking, reading, and singing in the church choir.

Her most recent series of novels, Ladies in Lab Coats, features women doctors in their quest to find true love.

Sally's website is www.sallywillardburbank.com. She loves public speaking about Alzheimer's disease or stories from her thirty-year career as a doctor.

Made in the USA
Columbia, SC
05 November 2023